PIONEER SPIRIT
Book One: Overland Trail

Earle Jay Goodman

Also by Earle Jay Goodman

DISCREET – Book One: Childhood's End
DISCREET – Book Two: Growing Pains
DISCREET – Book Three: Round Up

PIONEER SPIRIT - Book One: Overland Trail
PIONEER SPIRIT - Book Two: Indian Affairs
PIONEER SPIRIT - Book Three: Wars and Rumors
PIONEER SPIRIT - Book Four: An Uneasy Peace
PIONEER SPIRIT - Book Five: White Indians
PIONEER SPIRIT - Book Six: Perilous Times
PIONEER SPIRIT – Book Seven: War Drums

To see photographs and maps of actual historical people and places
during the time of Connal Lee's story, please visit:

https://goodmans-pioneer-spirit.blogspot.com

"...and the desert shall rejoice, and blossom as the rose."

Isaiah 35:1

PIONEER SPIRIT
Book One: Overland Trail

Earle Jay Goodman

Dedication

Boca Raton, Florida
2018

    I dedicate this book with love and gratitude to my wonderful parents and grandparents, on both sides of my family, who raised me on the stories of my great and great-great-grandparents, some of the earliest pioneers and settlers of America's Intermountain West in the mid-1800's;

    and, to my friend and advisor since 1973, mentor, and de facto book editor, Edward P. Frey, Esq. – Thanks, Ed;

    and, last but not least, to my first real love since 1979, then business partner, then domestic partner, and now married partner, James John Goodman. You are the light of my life. I love you, Jim.

                        ---Earle Jay Goodman

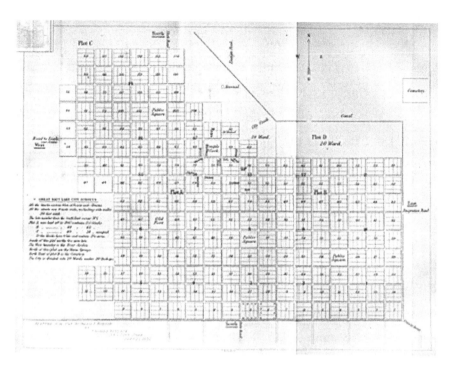

*Map of Great Salt Lake City
in the time of Pioneer Spirit.
The original City stretched
from 8th North to 9th South,
and from 9th West to 8th East,
for a total of 135 Blocks.*

*Population in 1860 Census:
Great Salt Lake City – 8,236
Salt Lake County – 11,295
Territory of Utah – 40,273*

Table of Contents

Chapter 1: Leaving the Ozarks Behind

Zeff wandered home exhausted after a hot day baking clay bricks in the family kiln. Trees lined the path between his home and the clay pit. His family's homestead and brick kiln nestled in the back mountains of the Ozarks, so far south in Missouri they could nearly reach out and touch Arkansas. They sold their bricks to poor homesteaders and farmers scattered around the mountains. A narrow wagon trail led to their secluded home, a good hike away from the barely cleared and graded county road. Zeff's dirt-poor family matched the poverty of all their hillbilly neighbors. They seldom saw anyone but family.

Zeff complained to himself as he strode along the red dirt path on his way home. *Another borin' day. Hot fer the end o' April. Work, work, work. And what've Ah got tuh show fer it? Barely enough cash tuh buy gunshot an' flour, thas what. Hardly ain't worth the effort. Oh, well, Ah have me a family tuh feed, now. Least-wise there's that. A new baby son. Thas somethin' good. Ah sure do hope Sister Woman has muh supper ready. Ah'm so hungry Ah could eat a horse!*

Zeff kicked his old boots against the sun-bleached boards of the porch to clean them of the clinging local red dirt. Barely nineteen, he looked older from working hard all his life. He shoved open the board door of the little log cabin he and his wife had built the year before. The rusty iron hinges squeaked. "I'm home, Sis." He automatically removed the leather belt holding his Bowie hunting knife and hung it by the door. He noticed his little brother's smaller knife hanging on a hand-carved peg on the wall. He gazed around his one-room home. "Where the hell are ya, Sister Woman? Why don't ya have supper cookin'?"

Zeff's entrance roused their two-month-old boy, who began crying and fussing. "Hey there, little Chester Ray, where's yer Maw now any hoots?"

He headed next door to his father's larger older cottage on the other side of a sagging barn looking for Sister Woman. When he walked by the open barn door, he heard the crack of a horsewhip, a muffled cry, then weak moaning. *What in tarnation?* Zeff rushed over to the unpainted barn and glanced into its shadowy interior. His slender young wife sagged against old ropes tied to one of the log columns supporting the barn's leaky cedar shake roof. They had only been married for thirteen months. He scowled angrily. "Hey there, Paw, what the hell're y'all doin' tuh Sister Woman? Let 'er go, ol' man."

Zeff's father snarled and cracked the whip again. A bloody red stripe bloomed against Sister Woman's faded calico day dress as she moaned pitifully.

"Whatcha doin' ol' man? Stop that right now, Paw. She's *muh* wife now. She's not yers no longer."

"Wull, she's still muh baby girl, an' she refused me when Ah needed 'er. Ah'm still the man o' the house, an' what Ah says goes! Obey yer parents. It's the first commandment, goddammit!"

"She's not yers no longer, Paw, she's mahn. Y'all done gave 'er away tuh me when we got married by that travelin' preacher man last year. Now, lay offen 'er, ol' man, or else!"

Zeff rushed over and yanked back his father's sweaty shoulder, then punched him in the jaw. As Old Man Swinton stumbled back, Zeff grabbed the bib of his ragged, filthy coveralls and jerked him up. Fumes of raw whiskey wafted around them. Zeff pulled back his right fist and knocked his father down with a hard punch directly to the nose.

Blood streamed down into the old man's scraggly beard. "Why yew ungrateful sonuva bitch, Ah'll show yew who's man o' this here house!"

Zeff leapt over him and began untying his petite, seventeen-year-old sister-wife. When he heard his father stumble to his feet, he spun around and landed a hard kick to the old man's protruding belly. His father dropped like a sack of beans and rolled around on the barn's dirt floor, moaning and cursing up a storm. Frightened of the temper of his thirty-six-year-old father, he kicked the side of his head. His old man had always been fast to turn angry and violent, especially when drinking moonshine, which he drank from sunup till sundown. "Sister Woman is muh wife, now, married in the eyes o' God. So, don't yew touch 'er no more!"

A lifetime of physical and sexual abuse by his sadistic father triggered Zeff's own Scots-Irish temper. He picked up the fallen driving whip and laid into his father. He vented all the pent-up hate of years of being beaten and forced to submit to his father's sexual lusts. He didn't stop until his father, who looked like an elderly grandpa, stopped moving. Panting to catch his breath, Zeff stepped back and inspected his bleeding wife, his younger sister whom he had married last year. Angry again at what he saw, he kicked the old man in the crotch hard enough to emasculate him. He snarled with a sneer on his face. "Fuck yew, ol' man. Screw yew an' yer heavy-handed ways. Fuck yew an' yer horrible demands."

Zeff leaned over with his hands on his knees, gasping to catch his breath. He heard his little brother sobbing in the corner of the dark barn. He glanced over to make sure his father hadn't hurt Baby Boy. Zeff sighed. Baby Boy sat hunched over in a fetal position to escape the awful scene of screams and blood. He had his arms around his knees with his head tucked down. His shoulders heaved with his sobbing. Since their mother passed away shortly after giving birth to Baby Boy, Zeff had tried to protect his little brother from their father's abuse. He hadn't always succeeded because his father often waited until he left for the kiln before going after Baby Boy, either physically or sexually.

Sister Woman moaned. Zeff stepped over and quickly untied the ropes binding her to the rough log beam. After she came loose, she flopped into his arms, limp, crying, gasping, and sobbing. Zeff picked her up over his right shoulder and carried her to the barn door. He looked over at his younger brother. "Come on home, Baby Boy. Y'all can stop yer blubberin' now."

Inside their little shack, Zeff carefully lowered Sister Woman onto their rough bed and rolled her onto her stomach. Their new-born son cried from his makeshift crib, an old peach crate lined with a tattered quilt. The noise distracted Zeff from tending to his wife's wounds. Knowing Sister Woman couldn't nurse the baby, he ordered Baby Boy to pick up the baby to stop his crying.

Zeff rushed out to their brick-lined well and dragged up a bucket of water as fast as he could turn the crank. He carried in the heavy bucket of water and knelt beside their bed. He had built the

13

bed himself from stumps of logs latched together with a spring of woven rope. It held a mattress Sister Woman had sewn by hand from cotton ticking and stuffed with raw cotton. He carefully peeled Sister Woman's dress off her sweaty body. She only owned two dresses, so he didn't throw this one away. He knew Sister Woman could mend the tears and soak out the bloodstains with a bit of effort. She had taken beatings from their cruel father many times before, only usually he didn't draw blood. Zeff picked up a rag from the rag bag and gently cleaned her back, carefully wiping up the blood seeping from seven crisscrossed stripes. The first time he touched her wounds with the cool dripping rag, her body tensed up. She screamed, then passed out.

Oh, me sweet little darlin' gal. Ah'm so sorry, Sis. Ah won't never let Paw touch y'all never again, no matter what! After he had her cleaned up as best he could, he spread a little healing Snake Oil salve on her wounds, then left her sprawled out uncovered over their bag mattress. Baby Boy placed Chester Ray back in his little crate crib. The baby began screaming his head off again, hungry, demanding immediate attention. He kicked off the flannel baby blanket. His flailing, chubby little limbs loosened his flour sack diapers to where they fell aside. The smell of baby shit filled the closed-up air of the warm, one-room shack. Baby Boy gingerly laid down beside his older sister. He gently placed his arm comfortingly against her shoulder, carefully avoiding the crimson welts on her back.

Zeff ran his hands through his shaggy blond hair, pushing the bangs back from his forehead. Zeff frowned as he picked up the soiled baby, placed him in the crook of his left arm then cleaned him with the same rag he used to clean Sister Woman. Zeff lay him down beside his comatose mother. Chester Ray began crying again, demanding his mother's tits. Zeff knew what his son needed, so he hightailed it to the barn to fetch some cow's milk from the settling pans.

When he entered the barn, he spotted his haggard father still sprawled where he had fallen. Zeff walked over and looked down at the sorry excuse of a man. His father's open lips exposed his broken, stained, and missing teeth. The man's shaggy red hair had turned gray around the edges. His scraggly beard and overgrown

14

mustache had turned gray with only a little red still showing. With a snarl, Zeff gave him another kick in the belly. "That'll show ya! Whatcha gonna do 'bout it now, Ol' Man? Y'all deserves tuh die fer beatin' on Sister Woman, ya worthless piece o' shit." He grabbed the rope used to restrain his sister-wife and tied up his vicious father.

With another big sigh, he picked up a tin ladle and scooped up a little milk and cream. Zeff returned to his shack and poured the milk into a bowl on their little homemade table. He picked up a clean rag, swished it in the bucket of bloody water, wrung it out, and dipped it into the bowl. He carried the saturated rag over to the baby beside his unconscious wife. Zeff let milk dribble into the baby's mouth every time he opened his lips to cry. When little Chester Ray tasted the milk, his lips pursed to suckle. Zeff twisted the corner of the rag and slipped it into the sucking mouth. He dipped the rag into the bowl of milk and fed his son until the child stopped fussing. Baby Boy sat up and watched, finally relaxing after the distressing afternoon.

At last, peace and quiet descended over the one-room hovel. Zeff glanced over at the cold fireplace, wishing Sister Woman had started supper. He spotted sliced vegetables and a cut-up grouse on the little table beside their cooking fireplace, but the fire had gone out. The pot hung in the fireplace as empty as his stomach. Seething with anger at his father's daily drunkenness and violence, he jogged over to the family house and kicked the door open with a bang!

When he walked in, he decided they couldn't stay on their father's homestead any longer. He had to escape with his wife, child, and little brother before his father woke up and took his revenge. His father might be an old man, but he still had his vigor and a wild temper. Zeff knew only too well. His father had stopped forcing Zeff to yield to his sexual demands after Zeff married Sister Woman, but until then, Zeff knew his father's heavy hand and lustful dominance nearly every day. And so did his little sister. It had begun less than a year after their mother died giving birth to Baby Boy twelve long years ago. Zeff had barely turned seven, and Sister Woman had been five when they lost their mother.

Driven by hunger and fear, Zeff grabbed a gunny sack and plundered his father's larder and nearly empty pantry. He shoved in a salted ham, a slab of bacon, and a round of moldy cheese. He spotted a tarred water bag and grabbed it, too.

Zeff rushed back to the barn and put a lead harness on the strongest of the draft mules his father used to deliver bricks. He rigged the long-eared mule with a packsaddle. He strapped his father's worn leather saddlebags on the mule's back and then tied the food and water bag to the saddle. With tugs and curses, he pulled the mule out of the barn and tied it up in front of his shack.

Zeff ran back to his father's filthy kitchen. He grabbed a nearly empty flour sack and shoved in a greasy cast-iron skillet and dirty cooking utensils. With a smirk of revenge, he grabbed his father's dented tin coffee pot and a bag of coffee beans. He snatched up a sack of flour and a small bag of salt. He tied everything on the big draft mule, then rushed into his hovel. He picked up the small cast iron cooking pot from the rusted swing arm inside his fireplace and strapped it onto the mule.

He scrounged around until he found another potato sack, then grabbed their clothes off the wooden pegs they used as their closet. He picked up the newly sewn pile of baby clothes and diapers and stuffed everything into the sack that still smelled of clean dirt. He picked up his hunting rifle and his dwindling supply of lead ball casting equipment. He tied the rifle onto the saddlebags and put the bullet supplies into the top leather pocket, ready at hand should he spot game along their way.

Zeff returned to the barn and rifled the pockets of his father's filthy coveralls until he found all his loose cash. He quickly counted out nearly five dollars in small coin money and gleefully shoved it into his own pants pocket. He glanced around for anything else that could aid their escape but couldn't find anything more to pilfer. With a snap of his fingers, he remembered the old flint tinderbox in his father's cabin. They would need it to start cooking fires as they traveled through the lush forests of the Ozark Mountains. He jogged over and found it next to a jug of homemade moonshine whiskey. With a gleeful grin, he grabbed up both. On the way out the door, he spotted his father's fishing pole in the corner and decided to take it, too.

Baby Boy looked up at Zeff when he came in from loading the mule. When Zeff sat down, he walked over and put his arm around his older brother's strong shoulders. Zeff pulled the cork on the jug and took a deep draw. The newly distilled white whiskey burned going down. He gasped, then smiled and settled in to wait until Sister Woman woke up so they could make good their escape. He held out the jug. "Here ya go, Baby Boy. Take a slug now. That'll put hair on yer chest."

Baby Boy bravely swallowed the harsh, raw liquor before he grimaced and began coughing. "Thanks, Big Brover." He then climbed up on Zeff's lap and laid his head on Zeff's shoulder. He had started his growing spurt not long ago, just before he turned twelve. He wouldn't be able to cuddle in Zeff's lap much longer.

Sister Woman woke up during the dark quiet of the night. She pulled herself out of bed with big moans and staggered out to the outhouse. When she returned, she crawled onto the mattress on her hands and knees. "Hey, Bubba. Can Ah have me a drink o' water?"

Zeff picked up his little brother, who had fallen asleep on his lap, and laid him down beside Sister Woman. "Sure, Sis. Here. Let me help ya."

After several long, slow sips, she pushed the tin cup away. "Thanks, Bubba." She tried to look over her shoulder to see what hurt so badly. "Boy howdy, but paw surely got me good, didn't 'e?"

"Ah'm sorry Ah didn't get back earlier from the kiln, Sis. Don't y'all worry, though. I laid 'im out but good as soon as Ah saw him whippin' ya. He's knocked out an' all tied up in the barn. Listen, Sister Woman, Ah've been thinkin'. Ah thinks it would be fer the best if'n we moved on an' found our own place tuh live, away from paw an' 'is mean ways. We should take Baby Boy, too, fer 'is own protection."

Sister Woman opened her eyes and looked at Zeff in the dim moonlight. She thought about it, then nodded her head once. She winced when the nod pulled the wounds across the top of her back and shoulders. "Yep. Ah suppose yer right, Bubba. When do ya wanna go, then?"

"Well, Ah think we should git outta here afore paw wakes up an' gits loose. We should probably leave in about a hour. Whaddaya think, Sis?"

Sister Woman struggled up to her hands and knees, wincing as the cuts and bruises on her back demanded she stop moving. With a sharp intake of breath, she whispered, "Let me git a couple o' things ready fer us so's we can leave."

Zeff patted her shoulder, leaned close, and gave her a tender little kiss. She felt clammy from sweating from the pain. "Rest easy, sweet little gal o' mine. Ah've got ever thin' ready. Ah already loaded up the mule. Try an' take a nap, Sis. I'll wake y'all up when it's time tuh go."

With a moan, she collapsed face down on the dirty mattress.

An hour before daybreak, Zeff checked on his father, still tied up in the barn. Satisfied they could make their escape before his old man regained consciousness, he woke up Baby Boy. Together, they helped Sister Woman stand up. Zeff carefully applied a little more of the echinacea tincture salve called Snake Oil, then bound up her wounds in scraps from the rag bag. They helped her into her other day dress. She sat down on the homemade chair made from tree branches while Baby Boy helped her put on her ankle-high work boots. She didn't have any other shoes. She typically went barefoot except in the coldest of winter.

Zeff saw that Sister Woman wouldn't be able to carry Chester Ray. After thinking a minute, he pulled out his old canvas rucksack and used it to jury rig a way to carry their infant son. He had made the backpack a couple years before to take hunting. He picked up Chester Ray and handed him to Sister Woman to hold. He took the scrap of quilt that lined the baby's little crib and lined the canvas bag of his rustic knapsack. He strapped it on his back and told Baby Boy to gently lower Chester Ray into the bag.

Zeff held out his hand and helped Sister Woman stand up. Zeff noticed her grimace. "Y'all gonna be all right, there, Sis? Can y'all make it?"

Sister Woman frowned in concentration. "Let's go, Bubba. Let's git goin' while the goin's good."

Zeff took hold of Sister Woman's hand. "Come on, Baby Boy. We're goin' out in the world tuh seek a better life. Let's git a move on."

Zeff grabbed the lead reins of the mule in his free hand and led his little family down the red dirt road. Half an hour later, they reached the county road running along the border between Missouri and Kansas. Dawn began lighting the sky when they stopped for a sip of water. Zeff dug out dry day-old biscuits from the gunny sack and split them between the three of them. Before they started back up, he picked up his rifle. He placed Sister Woman's hand on the heavy-laden packsaddle. "Here ya go, Sis. Hold on here tuh help ya walk. Come on, Baby Boy, back on yer feet. We's gotta hunt us up some food while we're a travelin'."

They took off walking due north on the dirt road. A little after high noon, Zeff spotted a cottontail rabbit beneath a pine tree and shot it. Baby Boy ran to retrieve it. Zeff noticed Sister Woman staggering along, clinging to the side of their mule, struggling to keep up. He knew she needed to stop and rest. He took the lead rein and pulled the mule off the road behind a cluster of large white oaks. Bushes of dogwood made a spectacular hedge of white four-petaled blossoms between them and the county road.

Zeff helped Sister Woman lay down on her side. She focused her mind on the vanilla-like perfume of the dogwood blossoms to distract her from the pain. Zeff unpacked the mule while Baby Boy dressed out the rabbit with his sharp hunting knife. Baby Boy took the rabbit over to Zeff and placed it on the grass. Zeff nodded his thanks. "Baby Boy, go scrounge us up some dry deadfall so's we can make us a cookfire. Ah'm gonna try an' find somethin' tuh flavor the pot. Then, when y'all get back, please joint the rabbit fer some stew. Y'all knows what tuh do."

Baby Boy nodded. Somehow, they managed to make a credible stew without Sister Woman. Zeff had found wood sorrel plants to spice up the broth with their leaves. Their root tubers cooked up like miniature potatoes in the stew. When they finished their early supper, Chester Ray began crying for his own dinner. Sister Woman didn't want to sit up. She hurt too much. With Zeff's help, she fed her baby while reclining on her side.

Zeff used their flour, sugar, salt, and baking soda the following morning and made pan bread. He fried it up in their iron skillet at the edge of the campfire, turning it occasionally so it would brown evenly. After they ate their fill, Zeff and Baby Boy loaded up the pack mule. Zeff pulled on his backpack with Chester Ray already inside, sucking his thumb. They hit the road. At midday, they stopped and munched on the remains of their soda bread. When they started back up, Zeff asked Baby Boy to carry his shotgun so they could hunt up some supper. This became their routine as they plodded their way north.

After a week, Sister Woman had healed enough to help them set up camp and prepare meals.

Chapter 2: Queen City of the Trails

Three weeks later, the filthy young family staggered into Independence, Missouri. The crowds of people and all the carriages, wagons, and horses crowding the streets intimidated them. Zeff led them back to the peace of the woods outside the city. They had never seen so many people in one place before. Sister Woman and Baby Boy pitched camp back off the road. Zeff built a cookfire of deadfall and lit it with the flint and steel from his tinderbox. Sister Woman found a spot of soft weeds where she made a bed for Chester Ray, then turned to cook supper. She didn't have much to work with. Zeff had shot a small gray fox late that afternoon, the only game they had seen all day. Baby Boy had used his sharp hunting knife to skin and clean it where it fell. Sister Woman set about cutting it up at its joints for the pot, humming tunelessly to herself as she worked. None of them cared much for fox meat. It usually ended up tougher and drier than venison from an old stag. Sister Woman let it simmer in the stew for hours, hoping to tenderize it a little. It turned out tough and gamey, but they ate it anyway.

They camped outside Independence for several weeks. Every morning, Zeff walked into town to find day work to earn money. Sister Woman tended their baby in the camp. Baby Boy hunted, never straying very far from their little campsite.

On Monday morning of their fourth week in Independence, Zeff joined a milling group of men looking for day work in the square before the courthouse. A man in his early thirties drove up in a small farm wagon pulled by two strong mules. When he neared the group of laborers, he stood up in front of his seat and faced the men. "I'm a blacksmith from the edge of town. I'm looking for a strong man to tend my fires and help me move my goods around as I'm working on them. It's hot hard work, but I pay well. Anyone interested?"

Zeff leaned against an oak tree while waiting for work, enjoying the shade. When he heard the man in front of the white picket fence surrounding the courthouse grounds, he jumped out into the sunlight and raised his hand in a big wave over his head, hat in hand. The blacksmith noticed him and waved him forward.

At first, the blacksmith felt put off by Zeff's obvious poverty. He figured a man must be awful lazy to be so poorly dressed and slovenly in his appearance. Zeff walked up with a big smile, holding his hand out for a handshake. "How do. Ah'm Zefford Ray Swinton. Ah ain't afeard o' no heat from a little ol' forge. Ah tended a brick kiln back on the mountain with muh family all muh life, so Ah'm not afeard o' no hard work, no way howdy."

The blacksmith smiled at Zeff's enthusiasm. He shook Zeff's hand, then pulled his glove back on as he looked Zeff up and down. He saw a country boy with a short, scrawny beard and stringy unwashed blond hair pushed back on both sides behind his ears. Zeff wore his only pair of dirty blue dungaree coveralls and a collarless shirt made from flour sacks. His scuffed and worn work boots looked shabby. Zeff had rolled up his pant legs into cuffs about four inches high. The pant legs ended a couple of inches above the ankles of his work boots. The bottoms of his muddy cuffs had become frayed and worn. Sweat stained his shapeless old felt hat. Despite his poor clothes, Zeff appeared to be strong and healthy. The blacksmith glanced around at the other men. He didn't see any other volunteers, so he gestured towards his rustic wagon. "Climb aboard then, Mister Swinton. Let's go to work."

After they sat down on the simple board bench at the front of the wagon, the blacksmith turned to Zeff. "My name is Jonathan Kressler, Mister Swinton. Since we'll be working side by side, please call me boss."

Zeff grinned agreeably. "Yessiree, Boss."

"So, Mister Swinton, tell me a bit about yourself. What brings you to Independence?"

In his heavy hillbilly accent, Zeff shared a brief summary of his life history. Zeff appeared to be thirty but said he was nineteen, which surprised Jon. Zeff explained how he took his wife, baby son, and little brother and set out to seek their fortune in the world, breaking free from his cruel, domineering father back in the Ozarks. It pleased Jon to hear Zeff wasn't a homeless vagabond. "An' what about y'all, Boss? Where does y'all's family hie from?"

"Well, sir, I was born in Hamburg, Germany, just over thirty-one years ago. I immigrated with my parents twenty years ago when

I was just eleven years old. We didn't speak a word of English at the time, but we soon learned. We eventually came west and settled down to farm here in Missouri. The land has been good to us. I met a lovely girl from Berlin, and we fell in love. That was, oh, about ten years back. She came to live with my parents and me. We are now the proud parents of three blond, bright-eyed little girls. We're still hoping to have a son or two. We work at it most diligently."

Zeff and Jon looked at each other with a grin. Jon winked and shook the reins over the backs of the two big draft mules. He soon turned onto a dirt track leading towards a big barn on a prosperous farm. Zeff saw horses and cows in a big pasture. They grew a large garden patch close by an attractive two-story farmhouse. Jon pulled the wagon up beside the barn and stopped. As Zeff climbed down, he noticed a young woman hanging clothes on a clothesline up by the house. The men worked as a team to remove the harness. Jon tied off the mules to a mature, sixty-foot tall cottonwood tree. Grasses and weeds grew along the ditch bank. Gesturing with his hand, Jon indicated for Zeff to enter the barn. Zeff surprised Jon when he suddenly jumped up and touched the bottom of the U of a rusted old used horseshoe hanging above the open door. It hung open side up to catch the luck. When Jon looked oddly at Zeff, Zeff shrugged. "Jest fer luck, doncha know."

Jon chuckled. "Horseshoes aren't just for your Irish luck, you know. They are good luck symbols for all blacksmiths. It's because we work with iron. Everyone knows iron resists wizardry and devilry. Come on in. I'll show you where we'll be working."

Jon showed Zeff around the smith located in an open lean-to shed attached to the side of the board and batten barn. He pointed to where he had piled charcoaled lengths of wood in an open bin near the forge. Zeff noticed another horseshoe hanging above the forge's massive brick hearth. With an embarrassed little grin, Zeff reached up and touched it. "Ah'm not superstitious, nor nothin', but Ah can use all the luck Ah can get these days."

Jon shook his head at Zeff's silliness and pointed at the forge. "Fill the hearth with charcoal and man the bellows, Mister Swinton. Let's go to work."

Zeff piled charcoal on top of the old ashes. He pushed down on a long lever braced on a crossbar over the huge leather and wood bellows. The other end of the handle lifted the lower paddle of the oversized bellows, forcing air out its small brass nozzle. The charcoal burst into flame, lit by the hot coals banked beneath the ashes.

Jon nodded. "Slow and easy does it, Mister Swinton. Keep the air blowing nice and steady there. Let me know when the flames burn out, and the coals begin glowing yellow and red hot."

"Yes, suh, Boss."

While Zeff worked the bellows, Jon pulled on a heavy leather apron and tied its bib close to his neck. The bottom of the apron brushed the toes of his work boots. Zeff quickly worked up a sweat from his physical labors so close beside the intense heat of the forge. It didn't take long for sweat to soak his shirt. He wiped the sweat off his forehead with his left hand while pumping the bellows with his right, then, a few minutes later, traded off hands. When the heat became so intense he could hardly stand it, he called out, "Hey, Boss. Ah thinks yer fire's hot, now."

Jon picked up a ten-foot-long strip of iron and inserted one end in the heat. After it began glowing, he moved the hot end to his big anvil and hammered it until it began curving down on the right. When he paused to heat the next segment of the band, Zeff's curiosity got the better of him. "Whatcha makin' there, Boss?"

"Well, now, the captain of a new Mormon immigrant handcart company that's forming up to go to the Utah Territory has commissioned a whole mess of iron tires for their carts. I'm building the bands to fit over their hardwood wheels, so they don't break traveling over rough ground."

"Oh. Ah see."

Jon pointed at several wood pegs in the side of the barn where several completed iron wheels hung, waiting to be mounted. "The carts have to last for the twelve or thirteen hundred-mile journey."

Jon picked up the hot iron band and put it back on his anvil. He picked up a three-pound hand-forged rounding hammer and set to work. The clanging of metal against metal didn't permit further conversation. Zeff focused on the job at hand, keeping the bellows

24

pumping and the fire burning white-hot. "Hotter, Mister Swinton. Faster if you please."

Zeff put his back into it. The heat soon flamed up to a roar then settled into white, red, and yellow logs of fiery hot charcoal. Jon put the tire back in the heat. "Take a breather, now, Mister Swinton. This's hot work."

"Y'all're tellin' me!"

Zeff backed away from the bellows and the forge's heat. He pulled a leather string from his pocket, pushed his damp hair back off his forehead into a sloppy ponytail, then tied it up off his sweaty neck. After Jon finished pounding the iron, he slipped it into the cooling trough, where it briefly hissed and steamed. Pointing wordlessly, Jon led Zeff over to a rain barrel at the corner of the barn's roof. He lifted a big tin ladle off a hand-forged nail above the barrel and dipped it in. He splashed the first ladle of water over his head to cool him down. The second went to a long drink. When he finished, he handed the ladle to Zeff. "Help yourself, Mister Swinton."

After they cooled down, Jon undid the bib of his apron and pulled off his damp shirt. The summer day and warm breeze had added to the stifling heat of the forge. Zeff followed suit. As they returned to work, Zeff couldn't help but notice a lot of burn scars, large and small, puckering Jon's otherwise smooth skin. Most of the scars appeared on his muscular hands and forearms, but he had other spots on his face, neck, and chest. Zeff had a few scars from flare-ups and hot cinders shooting out of the smoke hole on top of his brick kiln. He knew the pain that created such brands on a man's skin.

By the end of the day, Zeff's stamina and uncomplaining nature had impressed Jon. Most of his hired help gave up and left before the end of the day. The men doused themselves several times from the rain barrel and pulled on their dry shirts. "Come along, Mister Swinton. I'll give you a ride back to Independence Square."

After re-harnessing the mules, they climbed up on the small farm wagon and sat down on the board bench seat. Zeff pointed south. "It'd save me quite a hike if'n y'all could drop me off over that away. Muh little family's camped jus' outside o' town, there."

"Not a problem." They rode on for a while in companionable silence, resting while listening to the clip-clop of the mules' iron-shod hoofs hitting the dirt road. "Want to work again tomorrow, Mister Swinton?"

They looked each other in the eye. Zeff nodded yes. "Good. The pay's a buck and four bits a day. Can you find your way here in the morning, or do I need to come pick you up?"

"Thanks, Boss, but muh own mule will get me back tuh yer place jus' fine. Never yew fear."

"Good. Let's start earlier in the cool of the morning, and we'll take a siesta in the heat of the early afternoon."

"Rightcha are, Boss."

Jon looked over at Zeff, whom he had begun to respect despite his impoverished appearances. "Call me Jonny, Mister Swinton."

Zeff smiled. "Then please call me Zeff, Mister Kressler."

They pulled up to Zeff's little campsite in the trees to the side of the road. Jon pulled back on both reins. "Whoa."

Baby Boy rushed over, always curious to know everything. Sister Woman sat against a tree trunk, nursing Chester Ray. Jon handed Zeff six silver quarters. They shook hands. Zeff waved as Jon drove off back to his farm. "See you bright and early, Zeff."

"Yep. Ah'll be there, Jonny."

Baby Boy ran up and grabbed Zeff's forearm. "Who was that? What did 'e mean? What were y'all doin' all the day long? Can Ah go with y'all tomorrow? Can Ah? Huh?"

Zeff shoved the boy away and took a seat in the weeds and grasses by the cookfire. "One question at a time, Baby Boy. One gol-danged question at a time. Ah'm plumb knackered out."

Zeff worked the next three days bending wheels with Jonny. A man brought in an oxen yoke that needed a broken pin repaired while he waited. Friday afternoon, the men finished their siestas in the shade of the massive cottonwood tree growing on the ditch bank beside the barn. They splashed their faces with rainwater and went back to work. Fifteen minutes later, sweat drenched Zeff again. He felt like he hadn't taken a break.

Later that afternoon, an older man rode up on a big piebald gelding. He looked like a working cowboy, only he wore clean clothes. Jonny stepped up and shook his hand. "Captain Hanover, this is my new assistant, Zeff Swinton, from down in the Ozarks where his family worked a kiln. Zeff, meet Captain Hanover of that Mormon handcart company I told you about."

The captain inquired about the progress of his tire order, then inspected those already made and hanging on the side of the barn. Jonny turned to Zeff. "Time to cool down, now. Go ahead and bank the fire."

The captain leaned against a cedar post near the forge, making conversation while Jonny and Zeff returned the tools to their proper places. Zeff swept the floor, anxious for the long, hot day to end. Jonny took off his heavy leather apron and hung it on a peg by the big brick forge. The captain joined them as they washed up at the rain barrel. After they pulled their shirts back on, they walked the captain over to his gelding and stood talking. Several minutes later, Zeff looked at the gray-haired captain. "Ah heard about the California Gold Rush. Ah'm interested in goin' out West an' seekin' muh fortune, Captain Hanover. Now, what can y'all tell me 'bout yer plans?"

Zeff gave the captain his undivided attention. Jonny listened in, curious himself. He'd been tempted to go out West to try his hand in the goldfields more than once. The captain hung his arm off the saddle horn and leaned against the big horse. "Well, let me tell ya, men. So far, we have a hundred thirty-seven men, women and children signed on. Nearly all of 'em are recent Mormon converts."

Zeff held up his hand. "Converts? What're converts, Captain Hanover?"

"What? Oh. A convert is what we call a man who left his old church and converted to our faith. They're pretty much all newly baptized Mormons who want t' join the saints in Zion down in Utah."

"Oh."

"So far, we have fifty-four handcarts makin' the core o' the train. Then we have ten horses and three young men t' be our scouts an' guards. We also have three teamsters drivin' big freight wagons.

Each handcart will carry a tent, blankets, and food with a little room fer extra clothes an' the like. The freight wagons will carry weapons, tool chests, an' lots more food, especially flour, as there ain't none t' buy while crossin' the wide-open plains. We always take food in barrels we can use t' haul water over dry stretches of the trail when needed. We'll also be drivin' a small herd o' twenty or so head o' milk cows with four adventurous boys headin' t' the goldfields in California who signed up t' herd 'em along."

"Sounds right interestin', Captain. Does a person have tuh be one o' those Mormon converts tuh join up?"

"Nope. Though most are. Most of 'em are immigrants from England, Scotland, and Ireland. Yep, we're a mighty diverse group, yet we're all of one mind an' spirit in the Lord's restored church. We have a couple of gentiles coming along, too, though."

"Gentiles? What're gentiles?"

"Well, that's what we Mormons call non-Mormons."

"Huh. If'n Ah wanted tuh go out West with y'all, what would Ah need tuh do, Captain?"

Captain Hanover gave Zeff a long hard look. "Come see me after church services Sunday afternoon. We'll have a chat. Bring yer wife an' children if ya got 'em."

"Yep, Ah've got me a wife, a baby boy, an' muh little brover, too. Where does we find y'all?"

"Well, the church doesn't have a meeting house in Independence anymore, not since the Saints left the county and relocated to Far West, Missouri. Since then, we have met in a tent on Temple Lot that the Church used to own. It's four blocks due west o' the courthouse on Independence Square. Ya know where that is, doncha?"

Zeff looked at Jonny with a smile, remembering that's where they had first met. He nodded his head. Captain Hanover pulled himself up on his tall horse and touched his gloved hand to the front of his big hat. "See ya Sunday, then. Thanks, Jonny. If it's all right with yew, I'll start sendin' the handcarts around next week t' get their tires mounted. I'll pay ya meself from the Church's Perpetual Emigration Fund. Thanks again fer takin' care of us in a timely fashion."

28

Zeff and Jonny waved as the captain rode away. Zeff untied his mule. "Well, let me go see what Baby Boy shot fer our supper tonight. I'll be seein' ya Monday mornin' first thing."

Jonny reached into his pocket and pulled out a handful of coins. He counted out six dollars pay for the last four days and handed it to Zeff. "Oh, thanks, Jonny. Y'all have a good night now."

"Bye, Zeff. Get some rest. You've worked hard this week, and I appreciate it."

That Sunday, Zeff led his little family into the center of town to the white canvas tent on a large empty field called Temple Lot. The property used to be owned by The Church of Jesus Christ of Latter-day Saints, often referred to by its shorter nickname of the Mormon Church. Zeff's family sat in the shade of a tree while they waited for church services to end. After the congregation departed, Captain Hanover waved them to come in. They took seats on pine board benches and met with Captain Hanover for nearly an hour. At the end of the interview, Captain Hanover extended them an invitation to join his handcart company, departing the last week of July. They planned to walk the Oregon Trail's nearly thirteen-hundred miles, arriving in the Promised Land of Zion around the first week of November.

When they finished the interview, the captain handed Zeff a list of trail provisions recommended by Brigham Young, which he had initially published in *The Nauvoo Neighbor*. The captain had reprinted the list on cheap newsprint paper. He picked up a stub of a raw wood pencil and placed careful check marks next to several items. "Note the need fer flour, sugar, salt, pepper, rice, suet, potatoes, saleratus an' beans. Beans travel well, so always take along plenty."

Zeff interrupted, "What's saleratus, Captain? Do y'all mean celery?"

"No, no. It's what's in bakin' soda. Yew know, sodium bicarbonate. Fer cookin' bread an' stuff."

Sister Woman understood and nodded her head.

The captain shook everyone's hands, welcoming them to the company. After they walked out into the bright summer sun, Zeff handed Baby Boy the shopping list. Baby Boy folded it and shoved it into a hip pocket of his dirty dungarees with a shrug. Zeff told Sister Woman, "We don't need no list o' things we need tuh travel on the road. Don't need tuh read someone else's idears. We knows what we'll need, don't we, Sis?"

She nodded as she propped Chester Ray up over her shoulder to carry him back to camp.

Zeff scoured the town after work each evening until he finally located a used handcart. It took nearly every penny he had saved, but he bought it. The seller included a servicing of black crude oil to lubricate the hubs of both five-foot diameter wood wheels, bound in rusted iron. With a lot of grunting, Zeff managed to drag the handcart back to their rough camp outside the city limits. He arrived with blisters on both hands, grumbling about how they would need to buy extra heavy work gloves for Sis, Baby Boy, and himself.

The other members of the newly formed handcart company spent their days lightening their loads and buying food for the journey. The ladies sold their cherished china dishes. They sold their family heirloom clocks guarded on the journey from their family homes in Europe. They wouldn't fit in a handcart. They shed many a tear as they bartered for food with their mirrors, silk dresses, travel trunks, and anything else not an absolute necessity. The Swintons didn't have anything to sell, but Zeff worked hard for Jonny Kressler to earn cash to buy their supplies.

On Friday, July the twenty-fourth, Zeff showed up early at the forge for his last day on the job. Jonny welcomed him with a big smile. "So, Zeff, your handcart train leaves Monday morning, right?"

Zeff smiled and nodded yes. He unbuttoned the shoulder straps on his dungarees and let the bib fall to his waist. He unbuttoned the three buttons on the top of his grungy cotton shirt, preparing to pull it off over his head. Jon placed his hand on Zeff's arm. "Hold up a minute, there, Zeff."

Zeff pulled his shirt back down and looked quizzically at Jon. Jon smiled. "I've got an idea you might have some last-minute things you will be needing for your trip. Am I right?"

Zeff nodded yes.

"So, what do you say if I take my rig and drive you on your day's chores. We finished the cartwright repairs yesterday, so I have nothing pressing on my schedule. Come on. I happen to know a farmer who could use a good work mule. I'll introduce you, and you can sell it. Afterward, I'll take you around to the general store so you can finish your provisioning. Then, I'll cart your goods and you back to your camp. How does that sound, Zeff?"

"Gosh darn, Jonny, muh friend. That's real nice o' y'all. Sounds great!"

Together they hooked up the draft mule team to the simple farm wagon Jon had driven when he hired Zeff. Half an hour later, Zeff shook hands with a farmer with the bushiest beard he had ever seen. The farmer counted out seven gold ten-dollar coins, the first gold Zeff had ever held in his hand. Zeff handed the farmer the reins to his mule.

When they parked the rig alongside the alley behind the general store, Jonny handed Zeff ten silver dollars. "This's your pay for this week, plus a little thank you and bon voyage gift for your family. Let's go buy the last supplies you'll need and get you delivered to your camp."

Zeff impulsively turned on the board bench seat and gave Jonny a one-arm hug. "Thanks, Jonny. Yer a real good friend, doncha know."

It took them several hours of haggling over prices and loading the farm wagon. By midafternoon, Jonny delivered Zeff and his supplies to his camp. After they unloaded the wagon, Jonny handed Zeff a small slip of paper. "Here's my post office address, Zeff. I know you don't read or write, but maybe you can ask someone at your destination to send me a note and let me know how you are doing and where you ended up settling down. Sometimes I wish I were traveling with you, having adventures exploring unknown places and building a future from raw land. Unfortunately, my wife doesn't want me to take our daughters into the wilderness with wild Indians, so I will stay here. I'll be thinking about you, though. Good luck, Zeff."

Jon waved at Baby Boy and Sister Woman, busy examining the new pile of supplies. "Good luck to you, too, Sister Woman and Baby Boy. Safe journey!"

As Jonny turned onto the road to head back to his working farm, Zeff saw him raise his hand in farewell. Zeff and Baby Boy both waved back.

Monday, the day of departure, finally arrived. They joined the handcart company in a large open meadow four blocks west of Independence Square at the temporary church tent. The captain walked up and shook Zeff's hand. "Since ya have little one's in yer family, I'm assignin' ya a place in the middle o' the company fer the protection o' the young'uns. Now, please join us over by the support wagons. I've got some words t' say before we depart."

Baby Boy noticed they had even loaded the milk cows with provisions for the company, strapped onto packsaddles.

While everyone sat under the tent's canvas roof or stood around in the early morning sun, Captain Hanover reviewed the simple rules of the company in a loud, carrying voice. "Take off yer hats an' bow yer heads, now." He gave a long prayer of gratitude for being gathered together with a common goal. Then he asked for the Lord's guidance and safekeeping as they set out for Zion in the distant Great Salt Lake Valley. "...in the name o' Jesus Christ. Amen."

Everyone but the Swintons said amen in concert after him. They all put their hats back on and shuffled off to take their places with their handcarts. Several handcarts had thin slats of hardwood bent over the front and back of the box with a white canvas tied over the top, rather like miniature prairie wagons. Zeff and Sister Woman had this kind of cart, so Chester Ray could ride out of the sun. Everyone had loaded their carts to overflowing, protected by squares of heavy canvas.

Zeff walked up and gave Sister Woman and Baby Boy an exuberant hug. He then grasped the handles on both sides of the cart and took off, following his neighbors. Baby Boy pushed from behind. Sister Woman carried little Chester Ray for the first few hours until he became too heavy. She placed the little boy on top of their stores in the three-foot by four-foot wood box. She then ducked under the side handles and took her place beside Zeff. They both pushed on the yoke secured between the two long handles, leaning their weight against it to pull their five-hundred pounds of meager possessions behind them. Silently, they departed Independence for places unknown.

None of them looked back.

Chapter 3: Walking to the Promised Land

From Independence, they dragged and pushed their heavily laden cart through the low rolling hills surrounding Kansas City. Zeff admired how they had laid out the big city's streets in grids, so different from the meandering animal track pathways of his home and neighboring villages back in the Ozarks. Brick buildings up to four stories tall lined the main thoroughfares. The Swintons had never seen buildings that tall before. Even the courthouse in Independence Square rose only two stories, not counting its roof and bell tower.

Baby Boy excitedly pointed at the twin stacks of big stern-wheeler riverboats plying up and down the mighty Missouri River, their paddlewheels churning up the brown water in their wake. Black smokestacks belched great clouds of black coal smoke into the clear summer air. Zeff watched a steam locomotive pulling freight and passenger cars on the other side of the river, dumping more oily coal smoke in the air. "Imagine, Sister Woman, how nice an' easy life would be tuh ride in a railroad train. Wonder how much that would cost. Wouldn't that be fine?"

Shortly after the handcart company crossed an enormous iron bridge over the Missouri River, they entered a vast prairie of low rolling hills and grassy plains, broken up with only a few thickets of cottonwoods and stunted red cedars. They slowly left civilization behind at a walking pace.

On their first night out away from civilization, the captain ordered the handcarts in the center of the train to pull up in a circle around their freight wagons, horses, cows, and draft animals. Then he directed the head and tail of the handcart train to circle around the inner circle, creating a double barrier to protect the children and livestock. Each party began lighting their small, individual cookfires and preparing supper. As the men lit the fires, the women visited the support wagons to receive their daily share of foods supplied by the Perpetual Emigration Fund: rice, salt pork or bacon, sugar, dried fruit, and one pound of flour.

Sister Woman had grown up without neighbors. Shy, she kept her eyes averted from the nearby campers. Later that evening, she set a cast-iron skillet over the hot coals just as Chester Ray burst into tears, raising his voice in a lusty, penetrating wail. A mature woman tending a cookfire on the outer circle walked up to Sister Woman. Sister Woman looked up, startled at seeing a stranger so close by.

The gray-haired lady greeted her with a friendly smile and held her right hand out for a handshake. "Good evening. I'm Sister Baines."

Sister Woman looked up timidly, then quickly glanced over to Chester Ray, screaming his head off on a tattered quilt in the grass. She offered a limp hand and barely touched Sister Baines' fingers before pulling back as if burned. "Howdy. Ah'm Sister Woman."

The neighbor lady pointed at Chester Ray. "May I give you a hand with your little baby while you finish cooking your supper?"

"Oh! That'd be very kind o' y'all, ma'am."

Sister Baines picked up the baby with one hand, carefully holding his head, and propped him over her right shoulder. She gently patted the child on his back to settle him down, cooing quietly into his ear. She smiled over at Sister Woman, watching her with a suspicious squint and frown. Sister Woman examined the middle-aged woman with braided hair neatly wound into a large bun. A black crocheted hairnet secured the bun in place. Sister Woman found it very attractive and wished she owned a hairnet. She couldn't help but notice Sister Baines had kept her face, hands, and clothing clean, even though she had just walked the same distance that hot summer day as everyone else.

Sister Baines gracefully sank down onto Chester Ray's small piece of quilt and tucked her legs to the side. "My three children are all grown up and married. It's just my husband, Gilbert, and me, now. I miss taking care of young children. We come from London Town. It's so nice to make your acquaintance."

Sister Woman began frying prairie chicken dipped in cornmeal. Earlier, she had picked a handful of bitter herbs, dandelions, lamb's quarters, and a handful of delicious pinecone mushrooms to wilt in the pan just before serving. While Sister Woman cooked, she glanced over at Lorna Baines and noticed a wedding ring with a

35

touch of jealousy. Neither her mother nor she had ever owned a wedding band. They couldn't afford such frippery.

"Now, tell me, dear. What's your Christian name?"

"Oh...uh...well, muh maw named me Effie, but Ah've only ever been called Sister Woman since Ah growed up. When Ah was a littlun, they called me Sister Gal."

"Well, dear, you may have noticed how Mormons address each other as brother or sister in the Lord's work and in God's family. So, it feels awkward for me to call you Sister Woman. It doesn't sound right to me. What's your married name, dear?

"Uh. It's Swinton. Effie Swinton."

"May I call you Sister Swinton? You may call me Sister Baines. Would that be agreeable to you, dear?"

Sister Woman squinted her eyes as she thought on it. She didn't like having a stranger changing her name. But she didn't want to be rude first thing off the bat. She shrugged and nodded. "Yes, ma'am. Uh, Sister Baines."

Lorna Baines pointed over at Baby Boy leaning against the wheel of their handcart, whittling a willow bark whistle. "Good. Now, what's the name of your son?"

"Chester Ray, muh firstborn, is the baby yer holdin' in yer arms, Sister Baines. That older boy over there's muh little brover, Baby Boy."

"I see. Very well. However, I do believe Baby Boy is a nick-name, isn't it? What is his given name?"

"Well, now. Let me think on it a minute. He's been called Baby Boy ever since he was borned. Oh, yeah. Muh maw named 'im Connal. Thas right. Connal Lee Swinton."

Sister Woman finished cooking and placed the hot pan on the grassy ground beside the small fire. She stood up and massaged her lower back. "Zefford Ray! Baby Boy! Come git yer supper, now!"

As the boys approached, Sister Woman reached out for Chester Ray. "Thanks, Sister Baines. Ah appreciate yer kind help tendin' Chester Ray while Ah was a cookin'."

"Oh, no problem. Let me know if you need anything else, Sister Swinton. I'm just right over there at the next campfire out. Good night, dear."

"Um, good night."

After supper, Zeff lay back exhausted, gazing up at the bright stars. The Milky Way formed a soft white band across the sky, with no moon to overwhelm its mild glow. Sister Woman snuggled up under Zeff's right armpit with Chester Ray asleep on her stomach and his head cradled between her small breasts. Baby Boy reclined on Zeff's other side with his legs crossed at their ankles and his hands pillowed behind his head. He saw a shooting star and sat up. "D'ja see that?"

"What?"

"A shootin' star. Thas what. Wow!"

"I missed it. Wait! There's another one."

Baby Boy laid down using Zeff's left arm as a pillow. "Hardly never see no shootin' stars. Ain'tcha supposed tuh make a wish on 'em or somethin'?"

No one answered him.

The handcart company followed Little Blue River's northwesterly course, never straying far from water. Baby Boy overheard a couple struggling with their cart behind them that day. The woman cursed the handcarts, calling them two-wheeled torture devices. The man assured her God had given them a handcart to teach them humility.

A couple of evenings later, they set up camp alongside the broad sluggish stream. It would soon guide them out of Kansas Territory and into the Territory of Nebraska. With such pleasant weather, Zeff didn't raise their small tent. The sound of running water in the creek tinkled like music just steps away. Baby Boy helped his older brother and sister set up their simple camp and then ran off to explore the creek bed. Zeff watched him scamper off, wondering where he found all his energy. Zeff and Sister Woman only wanted to sit down and rest after walking all day.

Baby Boy stopped and gazed into the flowing waters. If he saw any fish, he would return with the fishing pole after supper and try his luck. He had overheard their fellow travelers discussing how the river ran with green sunfish, which made for good eating. After he rounded a curve out of view of the camp, he paused to pee in the river. Small rocks worn smooth by the running water lined the creek. He picked up a couple of flat rocks and skipped stones, dawdling on his way back. The river current ran too rough to really skip stones, but he didn't care. He enjoyed the mindless fun of testing his skill at throwing horizontally.

When Zeff finished setting up camp the next evening, he sought out Captain Hanover. The captain had a stern look with a permanent crease between his bushy eyebrows from squinting in the sun. The stocky man had strong muscles from a lifetime of hard physical labor. When not guiding Mormon converts across the plains, he made his living ranching on a big spread south of Provo. Zeff later learned he had retired as a captain in the Mormon militia and had fought in the Fort Utah War.

Zeff walked over to the company's captain sitting beside a stone ring around his camp fireplace. He arrived as the captain's young third wife began cooking. She appeared young enough to be the captain's daughter. His first wife had grown too old for the rigors of travel, so she stayed home with her adult children and myriads of grandchildren to run his sprawling cattle ranch. His second wife had too many young children, so she stayed home to supervise the captain's farm on Hobble Creek next to his cattle ranch. The captain had established each family in their own home on the border of the two properties, within easy walking distance. His youngest wife had the strength to make the two-way trip and take care of him. She hadn't yet born any children, though not for lack of trying – which kept the captain quite content during the travails of their journey. She lived with the captain in his first wife's home. The captain would give her her own home once she began bearing children.

Zeff touched the brim of his hat as he approached. The captain nodded gravely, then waved his hand towards a stump of a log beside him, inviting Zeff to have a seat. Both men had sweat stains drying on their long-sleeved shirts, circling their underarms, and trailing down their chests and backs in narrowing V's. Sweat stained their hatbands. The temperature had climbed to nearly ninety degrees as they labored for hours under the day's intense summer sun.

"How're yer hands doin' there, Brother Swinton? They gettin' used t' pushin' an' pullin' yer cart, yet?"

"Yes, suh. Sure 'nough. The blisters're mostly gone at last. Our hands're gettin' pert near as tough as our work gloves."

They both smiled and nodded. Zeff sat with his elbows on his knees, looking down at his hands. His hair fell forward like a dirty blond veil. He didn't know how to start a conversation. Having lived such an isolated life in the backwoods, he had never developed the skill of making small talk. A breeze blew sweet-smelling cedar smoke into his face. He looked up to find the captain's eyes on him. "So, what can I be doin' fer ya, Brother Swinton? Didja have somethin' ya wanted t' ask me?"

"Yes, suh. Ya see, back home in the mountains, Ah hunted ever day, startin' soon as Ah could carry me a shotgun. Course, we had plenty o' game in the woods along the creeks an' rivers. Ah'm of a mind that Ah'd like tuh fetch some fresh food fer our pot. Ya see we're used tuh fresh meat, not yer salted meats like from the support wagons. Now, Ah've spotted some game in the trees along the trail, but none're close enough fer huntin' afoot. Back home, Ah never had tuh walk very far from home, an' Ah found plenty o' game. It's different out west here on these barren plains, though."

The captain nodded his agreement as he gazed around at the undulating grassy landscape on both sides of the river.

"Here, a man needs a ride so's 'e can get tuh the game an' then, tuh bring it back tuh camp."

"Yep."

"Ah seen some antelope earlier in the day. Bound tuh be some deer an' turkeys back in the trees."

"Uh-huh. Probably so."

"So, Captain Hanover, could Ah please borrow me a horse or a mule so's Ah can get in a little huntin' afore it gets too dark?"

Captain Hanover nodded once, struggled to his weary feet, and beckoned for Zeff to follow him. The company possessed ten saddle horses and four saddles. They kept the horses by the freight wagons and draft animals in the center of the camp at night. The captain pointed at a dark brown mare with black points. She stood saddled as she drank from a noisy feeder creek running through the camp. "Take that one, Brother Swinton. Let's see what ya can do."

"Why, thank yew, Captain Hanover, suh." Zeff jumped over the creek, tightened the cinch, and climbed into the saddle. He turned the horse towards his handcart, where Sister Woman and Baby Boy worked preparing supper. When he rode up, he waved at Baby Boy. "Hand me muh rifle an' bag o' bullets. Ah'm gonna try fer some prairie chicken or maybe a pheasant fer our supper. Ah won't be gone long."

"Can Ah come?" Baby Boy looked up at his older brother anxiously, pleading with sad, puppy dog eyes. "Can Ah come, please? Please?" He jumped up and down, excited to go along, nodding his head yes.

Zeff scowled impatiently. "Well, grab a rope, an' let's go afore it gets too dark tuh see. Get a move on!"

"Yippee!"

Baby Boy retrieved a small coil of rope from the handcart and shrugged his arm through it to carry on his shoulder. He grabbed Zeff's hunting rifle, slung it over his back, and picked up the little canvas bag of bullets and shot. Zeff reached down a hand and hoisted Baby Boy up behind him on the back of his saddle. Baby Boy wrapped his skinny arms around Zeff's slender waist, then waved goodbye to Sister Woman with a big smile on his face at riding.

An hour and a half later, the two great hunters returned to camp. Two pheasants, three prairie chickens, and a couple of quails hung off the saddle horn, their legs tied together with a piece of twine from Zeff's pants pocket. Baby Boy toted a wild turkey on his back, holding its legs over his shoulders. Its five-foot-wide wings flopped open upside-down, bouncing beside the boy's slim back to the rhythm of the horse's footsteps. Sister Woman picked what she wanted to cook for the family, plus a pheasant to share with her new friend, Lorna Baines. Zeff and Baby Boy took the rest of the game over to the captain's campfire. "Hey, Captain. Thuh huntin' ain't too bad 'round these parts if'n y'all knows where tuh look. Could anyone in the camp use some fresh meat?"

"Why, thank yew kindly, Brother Swinton. Mighty neighborly of ya. In fact, hardly any of us have had fresh meat fer a while now. Thanks fer thinkin' o' yer neighbors." He turned away to distribute the game to his followers, then stopped and turned back. "I'll have one o' the boys cast some bullet slugs fer ya t' replace what ya used up. We've got buckshot in the wagons when ya run low, too."

"Mighty kind o' y'all, Captain. Thanks."

"Thank yew. The ladies will appreciate havin' some fresh game."

"Maybe Ah could do this again tomorrow, soon's we set up camp at the end o' the day."

"Sure thing, Brother Swinton. Good idea. Yer welcome t' borrow a horse whenever ya need one."

Zeff and Baby Boy became the unofficial hunters of the small handcart train, which made them very popular. Many immigrants came from places like London and Copenhagen, where they never learned how to hunt and butcher. They appreciated having experienced hunters in their group. Zeff and Baby Boy brought in fresh game every day, fowls, deer, antelopes, and even a Buffalo calf to help feed the camp.

Neither Zeff nor Sister Woman had ever had any religious instruction. They found the customs of these devout Mormons strange. Every morning they watched as everyone knelt beside their bedrolls in prayer before they began their day. Then, each family group said a blessing on the food before eating breakfast. As soon as they broke camp, the captain led them in prayer, asking God for a safe and successful day's journey. After a while, he began inviting other men in the company to lead their morning prayers. Everyone said a blessing on the food at their noon-day rest and again at supper. The Swintons watched all bemused as everyone in the camp knelt at night beside their blankets before turning in. They just shrugged, snuggled into their dirty quilts, and made love as quietly as possible.

Everyone in the company lacked worldly goods. Most barely owned a change of clothes, a few blankets, cooking tools and a souvenir or two from their lives in the old country to remind them of home and family. One young lady cherished a cutting of a wild rose she had brought with her from her mother's cottage in Ireland. Zeff

41

and Sister Woman had grown up the poorest of them all, yet they didn't know it. They knew no other way. Just as Zeff and Baby Boy shared the food they trapped, shot, or fished out of the rivers, the others in the community shared their meager possessions and good fortune among the company. They didn't leave anyone out. Everyone felt a growing sense of community through their shared travails.

They rested from walking on Sundays. The captain conducted sacrament services in the early morning, leaving the afternoons for the ladies to launder their clothing while the camp relaxed. The captain invited the Swintons to join their congregation, sitting in a big circle. While they didn't understand much of the speeches and rituals, like passing around little pieces of broken bread called the sacrament, they enjoyed listening to the hymns. They quickly learned to join the chorus in a firm amen at the end of prayers.

After two weeks on the trail, everyone developed new muscles and endurance. The work didn't seem so onerous as when they started out. Zeff and Sister Woman had been skinny to begin with. Their bones and muscles became more sharply defined as they lost weight. It showed on their faces. Baby Boy grew more muscular and taller as he continued his growth spurt. His muscles didn't hurt so much from walking and pushing the handcart, as they ached from his bones growing bigger. He sprouted pubic hair, which he found amusing. He liked to see himself growing up and becoming hairier like his manly older brother.

Chapter 4: Classes on the Trail

One evening after supper, Lorna Baines strolled over, her travel bonnet still on her head. Zeff began to stand up, but she waved him to stay lounging on the sod. "No, no, Brother Swinton. Don't get up." She crossed her ankles and sank gracefully to the ground beside Sister Woman, who sat nursing little Chester Ray. "Sister Swinton, the captain asked me to start a school for the youngsters every evening after supper since I taught school back in London Town for many years."

Sister Woman nodded her head. "Well, that explains it then!"

"Oh? Explains what?"

"Why, the fine way y'all have with yer words."

Lorna Baines chuckled and shrugged modestly. "So, I wondered how much schooling you have had and if you would like to join my evening classes."

"Oh! Well, Sister Baines. Ah've never had me no schoolin'. None a tall. We lived back in the woods, doncha know. Muh Maw an' muh Paw neither one knowed how tuh read nor write, so there weren't no one tuh learn us."

"Oh, my! That's just plumb awful, Sister Swinton. None of you know how to read or do your additions and subtractions?"

"Nope. 'Fraid not."

"Well, I do so hope you will join my little classes. You, too, Brother Swinton. And you, too, Baby Boy. It's important to know how to read and write in this world. You need to be able to make calculations so men don't take advantage of you in your business dealings. I'll fetch you along tomorrow after supper for your first lessons, all right, dear? How does that sound?"

"Oh. Ah don't knows, Sister Baines. Ah'm a little old tuh learn new stuff, doncha think? 'Sides, Ah'm a maw, now, not a little kid."

"Now, dear, some of the students will be older than you, and several will be bigger than you, but we all need to improve ourselves each day. Size and age don't matter. Learning matters. Please do join us. Please?"

Sister Woman looked over at Baby Boy enthusiastically nodding his head yes. Then she glanced at Zeff, who sat frowning, shaking his head no. Sister Woman shrugged. "Ah guess Ah'm ready. Ah always wondered what it would be like tuh read an' write an' do calculations."

That evening as the little Swinton family sat around their dwindling fire, they heard someone strumming a banjo. After the player warmed up his fingers and tuned the strings, he began playing popular folk songs, singing the words as he played. When he started *Oh! Susanna* others joined in singing the chorus. When the song finished, Baby Boy heard soft applause from the campfires surrounding them. The banjo player began singing *Jeanie with the Light Brown Hair*. A flute began accompanying the man's singing to Baby Boy's delight. The singer went on to play *Camptown Races*. His small audience sat up and clapped along with the driving beat. By the second stanza, everyone enthusiastically joined in singing Doo-dah! Doo-dah! They all enjoyed the songfest. He wound down his sing-along with *Slumber My Darling*. The song ended with a soft, fervently sung, "And pray that the angels will shield thee from harm."

Baby Boy laid back down and snuggled up beside Zeff with his arm over Zeff's chest. His hand rested on Sister Woman's arm on Zeff's other side. Warm and comfortable, he drifted off to a dreamless sleep.

The following evening, they heard a handbell ringing from the wagons in the center of the camp. Sister Woman stood up from scouring her fry pan with a fistful of damp sand beside the river. She spotted Lorna Baines standing on the tailgate of a freight wagon, ringing a little brass bell on the end of a wood handle. Always curious, Baby Boy jumped up to see. They heard Lorna Baines' clear voice. "School starts in five minutes. Don't be late! It's time to start class."

Sister Woman picked up Chester Ray and propped him over her shoulder, then grabbed Baby Boy by the hand. "Let's go see what it's like tuh learn stuff. Come on."

They arrived to find Lorna Baines sitting on the freight wagon's open tailgate, smiling a welcome to each new arrival. The group consisted of a few older teenage boys, a young teenage girl bigger and taller than Sister Woman, and seven young children who appeared to be between five and ten years old. Sister Woman and Baby Boy sat down on the ground Indian style, where they had a clear view of Lorna Baines.

Baby Boy shyly glanced around at the other boys. He had seen them during the first two weeks of their journey but hadn't yet spoken to any of them. The older boys stood taller and brawnier than Baby Boy. The little kids squirmed and fidgeted while their mothers watched from behind the impromptu outdoor classroom. Lorna Baines stood up. The talking settled down. "For those who may not know me yet, I'm Sister Baines. I taught school in a little country school in Dunstable, just north and west of the great city of London. Now, if you know your ABCs, please raise your hands."

She stopped and noted that all but the youngest boys and the Swintons had their hands raised. "Excellent. And how many of you know how to read?"

One of the younger girls and the older teens raised their hands. "How many are good spellers?"

Only one older boy and the teenage girl raised their hands. Lorna spent a few more minutes asking how many knew addition, subtraction, multiplication, and division. Only the three oldest teens still had their hands up by the end of the questions. The teenage girl had raised her hand for everything. Lorna asked her to take aside those who could read and lead them in reading aloud from *The Eclectic First Reader for Young Children*. She handed the book to the girl with an encouraging smile.

Lorna Baines then invited the toddlers and the Swintons to step over to the other side of the wagon. She pulled out a small handheld slate in a raw oak frame. "Now, children, let's start with the alphabet. These are the letters that make all the words. It's where you start to learn how to read and write."

She drew a capital A on the chalkboard. "This is the capital letter AY. Say it after me."

She heard mumbling of AY's from the small class.

"It can be pronounced in different ways, depending on its usage in a word. It can sound like AH, as in father, and like AA, as in

45

exact. It can also sound like AW, as in fall. Then, the basic AY sound as in able and share."

She wiped the chalkboard with a rag and wrote a small letter a. "This is what the letter AY looks like in lower case." She patiently took them through all the letters. When she reached Z, she concluded for the evening. The sun had nearly set in the west, casting long shadows across her small class. "I'll see you all tomorrow at the same time. Well done, everyone. Goodbye and goodnight."

The next afternoon the train stopped a bit early when they arrived at an ideal campground often used between the Overland Trail and the river. Since he had time before supper, Baby Boy decided he felt like fishing and didn't accompany Zeff on his hunting expedition. An hour later, he returned with a couple of largemouth bass and half a dozen smaller green sunfish, already cleaned by the riverside. Sister Woman happily took the sunfish. Baby Boy picked up the bass and carried them over to Sister Baine's campfire. "Hiya, Sister Baines. Would y'all like some fish tonight?"

"Why, how thoughtful of you, Brother Connal. Thank you."

"Baby Boy."

"I beg your pardon?"

"Muh name's Baby Boy."

Lorna Baines paused and looked closely at the scrawny fisherman in front of her. She reached out and picked up the bass by their gills. "Surely, Baby Boy is your nickname. Didn't Sister Swinton tell me your mother named you Connal Lee?"

"Yep. Thas right. But Ah'm called Baby Boy."

'Oh, all right. Baby Boy it is then for now, anyway. Thank you for these lovely fish. Quite a catch!"

"Yer welcome."

"So, I'll see you later in class, right?"

Baby Boy had started to turn away, but he paused and looked at Lorna Baines with a puzzled frown. "Why?"

Lorna Baines then looked puzzled herself. "Why? Well, so you can learn your ABCs."

"Don't need yer class no more fer that, ma'am."

"Oh? And why not?"

"Cause Ah learnt 'em last night."

"You learned the entire alphabet?"

"Yep."

She tossed the fish down on the sod, delicately wiped off her fingers on her long apron, folded her arms, and gave Baby Boy a challenging stare to prove it.

Baby Boy reacted by folding his arms, standing up tall, and reciting, "Ay, bee, cee, dee, ee, ef, gee." After a second deep breath, he concluded, "...ex, wye, zee."

As he recited the alphabet in order without missing a letter, Lorna Baines' eyebrows rose higher and higher. A smile broke out on her face. When he finished, she clapped her hands delightedly. "Oh! Well done, Baby Boy. Well done. And you learned that just from yesterday's one class?"

"Yep. Ah guess y'all're a good teacher, Sister Baines."

"Well, I declare. You certainly are a fast learner. Come to class this evening anyway, Baby Boy. I'll give you a board of tree bark and a piece of charcoal. You can practice writing the letters as I write them. I will need to review the alphabet for those in the class slower than you, so you might as well use the review to practice writing. How does that sound, young man?"

"Well...Ah guess." Baby Boy frowned. He didn't look forward to sitting with little kids after supper each night. That evening, he showed up and learned how to block print the alphabet in capital and lowercase letters.

Later, Baby Boy sat gazing into the crimson embers of their dying cookfire, reviewing the alphabet and thinking about reading and writing. From somewhere across the camp, he heard a flute playing warmup scales, first up, then down. After a quiet pause, the flutist began playing a lovely tune, the loveliest melody he had ever heard. Days later, he met the young Irish woman who loved to play Mozart on her polished wood flute.

The company camped a bit early that Saturday so everyone would have time to bathe in the river, their weekly routine, getting cleaned up for sacrament service on Sunday. Baby Boy joyfully leapt up on the back of the mare Zeff borrowed. They returned later with a wild turkey and three fat squirrels, dragging a young doe behind the horse. Zeff knew Sister Woman liked squirrels because

47

they reminded her of home, so he dropped them off at their cookfire. Zeff and Baby Boy took the turkey and doe over to the captain's campfire. Zeff pointed his thumb over his shoulder at the deer behind them. "Howdy, Captain Hanover. Baby Boy did some really good shootin' today. Lookee here!"

Captain Hanover stood up and walked around them to admire the doe. "Hm. One clean shot. You sayin' the boy did this?"

"Yep. Baby Boy's been a straight shooter since 'e was ten years old. 'E's even better, now. Course, 'e don't get much practice in 'cause we's only got one shotgun a tween the both of us."

The captain gave Baby Boy a stern look. "Yew, come with me."

The captain marched through the encampment to one of the freight wagons parked in the center of the two circles. Zeff followed him, leading the horse dragging the large doe behind it. The captain rooted around in the back of the wagon and then pulled out a waterproof canvas bag containing a long, thin wooden box. He handed it to Baby Boy with both hands. Baby Boy accepted the package. He knelt down, placed the box on the ground, stripped off the canvas bag, and opened the lid. "Look, Zeff. A brand new huntin' rifle. Oh!"

"Ya have permission t' borrow it fer the duration o' the trip, Baby Boy. Do ya know how t' clean an' maintain a shotgun?"

Baby Boy nodded. A huge grin broke out on his face. "Wow! Fer me? Zeff, look! We can both hunt now. Yippee!"

Baby Boy leaned over and began expertly stripping the rifle without any hesitation. He ran his hands lovingly across the beautifully varnished stock and blackened steel barrel. He checked the magazine to make sure it didn't hold any bullets. He quickly reassembled the rifle and stood up, grinning. "Thanks, Captain. Ah really 'preciate the loan. Ah'll take good care of it fer y'all."

"Yep, I do believe ya will, at that."

Baby Boy took off jogging towards their camp to show off his new rifle to Sister Woman. The captain helped Zeff untie the doe and take the saddle and bridle off the young mare. "Ya say Baby Boy's been a good shot from the beginnin', Zeff?"

"Yep. Thas right. Muh Paw called 'im a hinstinctive shooter. He hardly even has tuh aim. He fires one-handed from the hip as much as with both arms extended like Ah shoots. Fact is, pert near ever thin' Ah've ever showed 'im since 'e was a little tyke, 'e picked up quick. Never had tuh repeat muhself, neither. Ah only had tuh show 'im somethin' once. All it ever takes with that boy. He's a fast learner, seems t' me like."

"I'd say. Lucky fellow. I can't wait t' see what he does with 'is own shotgun."

"Y'all won't be disappointed, Captain."

"Thanks fer the meat, Brother Swinton. We'll butcher up this pretty doe an' share the meat around. Have a nice evening."

"Bye, now."

"Good night.

"Thanks again."

That evening Baby Boy cuddled the rifle in his arms as he laid down with his back against Zeff. He heard the eerie call of a wolf far out across the plains. A few moments later, he listened to a mournful howl from farther away, answering the first wolf. Smiling, he drifted to sleep, dreaming about hunting with his own rifle.

As the journey passed westwards through the plains of Nebraska, the handcart train followed the old trail of mountain men, explorers, and fur hunters. Later, men headed to the California gold rush, and the Mormon pioneers had cleared the road even more. The company entered a drier, more desolate land.

Zeff found the grassy open plains along the Overland Trail strange and lifeless. Used to having his horizons mere feet away, the wide-open skies made him feel small and insignificant. He had never seen such a big sky, a blue dome running from flat horizon to flat horizon. He felt distinctly uncomfortable walking the treeless plains, nervous and anxious. Once he entered the shallow swales alongside the waterways, often lined with small trees, he could relax and hunt. Zeff and Baby Boy had to travel further and further away to bring fresh meat to the camp. They worked diligently every evening without fail.

A few days later, they pulled up and camped outside of Fort Kearney. Before their group prayer that morning, Captain Hanover had explained how the fort served as a rest stop and resupply station, not a defensive fortification for fighting Indians. He told everyone who had letters to take them to the post office in the fort. "It's the last one yew'll find fer a couple o' weeks after this."

Baby Boy saw two clapboard buildings, each two stories tall, surrounded by young trees, sod huts, military tents, and a couple of tipis. The fort also maintained large herds of livestock so travelers could trade their tired beasts of burden for fresh horses, oxen, donkeys, mules, and milk cows. Several of their company visited the general store and post office.

The captain rode to the general store in the Fort with his three support wagons. The night before, the teamsters had given him a list of items they needed. He had drawn down money from a bank in Independence for the immigrants of his company from the program set up by The Church of Jesus Christ of Latter-day Saints in 1849 to help finance members' long, expensive journeys to Great Salt Lake City. The church called the program the Perpetual Emigration Fund. The recipients all promised to repay the fund in money or goods so the fund could help future members.

The captain heaved a big sigh of relief to find the Fort stocked with generous supplies of bacon preserved in barrels of bran. He bought all the dried fruit leftover from the prior fall's harvest, though he had wished for much more. The store didn't have enough salted pork, so he purchased smoked hams, even though they cost more. When he had everything properly loaded and secured, he sent the wagons back to camp while he asked about the conditions of the trail ahead of them.

The land they traveled through after leaving Fort Kearney did not have forests or even scattered trees with wood for burning. They hadn't seen any coal since leaving civilization back in Kansas City. Captain Hanover patiently explained how previous travelers had learned to pick up buffalo chips to burn for cooking fuel. Several of the ladies looked at each other, their faces puckered in distaste. "It's not as bad as all that. Try it. They're clean t' handle an' better than eatin' cold food an' raw meat."

That evening the ladies and children of the company spread out into the flatlands around their campsite. They picked up all the buffalo chips they could find and placed them in their aprons or under their arms to carry back to their campfires. The chips burned with little flame and needed frequent stoking to stay hot. Lorna Baines delicately called the dried piles of feces Plains Oaks. Burning buffalo poop didn't bother Baby Boy at all. He thought they smelled like burning grass, not like animal manure. Sister Woman liked how the fuel burned hot with no sparks. The next day Lorna Baines joked with Sister Woman how she didn't have to use pepper on her steaks when she fried them over Plains Oaks.

Chapter 5: Stormy Weather

The grasslands stretched flat as a tabletop in all directions. A day's march away, Captain Hanover became concerned when he noticed dark clouds on the western horizon in front of them. He ordered everyone to make camp early and put up their tents before doing anything else. "We might be in fer some severe weather, Brothers an' Sisters."

Before they had all the tents erected, a strong gust of wind blew through the camp. Hats and unsecured tents blew away, causing everyone to scramble. The sky darkened ominously. Baby Boy watched, concerned, as he saw an enormous curving band of clouds drawing ominously nearer and lower. Suddenly, a ray of light showed on the distant flat horizon. Overhead, a massive lightning strike shot across the purple-gray clouds, appearing to jump from left to right as well as down from the heavens. Rumblings of thunder grew louder and more bombastic by the second.

Splat! Plop! Baby Boy and Zeff jumped when they heard a chunk of frozen ice strike the ground. It bounced over and landed on the little tent they struggled to erect in the wind. "Quick, Sis, git yerself an' Chester Ray in the tent, now!"

A jagged piece of hail as big as Chester Ray's pudgy fist struck Baby Boy's face. "Ouch!" He put up his hand to touch where it hit his cheek. His fingers came away bloody.

"Git in the tent! Git in the tent, now!"

They all ducked in. Sister Woman lay down and curled herself around Chester Ray, eyes wide. More and more hailstones struck the canvas of their shelter. Zeff pushed Baby Boy over next to Sister Woman, then threw himself over the huddle to provide another layer of protection. They heard people crying out in alarm and pain as the noise and onslaught grew louder and more intense. Within minutes, white ice covered the ground. The noise became quieter and softer. Baby Boy raised his head to look out the little peaked opening of their tent. "Hey. It's rainin', now. The hail stopped. That sure was the biggest hail Ah've ever seen."

"Me, too, Baby Boy." Zeff pushed himself up on one arm so he could see out. "Sure 'nough. Now it's jus' a rainin'. Great. Jus' what we need."

The wind, lightning, and thunder increased, growing louder and louder. Water began flowing into the tent, soaking along the sod floor. They sat up, resting on their knees, trying to keep dry. After the severe dark clouds of the storm front passed by, the rain settled into a steady drizzle. The sky brightened, but low gray clouds sat above them for as far as they could see. The setting sun brought no let-up in the rain.

Hunger finally motivated Zeff and Sister Woman to try and build a fire. Unfortunately, the rain had soaked the small number of buffalo chips they had gathered. They wouldn't take a spark. Bored and hungry, Baby Boy crawled out and stood up in the rain with water flowing down his face. He peered around but couldn't spot any fires in the camp. Sister Woman turned to their handcart. Zeff held up the canvas cover while she rummaged inside. She found a wedge of Johnny Cake leftover from breakfast and a small venison steak from supper the night before. She served the cornbread with a small drizzle of molasses. Baby Boy felt glad to have something to eat, cold and stale or not.

The rain poured steadily all night long. Everyone in the camp woke up damp, chilled, and miserable. Without fires, they couldn't cook even the simplest porridge or beverage. The sound of constantly drumming rainfall dulled their senses. They couldn't determine the time of day. Captain Hanover strolled over to the support wagons, trying to find something he could offer his company to eat. But everything they carried, like salt pork, flour, onions, and beans, required cooking before it could be eaten. He gave up with a shrug. He checked his pocket watch and began walking around the soggy camp. "Sorry folks, there's no breakfast till we get outta this rain. Mornin' prayers will be in thirty minutes. Strike yer tents an' get packed up. We're movin' out. Watch yer step, now, as the ground's mighty slippery."

They all felt miserable as they set out that morning. Baby Boy scowled. "Muh stomach's a touchin' muh backbone."

Nobody responded. They all felt the same. They stopped as close as they could estimate to midday and huddled together under the gloomy skies. Those ladies who could find food already prepared shared it. Everyone received a small portion. The small rations did not relieve their gnawing hunger. The cowboys distributed a small drink of fresh milk to everyone. Captain Hanover prodded them to move out. They manned their handcarts with a great deal of grumbling.

The rain tapered off that afternoon. Several of the women and children began shivering, despite the exercise of pushing their carts in the mud. Captain Hanover walked through the camp. "School's canceled fer tonight on account o' Sister Baines slipped an' sprung 'er ankle this afternoon. Plus, there's no light t' see by."

With nothing dry to burn, the entire camp went to bed hungry. Again. The sheer physical energy expended pushing a heavy load across the wilderness for a long day left them burning their bodies' fat and energy reserves. Hunger gnawed at them as they curled up in their damp blankets. The three Swintons hugged each other to share bodily warmth.

The following morning, a couple of the more experienced woodsmen managed to start two small fires. Captain Hanover asked the ladies to pool their resources and make enough Lumpy Dick for everyone. Soon the bedraggled ladies began sprinkling flour over small pots of boiling milk, a little bit at a time. They carefully pushed the flour into the milk so it became lumpy, careful not to stir it. About fifteen minutes later, it thickened up like porridge. They served it up with butter and a pinch of salt. Baby Boy scowled as he dug in. "Ah hates Lumpy Dick without no jam or honey like at home."

Sister Woman patted him on the back. "Eat up, Baby Boy. At least ya won't go hungry this mornin'. That stuff sticks tuh yer ribs it does."

After eating the entire bowl, the Lumpy Dick sat like a stone in Baby Boy's stomach until midafternoon.

The minute they set up camp that evening, Zeff and Baby Boy borrowed two horses and rode out, determined to find real food. It took them a good quarter hour's cantering before they came upon a

54

small cluster of bison. They each shot a calf. The startled bulls turned and watched, angry at the noise, snorting in a threatening way. They scraped at the ground with their big front hooves as though preparing to give chase. The cows and calves scattered. When Zeff and Baby Boy arrived in camp an hour later with two calves cleaned and ready to skin and butcher, a great cheer went up among their neighbors. Everyone pitched in to butcher them. Within hours, each campfire began frying, roasting, or stewing the dry lean fresh meat. After they ate supper, Baby Boy patted his stomach. "Now, that's more like it!"

The following morning dawned clear, dry, and sunny. Captain Hanover ordered everyone to spread out their tents, canvas cart covers, and wet clothing to dry so they wouldn't sour and mildew. The condition of their wet belongings secured so carefully in their handcarts dismayed everyone. They couldn't do anything with wet sacks of flour. They spread out their stores of beans, onions, and rice to dry out, hoping they wouldn't sprout and go to waste. They also did their best to dry out the salt and sugar. By the end of the day, everyone felt much more comfortable wearing totally dry clothing. It also helped to have dry fuel to burn. They all enjoyed three good meals to help them recover from their involuntary fasting for nearly two cold and dreary days.

A few days after the hailstorm and rain, they pitched camp beside one of the many nameless meandering creeks running parallel to the broad Platte River. Sand dunes covered with small bushes and grass separated the feeder streams. Early the next morning, before the sun popped above the horizon, a woman's piercing scream startled Baby Boy awake. He sat up abruptly. He heard the slap of running boots dodging through the sleeping camp. He stood up and glanced around. He saw Captain Hanover and three other men converging on the other side of the encampment from the Swintons.

Baby Boy jerked on his worn boots, grabbed his shotgun, and hightailed it over to the source of the excitement. He found a young woman sobbing in her husband's arms. Captain Hanover leaned over to inspect the small tent where the couple and their three-year-old boy had made their bed. He didn't find any sign or track of the missing child. The captain rose to his feet, raised his right hand up in the air, and waved it in a circling motion. "Gather round, men. We've got ourselves a missin' baby boy. He couldn't have walked too far since he's only three years old, so spread out. Let's find 'im fast so we can get underway on schedule this mornin'.'"

By the time he finished his instructions, more men and boys ran up, shirts unbuttoned, hats left behind. The ladies took longer dressing but joined the search as fast as they could. Baby Boy heard voices calling out as they dispersed in all directions, "Sammy! Sammy! Where are ya, boy?"

Baby Boy walked directly south to the edge of the wide brown river, wondering if the musical sound of running water had attracted the boy. He turned right and waded across the side eddies, searching the beach for small footprints in the damp sand. A few minutes later, he heard Zeff call his name. He turned around and waved. "Here Ah am, Zeff. Ah'm over here, up-river a bit."

Zeff strode up with his loaded hunting rifle braced on his shoulder. Baby Boy turned around in place, shouting, "Sammy! Where are ya, Sammy?"

Zeff placed his hand on Baby Boy's shoulder and squeezed it. "Shh, now. Let's listen a spell. Walk light like Ah taught ya when huntin', all right, Little Brover?"

Baby Boy nodded silently.

They stealthily hiked further west along the river. Zeff noticed low branches rustling at the base of a cluster of wild chokecherries. The bush grew down to the ground a few feet north of the riverbank. He held his forefinger to his lips and looked at Baby Boy, who nodded. They both crouched down and crept closer, listening for the sound of an animal or a young boy in the small bushy trees. Clusters of white flowers grew alongside ripening purple-blue berries on the dense bush.

They spotted low branches moving again. They froze.

The next thing they knew, a great tawny cougar crept backward out of the bushes, dragging a partially eaten corpse in its mouth. Zeff brought his rifle up to his shoulders. The cougar either saw or heard the movement. It spun and crouched, ready to defend itself. Baby Boy trembled when he saw the great mountain lion, larger and heavier than his ninety-pound body. He froze. The cougar growled, snarling a challenge and a threat. Zeff lowered his rifle and took careful aim.

Blam!

The cougar dropped where it crouched.

Keeping his eyes firmly on the fallen cat, Zeff reloaded a slug as fast as he could, careful not to fumble in his haste. Zeff and Baby Boy walked closer, shotguns loaded, aimed, and ready, worried the big beast might have some fight left in him. When Zeff saw the partially eaten remains of a young child wearing scraps of clothing, he grabbed Baby Boy's shoulders and turned him away. "Best not look, Baby Boy."

Zeff made sure he had killed and not just wounded the cougar, then took off his shirt and wrapped up the sorry, bloody bundle. "Baby Boy, we'll come back with a horse fer the mountain lion. It's too big fer us tuh handle on foot. Let's get back tuh camp with the sad news, okay Little Brover?"

"Ya mean the little baby's daid?"

"Yep, Ah'm afraid so. Ain't much left of it, the poor little thang."

Zeff handed Baby Boy his rifle before he picked up the tiny bundle. As they neared the camp, Zeff stopped. "Run ahead, Baby Boy, an' fetch the captain. He'll know what tuh do, ya know, how tuh break the news tuh the parents. All right, Little Brover? I'll wait here fer ya."

Baby Boy nodded as he took off jogging along the riverbank in his leaky wet boots, shotguns bouncing in both hands.

No one had seen any trace of the missing child. The ladies gathered around the distraught mother, huddled in front of her tent, sobbing. Her husband returned from walking down the river. He figured if his son had drowned, his body would have washed ashore downstream. He knelt down beside his wife and hugged her tight. Over her head, he watched Baby Boy jog up to the captain and gesture towards the river.

Baby Boy guided Captain Hanover and Mr. Bohannon, the little boy's father, back to Zeff beside the river. "Oh, no! Not Sammy! Please tell me that's not Sammy. Please!"

The young father staggered over to Zeff. Zeff stood up and held out the cloth-covered bundle. Zeff, the captain, and Baby Boy stood around with tears in their eyes as they watched Sammy's father's trembling hand hesitantly turn down the edge of Zeff's shirt. When he saw his little boy's partially eaten face, he collapsed to his knees, clutching the body to him. "Why, God? Why?"

The young man bowed his head over the little corpse and sobbed. When the weeping began to ease, Captain Hanover, now in the role of bishop, grasped the kneeling man's shoulders and helped him up to his feet. "Come, Brother Bohannan. Let's go back t' the camp. Yer lovely wife's gonna need ya now more than ever."

Mr. Bohannan staggered to his feet. He held the lump up over his shoulder like he had held his baby so many times over the past three years. The captain held his elbow and guided his staggering steps east towards the camp. Captain Hanover asked Baby Boy to run ahead and announce they had found the lost child. As Baby Boy took off jogging towards the camp, he called out, "Spread the word we won't be movin' out as planned."

By the time Zeff, the captain, and Mr. Bohannan arrived, everyone in the camp had gathered around to lend their support to the bereaved young couple. The ladies helped Mrs. Bohannan stand up. They supported her when she nearly fainted upon seeing the bloody shirt carried on her husband's shoulder. The neighbor ladies gently took the baby's remains out of Mr. Bohannon's arms so they could prepare him for burial. Mr. Bohannon adamantly refused to allow his wife to see their child's remains. He assured her their little son had died quickly, but his remains were a horrible sight, mauled by a ferocious cougar.

Mr. Bohannon only hoped his dear little son had died quickly.

Mrs. Bohannon collapsed onto a log bench beside their little cookfire, her face cupped in both hands. The captain walked over, placed his hands on her bowed head, and gave her a silent blessing. Mr. Bohannon sat down and pulled his wife into his chest, where she cried until her tears ran dry. They sat there stunned, not knowing what to do. An hour later, the captain invited them to join him at the newly dug grave.

While the men dug the grave back away from the river on dry land, the women busied themselves preparing a potluck breakfast.

The captain conducted a solemn service by the tiny open grave. He led his little congregation in singing the hymn *How Great Thou Art*. He closed with a short, heartfelt prayer, then gestured towards the men standing by with short spades in their hands. Mr. Bohannan put his arm around his shaking wife's shoulders and gently pulled her away as the men filled in the grave. She kept turning back. She didn't want to leave her little baby boy in a hole in the ground. It broke her heart.

Everyone gathered quietly at the camp center for the funeral dinner. Everyone's thoughts turned to their own mortality, to the dangers of their lives on the trail. Poor Mrs. Bohannan felt such guilt for not watching her boy child more closely during the night she couldn't stop crying to eat.

The events of the morning left Baby Boy feeling sad. He didn't feel like taking part in any more killing, so he didn't join Zeff for their evening hunt. He took their simple fishing pole and walked downriver where he could be by himself. He spent the afternoon fishing quietly. The silence slowly renewed his soul after the emotionally distraught morning.

No one went back for the dead cougar's pelt.

Following the North Platte River, they reached the little town of North Platte with the western terminus of the Union Railway. Baby Boy had seen nothing but flat, grassy plains on all sides. What few trees he saw in the shallow swales had grown stunted and scrawny. Sometimes Baby Boy could see the sky and the horizon beneath the legs of people, horses, and cows. What trees the company encountered grew along both sides of the shallow, broad North Platte River.

Zeff and Baby Boy concentrated their hunting efforts along the riverbank, teaming with wildlife. Unfortunately, the waterside also teemed with mosquitos, excited to find a source of protein for their eggs in warm human blood. Baby Boy felt like the prey rather than the hunter by the time they secured their kills.

A couple of days' journey along the north bank of the North Platte River, Captain Hanover rode out in advance of the company. He soon galloped back to the train, waving his big hat overhead and shouting, "Round 'er up, folks. We're settin' up camp right here. It's gonna be a bit of a wait, too. There's a huge herd o' buffalo makin' their way towards us. Probably gonna take a couple o' days fer 'em t' clear out o' the trail."

As soon as Baby Boy heard the captain's orders, he ran ahead to see the bison herd. They had seen scattered clusters of buffalo before, but mainly off in the distance. They had passed by a few lone groups of a bull, a couple of cows, and some calves from time to time, but nothing prepared them for the scene unfolding before them. Over the rest of the day, a wave of dark brown animals ambled slowly over the land with their heads down close to the ground, grazing on the lush prairie grasses. They drew nearer the camp, one unhurried step at a time. The travelers couldn't see anything beyond the massive herd to the north, west, and south. The enormous animals broke over the land like a slow-moving wave of cold molasses, passing within a stone's throw of the double-ringed camp.

The few men with weapons congregated along the northwest edge of the camp, ready to defend the company from any incursions or rogue beasts. The bulls' shoulder humps over their forelegs stood taller than the tallest man in the company. Their bodies grew an unbelievable seven to twelve feet long from nose to tail.

Zeff and Baby Boy stood guard that evening after supper. "How on earth are we supposed tuh stop somethin' that huge if'n it decides tuh charge us, is what I wanna know!"

Baby Boy swatted at mosquitos buzzing around his face and bare ankles. "How're we supposed tuh stop somethin' this itsy-bitsy, is what I wanna know!"

They looked at each other and grinned, although both their grins appeared more like grimaces.

After they stood their watch, they settled in to wait for the buffalos to clear their path.

Chapter 6: Buffalo Hunt

The grazing herds gradually thinned out two days later, leaving the field strewn with bison dung and the grass cropped nearly to the ground. One of the men standing guard duty at the edge of the camp pointed north at a mounted troop of Pawnee warriors. "Look. Lookee there!"

People stood up and watched warriors riding towards stragglers behind the main body of the vast buffalo herd. They listened for war cries but heard nothing. The native Indians come to a halt surrounding a small group of foraging cows and older calves. After a long pause, one of their leaders stood up in his saddle and waved a war spear decorated with rows of dangling feathers over his head. Suddenly, but silently, all the mounted warriors darted towards the buffalos and began shooting their bows, aiming their arrows into the animals' flanks. Their flint arrowheads punctured the great arteries that fed the bison's strong hind legs. The wounds bled copiously, staining their lower legs a glistening red. Within minutes, weakened from blood loss, the incapacitated beasts sank to the ground and fell onto their sides. The warriors moved in to finish them off. Careful not to puncture the valuable hides with sharp arrowheads, they aimed primarily at the fallen beasts' heads and lower legs to complete the kill.

When Baby Boy heard the alarm from the camp's periphery, he jumped up, grabbed his rifle, and jogged over to see for himself. He pushed his way between two tall men, earning a shove from the one whose arm he jostled. He eagerly turned his head from left to right, taking in the sight of the brave warriors hunting the bison. The prey, so much larger than the hunters, reminded him of small blackbirds chasing off a raven several times larger. He spotted women and children running towards the fallen beasts from further north and pointed at them with his shotgun. "Look! Who's that? What're they a doin' over that away?"

Puzzled, he took a step forward. He shaded his eyes with his hat held in his left hand to see more clearly. With a flick of his head, he tossed his unruly hair out of the way and watched women and children running towards the downed animals. The women wore buffalo skin moccasins, knee-length skirts, and loose smocks made of doeskin. Their youngsters wore breechcloths, if anything, as they ran barefoot over the grassy plains.

The Pawnee women and children led dozens of large dogs dragging travois behind them, laden with tools and supplies for butchering the bison. The dogs had tawny tan fur with black tips and sported white legs and underbellies. Their large ears stood up erect and alert as they labored to drag their heavy loads.

In the Pawnee Nation, the men hunted, and the woman butchered. The men and women in the handcart company shook their heads in amazement as they watched the teamwork. The women efficiently skinned the top side of the enormous carcasses with obsidian knives. After they peeled back the pelts, they cut away the meat in long thin strips to be smoked for winter. They loaded everything on the dog travois to transport to their camp. The women and girls carefully saved the sinews and bones for making weapons and tools. When they completed butchering the top half of the carcass, young men rode up on horses. They tied rawhide ropes to the two legs still intact on the bottom side of the heavy body and dragged the corpse over so the women could reach the other side. After a lot of work, they completed skinning the beasts. They carefully folded up the valuable pelts to tan for blankets, tipis, and clothing. They worked quickly and silently as their men, mounted on horses, stood guard.

When the captain heard the alarm, he stood on the seat of a support wagon to see over everyone's heads. Captain Hanover watched for several minutes. When he noticed warriors separating themselves from the main party and riding towards their camp, he became alarmed. Adrenaline flooded his system. He shouted out to the men around him, "What's this, now? Grab yer arms, men. Be alert!"

The captain jumped off the wagon and landed with a hard jolt to his knees. He retrieved his new lever rifle, then jogged through the campfires to the side of the camp closest to the on-coming riders. He stepped in front of his men, cradling the big rifle in his left arm, and loaded a bullet. He pushed his big hat up off his face to see better.

The warriors approached at an aggressively fast gallop. The captain set aside his office as their spiritual leader and assumed his role as the camp's military captain. He shouted his orders to the men around him. "Don't no one say nothin' but me, not even to each other. Don't no one shoot off yer weapon unless I order ya in no uncertain terms t' do so. Don't nobody dare start nothin' here, or we're all in fer it! Don't even move a finger! Does everyone understand?"

He heard a mumbling of agreement around him. The camp's amateur guards closed rank, lining up behind Captain Hanover. They all watched the approaching warriors with their weapons clenched in sweaty hands. The women frantically scurried about, collecting their children around them. They ran to the center of the camp and huddled behind the freight wagons, hugging their children to them.

Captain Hanover strode up next to Baby Boy, who had taken the closest vantage point. Baby Boy's curiosity had overcome his caution. He just had to see these natives up close. Two nights before, Captain Hanover had told Lorna's class about the Pawnee Indian Nation. He described how they lived in lodges made from sod and farmed the land around them for a season, then moved on to a new camp, following the herds and the seasons, nomads, farmers, hunters, and fierce warriors.

The captain shoved Baby Boy behind him out of his line of fire. Baby Boy's eyes grew round as he watched the Indian braves rein in their horses and stop forty feet away. They each held a bow in their hands with an arrow nocked, ready to shoot. They spread out, making a straight line of defense. They didn't aim their bows at the camp, but their presence worried everyone. Three warriors rode forward at a steady walk, leaving the rest spread out in a line behind them. The oldest man, wearing a long war bonnet, obviously the Chief, pulled ahead of the other two and led them closer. One of the Chief's attendants wore the uniform of an army scout with eagle feathers in his cap and buffalo skin moccasins rather than boots.

As the three fearsome warriors drew near, Captain Hanover stepped forward three paces, stopped, and raised his right hand in greeting. The Pawnees stopped twenty feet away, easily within hailing distance. Baby Boy stared in fascination at a proud, handsome warrior sitting on a muscular war stallion at the Chief's right hand. He had a darkly handsome face with a strong nose, prominent cheeks, and full lips turned down in a sneer. His hair appeared most bizarre to the young boy. The warrior had shaved his eyebrows and scalp bald except for a strip of hair running along the center of his skull from his forehead to his neck. He had attached a narrow scalp lock made from the white fur of a deer's tail to his hair, held in place by small combs carved from antlers. He had stiffened the scalp lock with fat and painted it a bright blood red. It stood erect like a crest, crowning his fierce visage, adding eight inches to his already considerable height. Three big eagle feathers had been tucked into the scalp lock at jaunty angles. The warrior wore only a buckskin breechcloth and moccasins. The bright summer sun highlighted the defined muscles of his strong shoulders, arms, chest, and abdomen.

The man fascinated Baby Boy. His masculinity took the boy's breath away as he stared wide-eyed at the striking, magnificent savage. The warrior's necklace of bear claws hanging from a thin ribbon of pale gray fur impressed him. The big chest plate only accentuated his smooth skin and lean muscles, making them seem, somehow, more naked and exposed. Above the bear claws, the man wore two rows of necklaces made of alternating white knucklebone-sized beads and tiny black porcupine quill beads. From both ears dangled earrings of small polished beads hanging from a thin thread of braided horse tail hair.

The imposing warrior held his bow loosely in his left hand. His right hand rested on the bone handle of a big throwing knife hanging in a leather sheath from an intricately beaded belt with his elbow held out at a cocky angle.

The Chief turned and spoke to the warrior in the army uniform. The former army scout stood up in his saddle and shouted in a carrying voice with a brief pause between each word, "Chief ask why you um here?"

Captain Hanover raised his hand again, took one step forward, and called out, "Greetings, friends. Greetings, Chief. Peace. We are only passin' through Pawnee land on our way west. We come in peace. We are only travelin' through."

The translator spoke to the Chief. "No. Why here? Now?"

"We have been waitin' fer the trail t' clear. The buffalos blocked us from continuin' on our journey."

"One night, yes. Two night, no. Three night, no, no, no! Must leave now! Not welcome Paw Nee land."

"I understand. Please assure the Chief that we will be leavin' first thing in the mornin'. We mean no harm. We do not intend t' stay any longer than we must. We are only passin' through in peace."

The Chief stood up in his saddle and raised his bow over his head in his left hand. He shouted out words nobody in camp understood, but they sounded angry. The warriors behind the Chief thrust their bows up and down over their heads as they screamed a fierce, ululating war cry, "Woo! Woo! Woo!" Their raucous whooping raised the hair on the back of Baby Boy's neck. He had never heard such a threatening sound before. The women and children behind him cried out in fear as they huddled in the camp's center. Baby Boy's attention remained locked on the big native with the tall red crest.

The translator rode forward several paces, leaned in, glared fiercely at Captain Hanover, then shouted at the top of his voice, "Chief angry. Must pay. Must pay three day. Must pay now."

Captain Hanover didn't know what to say, so he said nothing. He continued standing there holding his right arm up in universal Plains Indian sign language that meant both 'greetings in peace' and 'friend.' Baby Boy involuntarily took a step back at the loud shouting. Fearfully, he peered to the right beneath the captain's raised arm.

"Chief say three day, pay three cow. Must pay um now!"

Captain Hanover lowered his hand slowly. He took a step back and stumbled into Baby Boy cowering behind him. Concerned, he gazed around at his poor little company of immigrants, untrained and poorly armed. Zeff jogged up with his old hunting rifle slung over his back on its rustic rope sling. He stopped behind Baby Boy and put his hands on the boy's shoulders, ready to lend the captain any help he might require. With a sigh, the captain's shoulders fell. He had no choice. They needed their cattle for food. But if he refused to pay the Chief's toll, the Pawnee warriors could decimate the camp within minutes of starting to shoot their powerful war bows.

The captain took a step toward the translator. "Agreed. I will bring the cows. Please wait."

Baby Boy watched as the translator informed the Chief. The Chief nodded once, turned his horse back towards the scene of the hunt, and rode away, his back straight and proud. Four of the riders in the rear guard fell in behind him as an honor guard.

Baby Boy stared fascinated as the warrior with the spiked red hair rode slowly closer, then stopped a mere ten feet away. Baby Boy still stood at the front of the camp guard. The warrior sat on his horse waiting for delivery of the payment with his eyes glaring at the impromptu guards. Baby Boy's eyes traveled up and down the fighting man's muscled bare legs and thighs gripping the sides of his war stallion. His eyes grew wider as they rose up over the ridged stomach and then raked up over the long sinewy neck bearing his handsome, imposing face.

The warrior's haughty attitude reminded Baby Boy of a day back in the Ozarks when he came upon a red-tailed hawk after it had killed a young cottontail rabbit. The predator carried its prey up onto a large branch over the forest path. It stood on one clawed foot with the rabbit clamped tightly in the sharp talons of its other foot. It lifted up its pointed down-curved beak as it gazed around with a proud, arrogant stare, challenging anything to try and steal its prey.

Baby Boy's spellbound eyes examined the warrior's lean face until he made contact with the splendid warrior's glistening dark eyes. The warrior stared back intently. Baby Boy couldn't pull his eyes away. He felt pulled on an invisible rope, drawn towards the glorious man sitting on the horse in front of him. He felt compelled to walk forward and yield to this impressive man. Unconsciously, he wanted the warrior to take him up on his horse and steal him away where he could be taught to be a brave warrior, like his new ideal, this strong, masculine brave. He leaned forward, preparing to take a step when he felt Zeff's hands hold him steady. He stared, hungry to memorize every detail of this muscular, ideal man before him. The fierce warrior didn't break eye contact, forcing his will on the young paleface who stood bravely before him, holding his own in the contest of wills. Baby Boy didn't dare blink. *Ah never knew a man could be so plumb beautiful.*

Baby Boy heard the captain leading the ransom through the camp. Still gazing deep into the warrior's unfathomable eyes, he nodded his head in both a greeting and an acknowledgment of his admiration of the warrior's perfection. His heart thrilled when the warrior gravely returned him the slightest nod.

The movement of Captain Hanover walking through the small group of guards, pulling three milk cows along by rope halters, drew the warrior's eyes from Baby Boy's, breaking the intense, hypnotic contact. Baby Boy sagged back against his older brother, suddenly feeling weak and small and helpless. He turned to watch as the captain and three cows walked through the line of guards on the edge of the camp. One of the teenage cowboys followed behind the cows, switching them on their rear flanks and back legs with a willow branch if they slowed down to eat the grass. Zeff and Baby Boy stepped aside so the captain could hand off the ransom to the uniformed Pawnee scout. He handed the ropes up to the soldier. "Paid in full. We come in peace. We leave in peace."

Before the former army Scout led the cows away, he leaned down and quietly spoke to the handcart company's captain. "You ride into war. Sioux. Crow. Arapaho. Shoshone. Federal Army. All fight um each other."

Captain Hanover stood stock still as the message sank in. "Thank you, Scout, for the advance warning. Go in peace, friend."

The scout led the cattle away at a slow walk, tugging on the ropes of the recalcitrant animals. The red-crested warrior glanced once more at the paleface youth, Baby Boy, then turned his horse and followed the three cow toll. The mounted guard who had stayed back during the confrontation fell in behind the striking warrior and the soldier, accompanying the cattle on the way north.

Unknown to the handcart camp, the tribe had a large lodge seven miles to the north, surrounded by fields cut into the sod of the plains near a rambling creek. Their main camp of tipis rose on the other side of the lodge from the fields the women and children cultivated to help feed the clan. The cows followed the burdened dog travois back to their base camp, northeast of the handcart camp.

Zeff and Baby Boy hugged each other in relief as they watched danger walking away, growing small in the distance. Baby Boy couldn't pull his eyes away from the departing warrior's broad muscled back. His right hand involuntarily rose to wave goodbye. He would never forget the intensity of the experience of locking eyes with a real man, a warrior's warrior in the middle of the great plains.

Captain Hanover turned towards the camp. "The danger's over folks. Put down yer weapons. Good work, everyone. Relax now an' return t' yer duties. Remember what the great Brigham Young has always said, it's cheaper t' feed the Injuns than t' fight 'em. We pull out at first light in the mornin'. Don't anyone stray from camp until we leave. I'm sure the Pawnee will be watching until we're well gone from here."

The captain set rotating night guards for the first time on their journey. The men grumbled about losing sleep, but they knew why it had to be done. Each did their duty in turn. After the camp fell silent, Baby Boy heard a violin play a lively piece by Vivaldi, followed by a sad melody. After the violin stopped the quiet, mournful music, Baby Boy lay back and stared at the stars until he drifted asleep.

As they walked northwest the following morning, Baby Boy pushed the cart from behind. He turned several times to glance back, hoping to catch another glimpse of the impressive Pawnee warrior.

Chapter 7: Literacy

During the next two weeks, they continued walking northwest along the north shore of the Platte River. Everyone kept their eyes open, focused on the horizon, on guard for Indians on the warpath. The captain kept everyone in a tight group, not spread out along the route like in the beginning. From time to time, the land rose in small rough mountains south of them across the river. On their side of the river, the ground spread flat as a tabletop.

When they camped at night, the captain ordered them into a tighter, more defensive position. He told them to keep their camp-fires small and extinguish them as soon as they prepared their suppers. He didn't want their fires to be beacons to any unseen adversaries during the night. Baby Boy missed the comfort of sitting around a fire in the evening.

Lorna Baines continued her classes every evening after supper except on Sundays. She taught the children how to join letters together to make words, preliminary to reading and spelling. Baby Boy caught on faster than any of them. However, he struggled with the concepts of silent letters. One evening after Lorna Baines dismissed the classes, he accompanied her back to her campfire. "Sister Baines, Ah understand words like think. It makes sense tuh spell it t-h-i-n-k. But thought? It jus' don't make no sense tuh spell it t-h-o-u-g-h-t. Why not spell it like it sounds? T-h-o-t?"

Lorna Baines smiled indulgently. She remembered having the same issues when she began learning to read. "Well, Baby Boy, t-h-o-t simply isn't the correct way to spell thought."

"Why not?"

"Well, just because. I don't think there's any reason. There's only a right way and a wrong way to spell it."

"Just because? What kinda reason's that?"

"I don't know, Baby Boy. Why is the sky blue?"

"Ah don't know. Why is the sky blue?"

"Just because it is."

"If'n Ah spelled blue b-l-u, y'all would understand me, right?"

"Perhaps, but it still wouldn't be spelled correctly."

"Ah'm sorry, Sister Baines, but Ah jus' don't understand."

"I know. I don't understand a lot of things either, young man. When I first began reading, I had to memorize the spelling of words like caught, colonel, and squirrel. Otherwise, I kept spelling them wrong."

"Those words're weird, Sister Baines."

"I know. So just memorize the correct spelling for now. It will become easier as you go along. So, how do you spell weird, Baby Boy?"

"Ah don't know."

"Try w-e-i-r-d. Repeat it back like in class."

"W-e-i-r-d, weird. Why's there a i in weird, anyway? That's jus' plumb weird."

"I don't know."

"Yeah, yeah. Ah know. It jus' is."

"Now you're learning! Good night, Baby Boy."

"Night, Sister Baines."

The following evening at the end of class, Lorna Baines lent Baby Boy her book, *The Eclectic First Reader for Young Children*. Baby Boy accepted it reverently, his eyes big with pleasure. He held it up to read the cover. He stumbled over sounding out eclectic but did just fine with the other words.

"Start reading it tonight and bring it back to class tomorrow. Ask me tomorrow about any words you couldn't read or didn't understand. I think you are ready to begin reading, Baby Boy. This book starts with easy words. It gradually adds more vocabulary and gets harder as you delve further into it. Take your time, and you will do just fine."

"Oh! Thank yew, Sister Baines. A real book. Wow!"

He ran back to their campfire to show Zeff and Sister Woman, all excited. They both complimented him for learning to read so well. Zeff complained that Baby Boy wouldn't be hunting much with him, what with his reading all the time. Baby Boy just smiled. He crossed his legs, sat down, and focused on reading. He read the first two pages, which listed the alphabet in lower case, upper case, and italics, and sample words using the letters. He turned the page to Lesson I, which had a woodcut illustration of a rat at the top of the page. Above the illustration, he read the words: a, and, cat, rat. Beneath the etching, he read: a rat, a cat, a cat and a rat, a rat and a cat. He surprised himself by reading all the words. He kept reading, delighted to be actually reading an actual book. The cat has a rat. The rat ran at Ann. Ann has a cat. The cat ran at the rat.

Baby Boy taught himself to read one lesson at a time. The light began fading by the time he reached Lesson XIV. He examined an illustration of a girl leading a blind old man. He read out loud, "This old man can not see. He is blind." Baby Boy had to sound out the word blind before he figured out the meaning. "Mary holds him by the hand. She is kind to the old blind man." He folded the book closed and laid back on the lush, grassy sod. His arms cradled the primer close to his chest. *Ah'm readin' sentences an' understandin' the words. Ain't that somethin'!*

From that point on, he made rapid progress, expanding his vocabulary and spelling skills, and taking joy in exploring his new abilities. He finished the fifty-two lessons in four days. Lorna Baines wanted to keep him interested in reading, so she searched for another book in the camp. She knew Captain Hanover carried a copy of the King James Bible and the Book of Mormon, but she thought they would be too much for a young boy just learning to read.

Finally, a young Irish couple offered her an old, well-read leather-bound copy of the popular adventure novel, *The Swiss Family Robinson or Adventures on a Desert Island.* Lorna felt thrilled at finding such a great first novel for Baby Boy. When she gave it to him, they sat down close beside each other. Baby Boy opened the book and began reading out loud. "The Swiss Family Robinson, Chapter One, Shipwrecked. Fer many days we had been tempest-tossed." Baby Boy paused and glanced over at Lorna. "What's tempest, Sister Baines?"

"A tempest is a really bad wind storm, Baby Boy. Keep reading. You are doing well."

"Six times had the darkness closed over a wild an' terrific scene, an' returnin' light as often brought but renewed distress, fer the ragin' storm increased in fury until on the seventh day all hope was lost. We were driven completely out o' our course; no conjecture could be formed as to our whereabouts. The crew had lost heart, an' were utterly exhausted by...uh, in-cess-sant – ah – incessant labor." Baby Boy looked up at Lorna Baines for approval for sounding out a long new word for the first time. She smiled and nodded with a gesture to continue. After about fifteen minutes, she saw he could manage with the book. She excused herself and went back to her cookfire and her husband.

Baby Boy's vocabulary and spelling skills expanded exponentially as he read. The story of young boys experiencing life so different from his drew him in. He only put it when it became too dark to see. When he finished, he returned it to Lorna Baines and asked if she had anything else for him to read. Once again, she asked around the company. She managed to scrounge up a beat-up copy of *David Copperfield*. Baby Boy absolutely devoured the book, fascinated with reading about another young boy growing up in such a different world from his.

When he finished and returned it, Lorna Baines solemnly handed him Captain Hanover's Bible printed on delicate thin paper. "Do the best you can, Baby Boy. The Bible can be hard reading. Sometimes it's not very interesting. But you will learn lots of new words and ideas. If you can't sound out or don't understand a word, bring it to me. I'm always right over there at the neighboring campfire."

"Thanks, Sister Baines. Ah kinda like readin', doncha know."

"Well, a great world of fine literature waits for you in civilization, but you'll have to wait until trail's end to find more books. I'm sure the pioneers and settlers in Utah will have novels they can share with you."

Baby Boy sat down and started reading, "In the beginnin' God created the heaven an' the earth." He felt a thrill he could read it. Doggedly he kept at it. He bogged down sounding out and understanding words like generations, Pison, bdellium, and onyx. Even Lorna Baines couldn't explain what bdellium meant.

Their journey led them into a drier stretch of flat land. Baby Boy went hunting by himself to explore what game he might find away from the river. He came across mounds of dirt around the entrances to prairie dog warrens. He rode towards the nearest colony, where he spotted a beige prairie dog with a white underbelly standing up tall. When Baby Boy came near the colony, the prairie dog squeaked out a high-pitched warning. Yip, yip, yip, yip! Its body jumped up with every bark. *Why that sounded jus' like a little dog barkin'.*

Within seconds, the rest of the pack scampered in from foraging around the colony and dove into the closest burrows, disappearing in a wink. He wondered if they made good eating. They looked like chubby squirrels, only without bushy tails. However, Baby Boy had never seen squirrels this big. They stood fifteen to seventeen inches tall when they reared up on their short hind legs to look around the countryside. They appeared heavy with a pear-shaped lower torso from the middle of their waists down to their rear haunches.

He rode his horse away downwind from the dozen or so burrows. He dismounted and tethered the horse's front legs so it could eat the grass but couldn't wander away. He loaded both rifle barrels with shot, then ducked down into a crouch. He slung his shotgun over his back on the simple rope sling he used for transporting it on horseback when hunting. With his hands on his knees for extra stability, he duck-walked towards the closest of the little dogs' bolt holes, keeping his profile as low as he could. When he approached shooting distance, he pulled the shotgun off his back, knelt down doggy-style, then lay down prone on his stomach on the ground. He cocked his right knee to stabilize his torso, lifted his head, and aimed the rifle at the dirt ridge above the burrow.

Minutes later, his quiet patience paid off. A chubby dog climbed onto the miniature cone of soil and gazed around on all sides. Baby Boy didn't dare breathe. A moment later, two more beige bodies clambered out of their bolt holes. He fired. The first dog flew in the air, tumbled back, and rolled along the ground for a couple of feet. Quick as a wink, Baby Boy aimed and shot again. Another direct hit. He smiled, delighted at having moving targets for his practice. He re-loaded and fired twice more before the colony dived back into their warren or scattered to the four winds, seeking escape from the deadly noise.

Baby Boy stood up, slung the rifle over his shoulder, and strolled over to retrieve his bounty. Holding two kills in each hand, he walked back to his mount. When he returned to the camp along the river, he dropped the kills on the rocky river edge. He pulled his hunting knife out of its heavy cowhide sheath at his waist and pulled a small bluish sandstone out of the pocket sewn into the front of his knife sheath. He spit on the whetstone to lubricate it, then placed it on his bent leg to hold it steady. With well-practiced movements, he lightly ran the edge of his steel blade along the stone, leaving a razor-sharp edge on both sides. He quickly skinned and cleaned the first prairie dog. He lifted it up and sniffed its flesh. *Smells jus' like a squirrel. Let's hope it cooks up the same. Sister Woman loves squirrel stew. Maybe they'll be good fer fryin', too.*

He finished cleaning them, tied a piece of twine from his pocket around their small necks, and hung them from his saddle horn. Sister Woman breaded them in cornmeal and fried them up in bacon fat, then sprinkled a pinch of salt and pepper over the pan. They all mumbled their approval as they ate the flesh from the bones for their supper. Sister Woman paused and looked at the drumstick the size of a chicken leg. "Bubba, this reminds me a bit o' pork or ham. Maybe 'cause it's fatter 'an squirrel meat. Right nice. Baby Boy, y'all can bring me all o' these here prairie dogs ya wants. Ah likes 'em!"

After Baby Boy finished eating, he took a stroll through the camp. On his way back, he passed Lorna Baines' campfire. She and her husband had just begun to eat. "Would you like to join us in a spot of supper, Baby Boy?"

"Why, don't mind if Ah do. Ah thanks y'all right kindly." When Baby Boy finished eating, he licked his fingers. Smiling broadly, he stood up. "Right tasty, Sister Baines. Thanks. Y'all have a good night, now, ya heah?"

He meandered back to the family fire. *Ah'm still hungry. Ah'm always hungry. Betcha anythin' if someone else offered me a third supper, Ah could eat it all an' still be hungry.*

Everyone in the company physically exerted themselves for long hours six days a week, walking while pushing or pulling their handcarts. They all burned up the food they ate as fast as they could

74

eat it. Everyone felt hungry, despite a diet high in animal fats. Most of the company had burned off their excess body fat, working thinner and tougher, with little or no reserves for lean times. Everyone paid attention to give the growing children extra servings so they wouldn't become stunted from malnutrition.

The following morning, Paddy, one of the older teenage boys who had signed on to tend the livestock, rode northwest, inspecting the route ahead. A large cluster of bison off to the side distracted him from watching the horse's immediate path. His horse's front left hoof stepped hard into a prairie dog's bolt hole. The mare crashed down, throwing Paddy flying over its shoulder as its leg dropped into the large hole. The horse thrashed wildly, trying to extract its leg, but only managed to twist and break it. The horse screamed in agony while it struggled unsuccessfully to remove its foreleg from the deep vertical burrow.

Paddy lay still on the ground.

The day's advance rider for the handcart train spotted the horse sprawled awkwardly on the grass two hours later. He approached the collapsed horse and found it still breathing. He stood up in his saddle and waved his arm overhead to attract the company's attention. Five minutes later, Captain Hanover galloped up on an unsaddled horse. When he saw their scout standing over the fallen horse, he pulled up fast. The captain jumped down beside the collapsed mare. As he dismounted, he spotted Paddy laying partially hidden behind mounds of dirt surrounding the prairie dog tunnels. "Go check on Paddy, Andy. I'll take care o' this poor animal."

Captain Hanover saw how the horse's front left leg had sunk nearly to her chest, leaving the broken leg trapped in the burrow. He knew he could do nothing to save the mare, so he reluctantly pulled his pistol and shot her between the eyes to put her out of her misery. When he pulled the trigger, he heard a man scream. He stood up and looked over to where Paddy lay sprawled on his stomach. He saw Andy hop around on one leg, then topple over and hit the ground. He ran over as fast as he could and crashed to his knees beside the youngster. Andy's face scrunched up in fear and pain. "A snake bit me, Captain. A rattler came up outa that hole over there an' bit me but good."

"Land sakes, boy! Lay still now. I gotta move fast."

The captain glanced around quickly to see if the snake still posed a threat. He didn't find any rattlers, so he immediately turned his attention back to Andy. He pulled out and opened his bone-handled pocket knife. Quick as a wink, he sliced up Andy's pant leg to expose the double puncture bite. Andy burst into tears. "I didn't hear no rattles nor nothin'. It jus' bit me like a lightnin' strike outa nowhere!"

The skin on Andy's leg began swelling into a bright red blood blister. The captain cut a deep X over the obvious two bitemarks with his hunting knife. He leaned down with a scowl of distaste and sucked on the bleeding wound. He gagged, spit out a mouthful of coppery red blood and yellowish snake venom, then sucked some more. He knew if he didn't suck all of the toxin out of the boy's leg, he wouldn't survive. After retching out several mouthfuls, he could only taste and see blood, so he stopped his distasteful ministrations. He jerked his kerchief off his neck and tied it tightly over the wound to stanch the bleeding. With one arm behind Andy's back, he helped Andy to his feet and led him over to the horse. Andy had trouble mounting up.

The captain left Andy clinging to the horse's mane and reins to keep his balance. Andy's right leg stuck out with its muscles seized up in pain. The captain rushed over to check on Paddy. He grabbed Paddy's shoulder and pulled him over onto his back. Captain Hanover saw he had broken his neck. The boy had stopped breathing. His skin felt cool to the touch. The captain shook his head sorrowfully, then returned his attention to the wounded boy on the horse.

When they reached the handcarts, Captain Hanover shouted for everyone to move closer to the riverbank and set up camp. The ladies of the camp cleaned up Andy, who appeared to be going into shock. They spread out his bedrolls and laid him down. He complained of feeling nauseous and weak. The ladies conferred with the captain. They decided loss of blood explained it. The captain thought he had managed to draw out all the venom in time. The captain stood up and gazed around the camp. He glanced over at their freight wagons. They didn't hold anything that would make a comfortable bed to carry a wounded man. He decided that bouncing across the plains on a hard bed wouldn't help Andy heal. He walked over beside one of the freight wagons and quietly asked the driver to take one of the boys and retrieve Paddy's corpse and the saddle from the dead horse.

After he watched them drive off, the captain asked three men to get spades from the freight wagons, move inland a bit off the trail, and dig a grave.

Zeff and Baby Boy borrowed two horses and took off riding upriver, hunting. They hadn't gone but a few hundred yards when they saw signs of a recently occupied campsite. They couldn't tell by the remains of fires and the churned-up tracks if they had been pioneers, gold hunters, trappers, or Indians. They had to go quite some ways before they came upon a small herd of antelope drinking from the riverbank. They each managed to shoot a young doe before the rest scattered at a run. They dragged the kills back through and below the camp to clean and butcher the meat without fouling the water used for washing, bathing, and drinking.

The Swintons had just finished eating their simple supper. Sister Woman sat nursing Chester Ray while Baby Boy cleaned their frypan and tin plates in the river. Zeff sat Indian style tending a nick on his big Bowie hunting knife, his head bowed over his hands in concentration. His tongue protruded childishly between his lips as he focused. He heard footsteps, looked up, and saw Mr. and Mrs. Bohannon walking toward them. He thrust his knife back in its heavy leather sheath and stood up. When Sister Woman saw him stand up, she also stood up, still nursing the baby held in her arms.

Mr. Bohannon held out his right hand to Zeff. "We never got properly introduced the other day, Brother Swinton, although I've since learned your names. I'm Jeffery Bohannon, and this is my lovely wife, Bethany."

Zeff shook his hand, then took a step back, reclaiming his personal space. All their eyes turned to Baby Boy as he walked up carrying clean dishes to store in the box of the handcart. Mr. and Mrs. Bohannon smiled a warm greeting to Baby Boy. He recognized them and returned the smile with a big nod. Zeff swept his arm around their little campfire. "Won't y'all have a seat?"

77

Jeffrey Bohannon looked at his wife, then shook his head no. "Thank you, but we don't want to intrude on your evening's rest. We just came by to thank you for helping us back on that awful morning when our dear little Sammy went missing. Thank you for finding him and returning him to us. It would have been horrible to never know what happened to him. That would have weighed on our minds for ages. At least this way, we had a chance to say good-bye. It was very kind of you to help."

Zeff shrugged, not accustomed to accepting gratitude. Baby Boy grinned and nodded as he turned to the cart and stored the pan and dishes in the box. Bethany Bohannon walked up and gave Zeff a light hug and kiss on the cheek. "Thank you, Brother Swinton. We will never forget your help finding our poor lost little boy." She stepped over to the cart and hugged Baby Boy. "You, too, Baby Boy. Thank you for your help."

"Ah, tweren't nothin'."

"We'll be moseying on then. We just wanted to stop by and introduce ourselves and thank you personally. Good night, all."

Zeff and Sister Woman mumbled, "Good night. Nice meetin' y'all."

Curious about the wounded teen he had seen brought back to camp earlier in the day, Baby Boy wandered over to the center of camp where Andy lay on the ground beside the big freight wagons. The poor boy looked pale and clammy. He laid shivering with quilts tucked about under his chin. One of the ladies of the company carried over a tin travel mug of broth to feed the wounded teen. A friend of hers accompanied her. They raised the boy's head and tried to spoon warm broth between lips squinched tight in a grimace of pain. They managed to get the boy to open his mouth. Before they could feed him any broth, they noticed bleeding from his gums. They gently lowered Andy's head back to his blankets and reported the new symptom to Captain Hanover. The captain turned away and muttered, "Damn it all, I thought I sucked all the venom out. I was sure I did!" After the ladies left, he said a silent prayer asking the Lord to help the boy survive the poison.

The other young cowboys and guards who had befriended Andy during their weeks on the trail took turns watching him during the long quiet night. A chorus of crickets sang against the backdrop of rippling water over in the river. Whenever Andy seemed calm and more lucid, they encouraged him to drink a little broth, milk, or water. Andy refused with a shake of his head, neither thirsty nor hungry.

When the morning sky lightened, the boys thought Andy looked better. But before they finished eating their cornmeal mush, Andy began convulsing, struggling to breathe. He tried to sit up, gasping for breath, then fell back. He died before they could even call out for help.

One of the boys ran to inform Captain Hanover. The captain returned right away. He knelt down beside the corpse and lifted an eyelid to see if it reacted to light. He leaned over and held his ear against Andy's chest, listening for breathing and a heartbeat. The boy lay dead.

His friends turned away, their eyes glistening.

The captain pulled on his responsibilities as their bishop and asked the gravediggers to dig yet another grave. Just before midday, the captain led his small congregation in a brief graveside funeral service. He shared two short eulogies followed by a quiet sermon about how all people will be resurrected with a perfect body through the sacrifice of the Lord Jesus. The group sang the well-known hymn, *Abide with Me*. The sweet, solemn melody left many a teary eye as the captain finished a dedication blessing on the two graves.

The captain stood up tall, plopped his hat back on his head with a pat, and resumed his role of captain. "We move out in an hour, Brother and Sisters. Grab a bite t' eat an' get packed up. Zion awaits us!"

The next afternoon, the company saw a large wagon train traveling towards them along the trail. Up until then, they had only seen a few army messengers riding east, back the way they had come. Captain Hanover ordered his company to pull off to the south and set up camp by the river. He rode towards the long train of enormous white-topped Conestoga wagons pulled by plodding teams of four oxen per wagon. Armed men rode point, left and right flank, and tail, guarding the heavily laden wagons with their rifles cradled visibly on their arms. Before the captain reached the lead wagon, a great bull of a man rode forward to meet him.

Baby Boy couldn't hear their conversation. He wanted desperately to know what they were saying. As soon as they parked the family handcart in their usual place in the formation, Baby Boy grabbed his shotgun and borrowed a horse. He tore off towards the wagon train, searching for Captain Hanover. The wagon train passed their campsite, then turned off towards the broad river. By the time he reached Captain Hanover, the sixty-seven great wagons had begun pulling around into a huge defensive circle, much larger than the double circle camp of the handcart train. He found it interesting how they placed their wagons in a horseshoe-shaped encampment with the open end facing the river.

Baby Boy waved as he approached Captain Hanover, still sitting on his horse talking to the corpulent wagon master. The captain nodded a solemn greeting to Baby Boy, who arrived in time to hear, "...be honored if you and your wife would join us for supper this evening after you set up your camp."

"Why, many thanks, sir. We'd be pleased t' join ya."

"We'll see you around dusk, then."

"Yes, sir. We'll be there. Come, Baby Boy, let's return t' our own camp."

They turned their horses and rode back west towards the setting sun at a good trot. "Who are they, Captain?" Baby Boy had to shout to be heard over their thundering horse hoofs. "Why're they travelin' east? What are they carryin' that they need so many guards with rifles? Where're all the women an' children?"

The captain turned and glared at Baby Boy, who immediately stopped asking questions. "Huh! These gobacks're fur traders headin' back t' Saint Louis with their loot. Their wagons're full o' fox, marten, mink, otter, an' beaver pelts, trapped by Injuns fer tradin'. The ladies love the soft furs. Beavers command a real high price back east an' abroad in Europe, as well, doncha know. They're used fer makin' felt an' fer their warm fur."

"Where did they get all the pelts, Captain?"

"Well, they mostly traded with the native Injuns. It's a very lucrative business, Baby Boy. It's been goin' on fer somethin' like a hundred years, now, which is why they know the Overland Trail so well, goin' both directions. I suspect they have all the guards because they're probably carryin' gold an' silver from the Comstock mines from the western side o' the Territory o' Utah. The mines transport most o' their ore west t' San Francisco, where it can be carried on sailin' ships t' the great cities of America. I dare say they have lined the bottoms o' their innocent-looking freight wagons with smelted ore beneath false bottoms. Of course, some of the men travelin' with them are returnin' because they're either defeated or discouraged by the hard country. Ya see, Baby Boy, we're headed towards a land o' wonder, promise, joy, an' boundless opportunities. But it's also a land o' dangers an' big disappointments. That's the West, fer ya."

"Wow. They mus' all be rich, then, huh? Jus' look at all the men an' wagons an' all their livestock. Wish we had us some oxens tuh pull our carts, don't y'all? Wouldn't that make life nice and easy? Well, thanks fer lettin' me know, Captain. Ah'll take off huntin' now afore it gets too dark tuh see. So long, Captain."

"Good huntin', Baby Boy. See ya in the mornin'."

Chapter 8: Scotts Bluff

They traveled towards a place called Scotts Bluff. Twenty-five years back, The Rocky Mountain Fur Company had abandoned a trapper named Scott at this place when he became ill and couldn't continue. All the maps and journals noted the major landmark. Its steep cliffs, barren hills, and high bluffs rose on the south side of the North Platte River, opposite the river from the Oregon Trail. The bluffs became increasingly visible over the next two days as they drew near. They pitched camp two days after they buried Andy and Paddy.

Later that evening, a woman with a clear soprano voice began singing hymns from the songbook put together by Emma Smith in 1835. One by one, other voices joined in. Some sang a pleasant counterpart to the melody that Baby Boy found quite enchanting. Someone added to the singalong by whistling. They ended with a peaceful song that meant so much to the Mormons, *Gently Raise the Sacred Strain.* Baby Boy loved hearing music and wished he knew how to sing or whistle.

During the night, several members of the company woke up with stomach aches that grew intensely painful very quickly. They began vomiting and discharging watery diarrhea soon after. Those not affected hustled to clean up the victims. They gave them drinking water from the river. Despite their good intentions, the oldest and youngest of those afflicted became so dehydrated that the skin on their hands and feet began wrinkling within hours of symptoms. In two cases, their skin turned blue. One older lady, Polly Winters, succumbed a mere fourteen hours after waking up with a mild abdominal cramp. By the end of the day, three more deaths shocked the camp. A dozen more took sick during the day and had to take to their beds. That night, a young mother died. Her baby daughter followed her just before sunrise.

The morning after the sickness began, Captain Hanover called those still healthy to gather around him. He stood on the back of one of the freight wagons to address them. "Brothers an' Sisters," he called out in his public, church-speaking voice, "it's clear that somehow we've been exposed t' the unseen destroyer, otherwise known as the cholera. Our cases over the past few hours have been so extreme it's probably the Asiatic cholera like what plagued the Oregon Trail back in the late forties an' early fifties. We now know that the cholera spreads from unsanitary conditions, like campin' in the garbage o' previous travelers an' drinkin' water infected by human urine an' feces. It's usually not found this far north, not anymore, but I'm sure that's what we're dealing with. Unfortunately, I've seen it before. The only advice I can give is t' take laudanum if ya got it, drink lots o' water, an' keep yerselves an' the camp clean. Only go t' the toilet downriver an' always drink from water pulled upriver from the camp. An' pray. Now, bow your heads an' join me in askin' the good Lord fer a blessing on the sick an' afflicted."

The captain said a long prayer asking for strength to overcome the sickness and keep going despite all the deaths among their party. While he led the group in prayer, many fell to their knees. Mothers grasped the hands of their husbands and children. Those who had already lost loved ones sobbed quietly in the background. A man bolted to his feet and ran for the riverside, where he crashed to his knees and vomited explosively. His wife gathered up her ankle-length skirt and ran after him. She held his forehead while he threw up. When he could stand, she helped him stagger back to their cookfire by propping him up with her shoulder in his armpit and her arm around his back. He collapsed to his bedroll. Six hours later, he died.

During the night, Baby Boy woke up Zeff, asking for a drink of water in a weak whisper. The sound of sobbing and crying as people mourned the passing of loved ones all around the camp disturbed their sleep more than once. The fast deaths from the cholera shocked everyone in the little handcart company.

Later the next morning, Baby Boy came stumbling back from fishing along the North Platte River. "Ah don't feels so good, Sister Woman. Muh muscles're all crampin' up. Ah thinks... Ah thinks... Ah'm gonna throw up." He crashed to his hands and knees and vomited beside the fire. An hour later, diarrhea cramped his lower bowels. He moaned and asked Zeff to help him get down to the river where he usually took his bowel movements. They were nearly there when he moaned and collapsed, held up only by Zeff's strong arms. Sister Woman saw them stagger and came running. They carried Baby Boy to the waterside and stripped off his boots and dungarees. He whimpered every time his bowels let loose with more watery diarrhea. Zeff and Sister Woman took turns washing Baby Boy's face and holding him up for a sip of water from a canteen filled from upriver. They gently washed his butt and legs clean of the distasteful liquids that looked like rice water and smelled like fish water. Sister Woman ordered Zeff to keep Baby Boy down by the river. She didn't want to expose Chester Ray to the highly contagious disease if he weren't already.

By the following day, Baby Boy's symptoms began lessening. He suffered through several more attacks of diarrhea, each one less severe and less debilitating than the previous. He had expelled so much liquid between vomiting and diarrhea he hadn't needed to urinate since the onset. None of the victims in the camp developed a fever. Baby Boy's skin turned clammy and cool. Sister Woman brought him soups and broths, insisting he eat to keep up his strength. He grumbled but ate. Despite all the fluids, he became thirsty and irritable. Zeff and Sister Woman patiently stuck by him, urging him to drink lots of water and broth.

At dawn the next morning, Baby Boy sat up and began taking an interest in the world. Sister Woman brought him pan biscuits and the last of their prior day's allotment of smoked ham from the support wagons. Captain Hanover stopped and chatted with Baby Boy as he made his rounds through the camp. He found Baby Boy sitting up, held in Zeff's arms as they rested beside the river. The captain joined them, sitting Indian-style on the gravelly riverbank. He smiled when he saw Baby Boy's clear blue eyes shining and alert, not hollow and unfocused like just the day before.

Zeff gave Baby Boy a little hug when he reached over to shake the captain's hand. The captain squeezed Baby Boy's shoulder. "Yer a mighty lucky boy, son. Looks like yer gonna pull through. Not everyone's been so lucky."

Zeff scowled, thinking of the tears during the night. "So, how're things goin' in the rest o' the camp, Captain?"

"Well, I'm sorry t' say, but we've lost eleven total t' the cholera. Many more have been taken ill, but, like Baby Boy, they're recoverin' slowly but surely. Some were hardly even sick. An' others died so fast I couldn't hardly believe it. They're all in the hands o' God, now, though. I'm glad t' see ya on the mend, Baby Boy. We need yer huntin' skills now, more 'an ever." He stood up and brushed off his pants. "We'll be havin' another funeral service at high noon if yer up t' joinin' us. Take good care now, Baby Boy. Bye, Brother Zeff."

"So long, Captain."

Later that afternoon, Sister Woman complained about feeling nauseous. Within an hour, she ran to the riverbank with her bowels cramping painfully. She experienced several bouts of diarrhea, but nothing too severe. That evening, little Chester Ray started discharging diarrhea, too. He also spit up much more than usual during the night. Zeff gritted his teeth and cleaned up Sister Woman and Chester Ray as best he could. Sister Woman nursed their little son despite not feeling well. Zeff made sure Sister Woman drank lots of water and fresh cow's milk. He really appreciated it when Lorna Baines brought them a small pot of venison stew so he wouldn't have to cook that night on top of all his nursing duties. He shared the tasty broth with Sister Woman and Baby Boy.

That evening, Captain Hanover stopped by to chat a moment as he made his rounds visiting each surviving member of his shrinking company. Zeff leaned against a small cottonwood tree trunk near their cookfire. Sister Woman held Chester Ray over her shoulder while she rested against Zeff's side. Baby Boy lay on the ground with his head pillowed on Zeff's thighs. He crossed his legs at the ankles in front of him. When he wriggled the big toe of his right foot, he could see it poking out the side of his worn-out boots.

The captain sank down to his knees and sat back on his heels. His hands rested on his knees. After the usual greetings, he stared into the flames of the campfire's cheerful blaze. "Brigham Young learned a lot o' lessons from the first immigrant handcart companies. The early companies thought they could make it through with only the supplies they carried on their carts. Used t' be that fully one outta ten o' the pioneers didn't survive the trail, what with sickness, accidents, foul weather, flooded rivers, robbers an', o' course, Injuns. They had some real tragedies during those first trips. One large company ran completely outta food. They also ran outta ammunition, so they couldn't even hunt. Starvation slowed 'em down t' where they got overtaken by snows in the pass when they tried t' cross the continental divide. Some poor souls froze plumb t' death right on the trail. Others starved t' death before help arrived.

"Another handcart company didn't have enough firepower t' fight off a pack o' mountain men who turned t' highway robbery. Those murderin' thieves set up a trading post where they sold all the goods stolen from the dead pioneers t' travelers who came along later. We've had more than one incident of attacks by renegade Injuns. Lots o' deaths by war bows an' arrows. That scoundrel, Chief Pocatello an' his renegade savages wiped out one entire handcart company an' stole all their goods. Plumb awful when Injuns go on the warpath. Now we know t' take freight wagons with extra food an' ammunition. We know t' bring along cows fer their milk an' in case of emergencies when they're needed fer their meat. Injuns an' thieves're still big problems, but at least we're better armed an' better prepared, now."

Baby Boy turned his head to look the captain in the eye. "Didja ever have t' fight Injuns, yerself, Captain Hanover?"

"Oh, yessiree, Baby Boy. On me first wagon train journey along the trail. It happened years ago, but I remember it like it happened yesterday. The Injuns didn't have many rifles or pistols back then, but their war bows inflicted mortal wounds when they rode their war horses in close to the camp. They sent many a soul t' meet their maker before we managed t' drive 'em off. Even though they were only a dozen or so warriors, they wore their war paint an' flaunted rows o' scalps on their spears when they threatened us. Later, we figured they were really tryin' t' steal our horses an' oxen an' cows. But we sent 'em packin' without any of our livestock. The trail boss sent out armed guards fer the rest o' the trip after that. He wasn't about t' take any more chances. It slowed us down a touch, but we finally made it down t' Great Salt Lake City in the Great Basin all in one piece. We were tired an' hungry, but all in one piece. Well, I'll be moseyin' on now. Have a good night. Glad t' see everyone on the mend."

Later that evening, the captain's rounds eventually brought him to the handcart of the young widower who had lost his wife and baby daughter the first horrific night of the epidemic. He encountered a sad and forlorn young man in his early twenties, mourning the loss of his wife and child. The bereaved widower stood up and solemnly shook hands. When Captain Hanover noticed his red eyes and haggard face, he looked at him more closely. "How ya doin' there, Brother Madison? Ya haven't taken down sick too, have ya?"

"No, Captain Hanover. Thank the good Lord. Please come and join me. Have a seat by the fire."

They both crossed their legs Indian style and sat down. Captain Hanover reached out, grabbed Mr. Madison's shoulder, and gave it a gentle, comforting squeeze. "I'm so, so sorry fer yer losses, Brother Madison. The cholera is a horrible thing doncha know. It doesn't have any regard fer any man's feelings. But, buck up, there, young man. Keep the faith. I'm sure the good Lord has a plan in store fer ya, includin' happiness once again, in yer very near future."

The depressed young man just shook his head despondently. "I might as well turn around, Captain. Without my sweet Dolly and my dear little baby Genny, there's nothing ahead for me now but sadness and loneliness. All our great plans and wonderful dreams for the future lie in ruins. I'm all alone after only two years with my wonderful Dolly, the love of my life, my sweet, sweet Dorothy. At least back home in Maryland, I have a mother and a little sister still living who care for me. I'm thinking maybe I should turn around and go back with the next group of travelers heading east."

"Oh, no, don't do that, Brother Madison. That's just yer sorrow an' yer loneliness talkin'. I know what yer goin' through, though. I had t' bury me second little family on me first journey along the trail. A young wife an' two little boys. I still miss their cheerful smiles. But, don't worry, son. Some day yer path will lead ya t' some cute young thing who will quicken yer heart, again, an' the two of ya will make a wonderful life fer yerselves in the bosom of the Church. Just you wait an' see. At least when we get t' Great Salt Lake City, ya can get sealed to yer Dolly an' Genny so ya can spend all eternity with 'em at yer side as part o' yer family. I'm sure they're waitin' fer ya up in heaven. Don't give up the faith, Brother. Yew'll get over this sad trial. Don't give up the faith."

"Captain, I just can't think clearly since their passing. Every time I go to do something, I see Dolly's clothes or the baby's blankets, and it hits me hard all over again. Each time I hurt as much as when they first passed through the veil. I just want to throw everything away, so I don't have to be reminded of what I'm missing every time I turn around."

Captain Hanover reached out and patted the young man's back, then let his hand rest comfortingly on his shoulder. They sat quietly for a few minutes, gazing into the flickering flame of the dwindling cookfire. "Well, young man. There's a few Sisters an' a couple o' little babies in the company who I happen t' know're hard up fer clothes, especially fer warm winter clothing. Please don't throw nothin' usable away. The nights're already gettin' chilly, an' we haven't even started the climb up t' the divide. It'll feel like full-on winter by the time we cross the Rocky Mountains an' head on down t' Salt Lake Valley, where it'll still be late fall. Perhaps ya could make something good come from yer sorrows an' misfortunes, Brother Madison."

After mulling it over silently, the sad widower nodded once. "Who do you think could make the best use of my wonderful Dolly's clothing, Captain?"

"Why, I think young Sister Swinton only has two poor, thin old dresses. No coats, jackets, nor scarves. She has a little baby, Chester Ray, who only has some sad ol' clothes she sewed up fer 'im from flour sacks. I know they could make good use of Dolly's an' Genny's nice things."

Feeling a sense of purpose for the first time since his wife died, the young man rose to his feet. He stretched his arms out in front of him with his hands clasped as he eased back muscles stiff from sitting on the ground so long. He moved over to his handcart and began rummaging through the wood box, tossing out articles of clothing one piece at a time. He held up Dolly's new long wool coat she had wrapped in brown paper and stored in the bottom of the cart against the change of seasons. He shook it out and handed it to the

88

captain. When he finished, he leaned over and picked up the clothes. He gazed sadly at the remains of his family's lives resting in his arms. He took a big slow breath and sighed with a shake of his head. "Give me a hand, here, if you would, please, Captain. Then maybe you could show me to the Swinton camp. I haven't met them yet, even though I know Brother Swinton and his little brother have shared the results of their hunting with us along the way."

"Why certainly. I'd be right glad to, Brother Madison."

His arms full of baby clothes, blankets, and diapers, the captain led the way through the center of camp to the Swinton cookfire. When Zeff saw Captain Hanover returning, he rose to his feet. Baby Boy popped up immediately, curious to see what the captain had in his arms. The captain nodded a greeting. "Good evenin', Brother Swinton, Sister Swinton, Baby Boy." With a nod towards the young stranger, the captain dropped his armful of clothes onto the ground beside a sleeping Chester Ray. "This here's Brother Madison. The poor man lost 'is young wife an' little baby girl the first night o' the cholera. He doesn't have any need fer their clothes anymore. We hoped maybe they would fit Sister Swinton an' Chester Ray."

The young man tossed his armful of clothing on top of the little pile the captain had made. He stepped up and shook hands with Zeff. "Nice to meet you, Brother Swinton. You too, Sister Swinton. Thank you for your generosity in sharing the bounty of your hunting over the past several weeks. I hope these things will come in handy for you." He bent down and picked up Dolly's new coat. "Dolly was saving this for later when it turns cold in the mountains, but..." His voice broke. He took a deep breath, then forced himself to speak through his tears. His voice trembled. "But...she won't be needing it now. Could you make use of it?"

Hesitantly, bashfully, Sister Woman reached out to receive the gift. She slipped on the coat and pulled the collar up close around her slender neck. "Oh! Brother Madison. Ah cain't believe it. It's beautiful! This's better 'an Christmas." She looked up with tears in her eyes. "Thanks. Ah thanks y'all so much. Ah've never had me nothin' so fine in all o' muh life!"

She burst out crying and buried her face in her hands. Zeff walked over and put his arm around her shoulders. "Ah thanks y'all too, Brother Madison, with all o' muh heart. Ah've been mighty worried about what tuh do fer coats an' all, 'cause we don't have none fer when it gets cold. Yer a godsend, Brother Madison. A real godsend."

Mr. Madison nodded and looked away, touched by how much his simple gifts meant to these fellow travelers. "Well, I'm pleased you can make good use of my poor deceased Dolly's things." He pointed towards the pile on the ground. "There are also some baby clothes we had for my sweet baby girl, Genny. They were made with a lot of pink ribbons and yarns for my little baby girl, but they will keep your little boy warm, regardless. He'll never know the difference. My mother and sweet wife, Dolly, sewed and knitted up all those clothes with lots of love and care before we left Baltimore to travel to Independence."

With a sad smile and a little wave, he turned and walked away.

"Thanks again, Brother Madison. Ah'm sorry fer yer losses. Yer a godsend." Zeff turned to the captain and shook his hand again. "Thanks, Captain Hanover. Ah cain't tell y'all how much we really appreciate it."

After breakfast, a bored Baby Boy wandered over to visit with Lorna and Gilbert. "Good mornin', Sister Baines. Good mornin', Brother Baines. How're y'all feelin' this mornin'?"

Lorna gave him a little wave with a big smile. "Good morning, Baby Boy. It's so good to see you up and around, young man. How are you feeling today?"

"A lot better. Thanks."

Gilbert patted the ground beside him. "Here, come have a seat beside me and rest a spell."

Baby Boy looked at Gilbert sitting on the ground, leaning back against the five-foot-tall wheel of his handcart. Baby Boy read the hand-painted words Lorna had painstakingly painted on both sides of their handcart – *Carpe Diem*. He pointed at the unfamiliar words and asked Gilbert what they meant. Gilbert read the phrase aloud. "That's Lorna's favorite quote from the ancient Roman poet, Horace. It's in Latin and means seize the day or enjoy the moment. In other words, don't worry about tomorrow, do the best you can right now."

"Oh." Baby Boy walked over, sat down next to Gilbert, and leaned his shoulder against Gilbert's arm. He watched Sister Baines tending a small cookfire. She settled a small Dutch oven in the coals, then sprinkled hot coals across the top of the lid. She stood up and smiled again. "There. That does it."

"Whatcha cookin', Sister Baines?"

"Oh, I'm taking advantage of the day free from traveling to bake a little treat. I felt like having cinnamon rolls this morning. Since I happened to have some raisins leftover, I decided to knead up some dough and do some baking."

Lorna stepped over and sat down on Gilbert's other side. He pulled her shoulders into a hug and gave her a tender kiss on her forehead. After a few minutes of companionable silence, Gilbert chuckled. "Remember trying to bake on board the ship, dear? What a disaster."

Lorna shook her head. She remembered all too well going up on a pitching deck to cook in the communal wood-burning stove used by everyone traveling in steerage. "Those were the worst six weeks of my life, dear. Absolutely and undoubtedly the very worst."

Baby Boy leaned forward to look at Lorna. "How come y'all were on a ship, anyway, Sister Baines?"

Lorna and Gilbert looked at each other with sad smiles. Gilbert gazed out into the distance as he remembered. "Well, Baby Boy, a few years ago, Minister Campbell of our little parish began preaching against what he called Mormonites. He declared that Joseph Smith was the prophet of the anti-Christ, sent to lure good Christians away from the true paths of faith and God's grace. He said that conversing with Mormonites would lead to the path to hell and damnation for all eternity. Now, I was raised a Calvinist and even studied divinity in my youth, but still, such declarations sounded forced and false to me."

Lorna glanced over at Baby Boy. "I grew up always searching to understand what God wanted of us as written in the holy scriptures. Somehow Minister Campbell's unpleasant speech bothered me. I didn't feel like he was speaking the words of the Lord that day."

Gilbert resumed telling their story. "A couple of days later, when I was in the Dunstable Post Office, I overheard two neighbor ladies talking. When I heard one mention Mormon Elders, I paid attention to their conversation. She told her friend she was going to go hear them speak that evening in the vacant horse barn on the edge of town. I told Lorna about it, and we decided to go check them out for ourselves. We were surprised at the size of the crowd filling the temporary benches in the shed. Shortly after we found a space to stand, leaning against a side wall, a nice-looking man around thirty years old and another clean-cut young man around twenty took charge. The younger one raised his arms and called out, 'Brothers and Sisters. Thank you for joining us this evening. May I present Elder Aaron Anderson of the Church of Jesus Christ of Latter-day Saints, a Mormon Missionary who came all the way from Great Salt Lake Valley in the far western American frontier of the Territory of Utah.' There was a small splattering of applause as the conversations quieted down.

"The Elder began speaking in very plain language, not orating like ministers are so inclined to do. He told the story of Joseph Smith having a vision from God. He told about Joseph Smith receiving golden plates from an angel, which he translated into the Book of Mormon. He went on and explained how Joseph Smith was called to be a modern-day prophet to restore the true gospel of Christ and to restore the true line of the priesthood. Two hours later, he invited the riveted crowd to bow their heads and join him in prayer. It sounded to us like he was actually having a conversation with God, not reciting a prayer from rote. He asked the Lord to answer our prayers if we were to heed the scriptures and ask if the message he had just related were true. After he said amen, he ended by quoting Matthew seven verse seven. Ask, and it shall be given you; seek, and ye shall find; knock, and it shall be opened unto you.

"Then the younger Elder spoke briefly. He told us that he knew in his heart that this message was true, that God lived, and that Christ was our savior. Well, Lorna and I were silent all the way home. We had so much to think about. The mere thought that God had chosen a prophet to reveal his words directly to the world like in the Old Testament gave me a thrill. I remember turning to Lorna and asking, what if it is true? What would it mean if we had a conduit to reveal God's wishes to us? When I said my prayers that night, I asked God to make his will known to me. The next day was Saturday. We discussed the story told in the meeting we had attended the night before. We made some inquiries and discovered the Mormons had a tiny chapel in Luton, four miles from where we lived.

"Sunday morning, we drove the buggy half an hour to attend their church service. Those same two missionaries were there. From that point on, we began studying with them and reading the Book of Mormon. A few weeks later, we asked to be baptized. We felt God had answered our prayers. The church's congregation was made up of modest, hardworking people, honest and friendly, always willing to help each other out. We felt welcome and wanted in their company."

Lorna leaned forward and gazed at Baby Boy. "You see, Baby Boy, there were many things about organized religions that bothered us when we read the Lord's words of love in the New Testament. We didn't like seeing how Christianity had become churches of power and wealth, pomp and circumstance. The way the Mormons took things back to the basics, actually trying to live by the teachings of Jesus Christ, spoke to us much more loudly than Bible-thumping from the pulpit."

Lorna stood up and turned her Dutch oven a quarter turn. Gilbert took over. "Within a few years, our little congregation grew. We built a new, larger chapel. Some time later, we all became interested in accepting Brigham Young's invitation to immigrate to America and join the Saints in building a perfect society in Utah. The other churches continued to preach against Mormonism and polygamy, working up a lot of prejudice and persecution. The older established churches felt threatened by the growing number of their congregation who converted to Mormonism. Pulpits declaimed the Mormons' growing political and economic power more and more fervently.

"Soon, our non-Mormon neighbors began shunning us. They stopped waiting on us in the workshops and stores. Their children taunted our children. They tormented and beat up our children at school, making their lives miserable. Finally, even though we had

93

heard the conditions of crossing the Atlantic were deplorable, even though we knew the difficulties of walking to Zion in the Utah Territories were harsh, we decided to join Brigham Young in building a perfect society in the State of Deseret.

"Our ward decided to sell the new chapel to help fund making the trip. Most everyone left as soon as they put their affairs in order. It took us a little longer than most of our Brothers and Sisters. We wanted to see our children grown and married before we left them. Our oldest son never accepted the teachings of the Elders, but our daughters were baptized. They both married good young Mormon men within the year. We are still hoping they will come join us, but for now, they are struggling to build their lives and careers in England."

They both fell quiet, thinking about their children left behind. Baby Boy leaned forward so he could see their faces. "So, how did y'all get on a sailing ship, then?"

"Well, I'll tell you. After seeing our second daughter married, we sold our house and most of our belongings. The Bishop arranged for us to get a loan from the Church's Perpetual Emigration Fund to help finance the journey. You wouldn't believe how much a ticket costs, even one in steerage, for a trans-Atlantic voyage. Finally, the day of departure arrived. We took the train from Dunstable to Southampton, where we boarded the sailing ship, *Ophelia*. It was a medium-sized merchant ship. We had been warned by the Brothers and Sisters of the Church not to expect too much. But frankly, we were horrified when we staggered down the steep steps to find our bunk in steerage. It was cold, so everyone still wore their coats and hats. The crowded room smelled of vomit from all the people who had already become seasick from the rocking of the ship while tied up in port. One dim lamp on a gimble cast roving shadows around the room like in a drunken nightmare.

"We found our bunk alongside the curving hull of the ship. It was only a meter wide. We were shocked. Then, I took all our luggage except a small Gladstone bag of things we would need during the voyage down to the hold. It was already full, nearly to the ceiling, with freight and luggage. I had to crawl along over the stacks of crates and trunks until I found space to leave our bags. What a stench from the bilge below!"

Lorna stood up and rotated her oven again. "Finally, I had to use the toilet. The Sisters hard warned me about ship's heads, as they call their toilets on-board. I walked to the front of the ship called the prow. Fearfully, I opened the door and stepped up two steps that followed the contour of the ship's hull. I could feel cold air blowing up through the hole cut in the dirty oak seat. The seat overhung the hull, so all the refuse fell below into the sea. Since the wind filling the great sails overhead blew from behind the ship, all the odors from using the heads located in the prow blew away from the ship. I was shocked at the filthy condition of the seat. With five-hundred forty souls on board *Ophelia,* including the officers and crew, we almost always had to wait in line to use the heads. If someone became seasick, which happened to nearly everyone at the beginning of the trip, they were encouraged to lean over the side rail rather than try for privacy in the head for their sickness. And that was only the beginning!"

Baby Boy did not yet feel well enough to go hunting, so the three spent the rest of the day talking about their adventures and misadventures on the high seas. Lorna explained how the ship provided food, but each steerage family had to cook for themselves on a communal stove up on the deck. Gilbert told about how all the passengers managed to share fleas with each other. They were all bitten and covered with tiny, nearly transparent eggs. They spent hours each day picking fleas off each other. Gilbert poked fun at Lorna, telling how she flinched every time she squeezed a flea full of blood and when she saw bloodstains left behind from squished fleas on their bedclothes. "We thought we would never reach the Americas!"

Baby Boy listened in wonder at their awful adventures on the crowded ship. Lorna served them all a hot cinnamon roll. Baby Boy ate two while he sat there spellbound.

Around midafternoon, Gilbert stood up to stretch. "Finally, six miserable weeks and four days after departing Southampton, we docked in Philadelphia. Lorna and I immediately contacted the small congregation of Mormons who still lived in Philadelphia.

There had once been a large congregation. But most members had accepted the invitation to move west with the church when they were driven out of Nauvoo back in forty-six. You see, after a lynch mob killed Joseph Smith in June of eighteen forty-four, vigilantes began burning the homes and farms of the Mormon farmers, determined to drive all the Mormons out of Illinois. Nauvoo had become the largest city in the state at that time. Their neighbors felt threatened by their success and growing political influence. Businesses were sacked and burned. Brigham Young and other church leaders soon realized they couldn't stay in Nauvoo under those circumstances. They abandoned the city and began a mass migration to the western frontier. Brigham Young invited all Mormons the world over to join their exodus.

"So, after we arrived in Philadelphia, we were invited to a church member's home. We stayed for a short time, just long enough to recuperate from the travails of passage by sailing ship. We had both lost a lot of weight and needed to recover our strength. We bathed and cut our hair to get rid of the fleas. Lorna felt embarrassed to have fleas in front of our new friends. We took time to launder all our belongings to make sure we were rid of all the fleas.

"With the guidance and assistance of the bishop of the Philadelphia Ward, we bought passage by rail to Baltimore, Maryland. There we transferred to a train going to Wheeling, Virginia. From there, we rode on a newly laid track that took us to Independence, Missouri. We arrived the last week of June. We sold the last of our non-essentials and all of our jewelry except our wedding bands and bought a handcart. We met you and this fine company and started the trek to Zion."

"Wow. Thas quite an adventure crossin' the ocean then crossin' the country. Thas a long way tuh go jus' fer religion, if'n y'all ask me!"

They all three stood up. Gilbert pulled Lorna and Baby Boy into a gentle hug. Smiling, Baby Boy pulled away and headed for supper at Sister Woman's campfire. "Bye, Sister Baines. G 'night, Brother Baines."

"See you tomorrow, Baby Boy."

It took Sister Woman and Chester Ray two more days to completely recuperate. The entire camp rested as they recovered their strength, mourned their losses, and buried their dead. They redistributed items from the carts the dead left behind. One of the teenage cowboys agreed to help a widow push her cart so she could keep her belongings and continue the trip. In the end, they abandoned five of the oldest and most worn handcarts at the side of the trail. During this time, Connal Lee finished reading the Book of Mormon.

That evening, Captain Hanover visited the Swinton campfire. He sat down Indian style. Connal Lee asked the captain where he had his home. The captain leaned back with both arms stretched out behind him for support. "I make me home along Hobble Creek a couple miles south o' the city o' Provo by Fort Utah. That's a day and a half ride south o' Great Salt Lake City. About forty-five miles.

"How did y'all come tuh live in Provo, Captain?"

"Well now, back in March o' forty-nine, Brigham Young called us an' twenty-nine other families t' colonize Utah Valley around the Provo River. When we arrived, we began buildin' the fort first thing. Brigham Young had recommended forting up each settlement as the best way t' assure our temporal salvation."

Connal Lee held up his hand. "Temporal salvation? What's that?"

"Oh, that's fancy church talk fer physical safety, doncha know. Well, so anyway, Chief An-kar-tewets warned us that trespassin' would be met with death an' destruction. Brother Carter thought the ol' Chief jus' wanted tribute fer bein' on the tribe's land. We finished buildin' the stockade an' named it Fort Utah. We built a high deck fer the twelve-pound cannon Brigham Young had brought from back east. We thought the noise alone would scare 'em. We didn't know, but unfortunately, we built the fort on the location o' the Timpanogos' annual fish festival. The Injuns objected that our cattle were eatin' an' tramplin' the seeds an' berries that fed their children. Because we fished the river with nets, we didn't leave much fer the natives. The Injuns got real hungry that first winter we were there.

"Then the tribe caught the measles an' died in large numbers. They blamed us fer bringin' 'em white man diseases. Hatred fed on

97

hatred. Well, that winter, the hungry natives stole nearly sixty head o' cattle. By January, we asked Governor Young t' protect us. He sent the Nauvoo Legion. Naturally, as a captain in the Legion, I fought with 'em. Brigham Young feared that if we lost Fort Utah, we wouldn't have our southern route t' California an' all the fertile valleys between Great Salt Lake City an' Los Angeles that he wanted us Mormons t' settle.

"Well, the legion ended up killing all the Timpanogos men. We took the women an' children captive and sent 'em t' Great Salt Lake City t' be servants so they could learn civilized ways. 'Course, most of 'em escaped as soon as they could, doncha know. It was all one huge mess, Connal Lee. War always is. There's really no honor in killin' our fellow men, even if they are cattle thieves. Time used t' be when we Mormons didn't believe in killin' the native Injuns, the descendants o' the Lamanites from The Book o' Mormon. But that changed over the years when they started resentin' us an' stealin' from us an' murderin' us."

Connal Lee gazed sadly at the captain. "Why can't we all get along without war and killing, is what I want to know." Zeff nodded his head in agreement.

They pulled out a few days later, having lost nearly a week to the cholera while camped across from Scotts Bluff. Baby Boy became uncomfortably aware that his boots were badly worn out. By the end of the day, the big toe on his left foot had begun working its way through the old dried-out leather, matching his right boot. He had inherited the boots already well used a couple of years back when Zeff discarded them. They were so big at first that Baby Boy had to wear two thick pairs of hand-knitted tube socks so they would stay on. Now, with him growing up, the boots had grown too small, even without socks. The backs of the heels had worn down nearly to the boot's sole. He knew they didn't have a cobbler in the company. They wouldn't find a town with a shoemaker until they reached the end of the trail.

The following day, he woke up with an inspiration. He had seen the Indian moccasins made from leather. He decided he would skin the next deer he shot and cure the leather into a form of rawhide to use to repair his boots. He envisioned somehow making a soft cover he could slip on over his worn work boots. He tried to figure out how to tie it on. He went to sleep worrying about the problem and awoke during the night with the solution. He would cut some of the rawhide into small ribbons and use them like leather laces on tie-up boots. It took several tries before he learned how to trim thin laces.

While he practiced tying the laces around the rawhide bag over his boot, Baby Boy realized he could use the existing boot top. He didn't need a bag to cover it. He made up his mind. He cut a slit down the front of his boots and opened them up in two halves to improvise lace-up shoes. Using the sharp point of his knife, he laboriously drilled two holes in each flap near the top. He figured he would string the laces through the holes and tie his boots closed that way. Trial and error required he puncture the open edges in several places to keep the boot securely tied to his feet, but it worked. Over the next four days, he perfected his new footwear. They didn't look pretty, but his feet now had room to grow.

That evening Baby Boy walked towards the pup tent to go to bed. Zeff sat just inside the low entrance on his quilts. He noticed how short Baby Boy's ragged pant legs had become, not even touching the tops of his ankle work boots. *Hm. Where the heck're we supposed t' find 'im some dungarees on the trail? Oh, well. Guess it's all jus' part o' growin' up.* Zeff watched as Baby Boy removed his modified boots before going to sleep. He noticed where the homemade laces had rubbed against the top of Baby Boy's feet and shins during the day, leaving them raw and red. "Good idea, Baby Boy. Now all ya need is a tongue fer yer shoes."

"Whaddaya mean, a tongue, Zeff?"

"Ya know. A strip o' leather shaped like a tongue that runs up inside the boot behind the laces. It keeps out the water an' protects yer skin, ya know, like on regular shoes."

"Ah don't know, Zeff. Yer ol' hand-me-down boots're the only shoes Ah've ever worn."

"Well, tomorrow, why doncha ask yer school teacher tuh show y'all her husband's fancy English hikin' boots. They lace up over a tongue."

After class the following evening, Baby Boy walked Lorna back to her cookfire like he usually did. When they arrived, he asked if he could please see her husband's hiking boots. Lorna frowned, puzzled. "Why I suppose you could, but whatever for, Baby Boy?"

"Zeff tol' me tuh make muhself a tongue o' leather fer muh lace-up boots, only Ah've never seen a tongue on a shoe, afore."

With a smile on her face, she asked her weary husband to take off his boot and show its tongue to Baby Boy.

"Why sure, now, and it will be a pleasure indeed for me to take off my boots now that the day's walking is done."

While Mr. Baines unlaced and removed his boots, Baby Boy sat down next to him and untied his own boots. He accepted the offered shoe without a word, only nodding his head in thanks. He studied the boot's construction and immediately saw how a tongue would help. Mr. Baines' boots had thick soles, but there wasn't anything he could do about his own thin soles. He mumbled to himself, "Don't have me no boot leather, but Ah suspect muh rawhide'll serve jus' as well."

Lorna watched Baby Boy with an amused look on her face. "Why, Baby Boy, whatever have you done to your poor boots?"

"Oh, ya see, Sister Baines, Ah was growin' out of 'em an' wearin' 'em out all at the same time. Ah had t' do somethin', or Ah would be walkin' barefoot in jus' a week or two."

"Well, aren't you the clever one? I declare! Did Brother Swinton help you?"

"Huh-uh. Ah figured it out all by muh lonesome. Zeff only tol' me about a tongue."

"Where did you find rawhide laces out here on the trail?"

"Why, Ah made 'em muhself, Sister Baines. Ain't no cobblers round here, that's fer sure."

"Such a smart young man. I confess I'm very impressed. You worked out a solution all on your own. You've got a brain on your shoulders, Baby Boy. I've said it before, and I'll say it again."

By the next night, he had lashed on two rough-shaped tongues behind the laces of both boots. He found the remodeled boots much more comfortable and warmer, too.

100

Chapter 9: Fort Laramie

For three long hard days, they journeyed westerly from Scotts Bluff, following the worn tracks of the trail until they arrived at Fort Laramie. The impressive adobe Fort used to be an important fur trading post of John Jacob Astor's fabulously wealthy American Fur Company to service the overland fur trade. The U.S. Army bought the facility eight years ago to protect immigrants on the Overland Trail, which some called the Oregon Trail and others the California Trail. Captain Hanover always referred to it as the Mormon Trail.

As Baby Boy plodded along, pushing the handcart, he couldn't help but notice how the shoes of many of his fellow travelers had begun showing extreme wear and tear like his.

They camped down alongside the river away from the sprawling Fort complex. When Captain Hanover walked by their cookfire, he congratulated Baby Boy. "Yessiree, Baby Boy. Yer more than halfway t' Fort Hall, now. A little more 'an halfway. Congratulations. Ya made it!"

The big modern buildings on the plateau leading north away from the old adobe Fort fascinated Baby Boy. The Fort perched above a bend of the Laramie River. Later he learned the new buildings housed the soldier's barracks, officer's quarters, stables, storerooms, a sawmill, workshops, a laundry, a bakery, and even a well-stocked sutler's store open to travelers as well as to the soldiers. An enormous parade ground stretched between the old Fort and the new buildings. Beyond the corrals and milk sheds along the Fort's periphery sat several clusters of tall tipis of Lakota Sioux and Arapaho Indians dotting the low rolling hills around the Fort.

As Baby Boy watched, a cavalry patrol rode away from the parade ground. They turned west, splashed across the Laramie River, and galloped away. He admired their dark blue jackets and sky blue pants with yellow stripes running up the outside of the legs. He wondered where they were going in such a rush. He noticed they all had bulging saddlebags and carried rucksacks on their backs with pup tents rolled up and lashed above them.

While the handcart company set up their usual double-ring camp, Captain Hanover invited a couple of the men to accompany him to the Fort to find out the road conditions ahead of them.

Zeff and Baby Boy borrowed two horses and took off riding along a meandering nameless feeder creek, heading back east towards the North Platte River. The men stationed at the fort had hunted the area close by so often they couldn't find any game. It took them a while, but they managed to bag two large snowshoe hares and three smaller cottontail rabbits. They returned after dark. Sister Woman welcomed the fresh meat, but she had already prepared their supper from beef doled out at the support wagons.

One of the milk cows had taken up limp and slowed them down. The captain ordered the cowboys to slaughter it, butcher it, and distribute the meat around as a special treat. Sister Woman had done the beef up proud, stewing their allotment with plenty of onions, potatoes, and wrinkled dried-out carrots that cooked up tender and tasty despite their appearance.

The Irish flutist played a quiet background of melodies for nearly an hour as full dark descended around them. Baby Boy thrilled to hear the lovely sound, so pure and clear. The Swinton family went to bed that night with their bellies full of delicious stew.

Late the following morning, Lorna Baines returned from the big general store at the Fort because she had run short of cash. All excited, she invited Sister Woman and Baby Boy to return to the store with her. "You won't believe it, Sister Swinton. The Fort is a most impressive community. It's almost like a real town, only it's all spread out. Their general store and trading post, where you can get almost anything you would ever want, is what the army calls the sutler's store. How they contrived to get goods out here, I can't even imagine. Bring some money, Sister Swinton. Let's go replenish our supplies. Baby Boy, they even have books at the trading post!"

"Books? Wow! Let's go!"

Baby Boy happily accompanied Lorna Baines shopping. He had never been shopping in a store before. Sister Woman carried Chester Ray in Zeff's homemade knapsack over her back, rushing to keep up with her enthusiastic friend.

They strode briskly across the low hills and waded across a couple of small streams. "When I was at the sutler's store earlier, the shopkeeper told me some seventy-five thousand souls have passed through here on the Overland Trail. Why I'm guessing there might be up to fifteen hundred soldiers, pioneers, gold-diggers, and homesteaders camped around the Fort just today alone. It's been a long time since I saw so many strangers. Isn't it exciting?"

Baby Boy nodded his head. "Uh-huh. It sure is."

Their fast march carried them past Captain Hanover, leading his three plodding freight wagons up to the storehouses to replenish their depleted reserves of food. Despite all of Zeff and Baby Boy's hunting, the company had emptied the wagons of nearly all their bacon, salt pork, suet, and lard. They had also run low on other things like baking powder and molasses. They had run entirely out of dried fruit of all kinds.

They climbed up onto the low plateau that held the spread-out Fort above a bend of the Laramie River. Lorna Baines smiled wistfully at Baby Boy. "You know what I miss the most since leaving my lovely stone cottage back in Dunstable, England? I mean, other than the lush little flower garden in front and my vegetable garden in the back?"

"No. What Sister Baines?"

"I miss a good old fry-up for breakfast."

"A fry-up? What's a fry-up, Sister Baines?"

"Why, young man, a fry-up is the perfect start for a perfect day. In a great big skillet, you fry up some bangers, which is what we call our breakfast sausages, along with some back bacon, half a fried tomato per person, some fried mushrooms, and fried bread. What makes it all come together is a couple of fried eggs with the yolks still runny enough to be used to dip everything in. A spot of jam or fruit preserve on the toast makes it an extra special treat. But the eggs, Baby Boy. The eggs! I haven't had eggs for breakfast since we left Kansas City. And oh, how I miss them. So does Brother Baines. At the sutler's store earlier this morning, I saw a basket stacked high with the loveliest speckled eggs. Only they cost three cents apiece. Imagine that! Back in Independence, you could buy a dozen eggs for ten cents. No, I simply must resist the temptation to foolishly lavish our dwindling cash reserves on fried eggs, however much I would enjoy them. They are simply too, too dear. But, oh, if only I could afford them, I would fry you up the best breakfast of your life. Would you like that, Baby Boy?"

"Oh, yeah. Ah, surely would, Sister Baines. All Ah ever gets is some hominy an' grits. Sounds right tasty, yer fry up does."

"Could Ah maybe get me some too?" Sister Woman asked, surprised how her mouth began watering at the thought of fried eggs and bacon.

"Of course, my dear. And I'll make us all a grand fry up just as soon as we reach Zion."

They entered the parade ground surrounded by the fort's buildings. Baby Boy gazed around at all the new two-story stone and adobe buildings and one-story sod buildings. A tall flagpole flying the American flag rose in front of the new white-washed army headquarters built outside the massive old fort. As Sister Baines led them past the army offices and barracks, Baby Boy stopped to read a hand-carved and painted wood plaque to the right side of the main entrance. He struggled to sound out a couple of the words. "First Contingent of Mounted Riflemen, E Company, Major Winslow F. Sanderson Commanding."

Baby Boy gazed wide-eyed at the group of young men, all dressed alike in heavy boots, pale blue trousers with yellow stripes up the outside of the legs, and short jackets of darker blue wool decorated with golden yellow braid on the sleeves and lapels. They all wore heavy belts carrying pistol holsters, knives, and leather pockets for ammunition and compasses. Some of the officers wore swords hanging off sword belts with thin straps over their shoulders. The sun sparkled on their brass buttons, polished brass belt buckles, and brass pommels on their sword handles, dazzling Baby Boy's attentive, curious eyes.

Still looking back at the soldiers marching step in step, Baby Boy followed Sister Baines through the parade ground. They walked up to the sutler's store, a low adobe structure as big as any storehouse back in Independence or Kansas City. They stepped into the dark cavernous room of the store. Baby Boy stopped to gaze around, surprised at all the barrels, crates, boxes, and shelves organized throughout the room. He didn't know where to look first. Indians mixed with immigrants and military personnel in a wild variety of clothing.

Lorna Baines headed directly to the side of the store with the dry goods. Baby Boy followed Sister Woman and stood listening as he studied everything around them, full of curiosity about the people and the great store, taking it all in. Lorna Baines picked up a bolt of fabric whose printed pattern caught her eye. She read the small note pinned on its edge. "Seventy-five cents per yard! Imagine that. I could have bought dress cloth like this in Independence for fifteen or sixteen cents a yard."

A mature, nicely dressed woman approached. "May I help you, ladies?"

Baby Boy lost interest in their negotiations and began wandering around the large store. So many things drew his eye. He had to stop and examine everything. Over to the right of the entrance door, back in the corner, he discovered a bookcase made of rough sawed pine shelves held up on unbaked adobe bricks teaming with books. He ran over, nearly bowling down a young mother holding a baby in one arm and a string bag of vegetables. He stopped in amazement and stared. He hadn't known so many different books existed. He stepped up closer and began reading the titles. He spotted *The Swiss Family Robinson* and reached out a hesitant hand to pull it off the shelf. Just then, a tall young soldier walked up and stood beside him. Baby Boy jerked his hand back, embarrassed. He feared the man would think he wanted to steal the book. The officer didn't pay Baby Boy any attention at all. He just stood there looking over the titles with his right hand resting on a shelf at eye level.

Baby Boy read a hand-printed card over the bookshelves: We Buy Sell Trade and Lend Books.

"Scuse me, suh. Does that sign mean Ah could borrow me a book tuh read?"

The twenty-year-old cavalryman, tall, dark blond, and clean-shaven, stepped back a pace and looked Baby Boy up and down. He frowned disdainfully. "Well, boy, borrowing presumes you will return the book when you have finished reading it."

Baby Boy looked down at the ground. "Ah wasn't a gonna steal it. Ah only wants tuh find somethin' new tuh read."

He glanced up at the soldier's clear, gray-blue eyes, fascinated to see he didn't wear a beard or mustache. Baby Boy hardly ever saw clean-shaven men. His abusive father back in the Ozarks had always let his straggly beard grow untrimmed. Zeff had a sparse scruffy, light beard on his face with a fine wispy blond mustache he could only see in bright sunlight. All the men and grown boys in the handcart company wore beards, many with long untrimmed mustaches. After all, who had time to shave on the trail? Baby Boy felt his own cheeks and jaws unconsciously as he stared at the hand-some man. The officer wore army pants and a wrinkled white shirt with long sleeves. Baby Boy had never seen a shirt so blindingly pure white. The soldier had casually tied a dark blue bowtie under the shirt's soft folded-down collar.

"Can you even read, boy?"

"Yep. Ah jest learned me how." He pointed over at Lorna Baines. "Muh school teacher over there taught me durin' the trip here. Ah just love readin' books, doncha know."

"Really. And just how many books have you read, then."

"Why, Ah read me two whole novels, an' Ah'm mostly through readin' the Bible. Though Ah don't always understand ever thin' Ah reads in the Bible, Ah mus' confess."

That got a chuckle from the man who stood a good foot taller than Baby Boy. The soldier looked down at the boy's earnest face. "Well, don't worry about that, young man. I don't understand everything I read in the Bible, either. I never have."

"Have ya read a lotta books, mister?"

"Yes. I've been reading all my life. I love reading, everything but the law, that is. Now, what two novels have you read?"

Baby Boy picked up the copy of *The Swiss Family Robinson* and showed it to the cavalryman. "Ah read this one first. Then muh teacher found me a copy o' muh favorite book, *David Copperfield*."

"But did you understand what you read, boy? Do you even re-member what you read?"

"Oh, yes, suh." Baby Boy held the tattered book to his heart and gazed earnestly at the soldier's bright eyes. "It's a great story about a brave mother an' father shipwrecked with their children on a desert island after a bad tempest. They were on their way t' Australia. It's mainly the adventures o' their sons, Fritz, an' Earnest, who was my own age when they got shipwrecked, an' Jack, an' Francis, who was only eight. Oh, an' don't ferget their big dogs, Turk an' Juno."

The soldier smiled and nodded his head. "Hm. It seems you do remember the book. So tell me, young scholar, what did you think of it? Did you read it all the way through?"

"Oh, yes, suh. Ah read ever single word. It was a great story 'bout livin' in a treehouse an' in a cave, cookin' all kinds o' weird stuff tuh eat. They even met a girl, Jenny, who was shipwrecked on the other side o' the island. Have y'all read it, suh?"

"Yes, young man, I have read it. And you are absolutely correct. It is indeed a great adventure story, just like Robinson Crusoe, who was stranded all alone on an island. I read both books when I was very young, too. Now, what else would you like to read?"

"Ah really don't know, suh. The Bible's jus' muh fourth book ever, not countin' the primer I read tuh learn muh words from, so Ah don't know many books. Sister Baines told me there's a lotta good books. She called 'em literature. But she said Ah'll have tuh wait till we gets tuh Zion tuh find 'em."

Lorna Baines walked up carrying a bundle of cloth neatly tied with string. She had two rolled army blankets tucked under her arm. Sister Woman, still carrying Chester Ray over her shoulders, frowned at Baby Boy. "Now doncha be botherin' this fine genelman, Baby Boy. Come away from there now, right this minute."

"But Sister Woman, look at all the books!" He turned pleadingly to Lorna Baines, "Look how many! Ah never knowed there was so many books in the whole wide world."

The soldier placed his left arm on Baby Boy's shoulder and held out his right hand to Lorna Baines. "Good morning, ma'am. I'm Captain John Reed of Company G, Sixth Infantry, at your service."

Lorna Baines shook his hand. "A pleasure to meet you, Captain. I'm Missus Lorna Baines. This is my friend and traveling companion, Effie Swinton, who prefers to go by Sister Woman. This intelligent young man is Sister Swinton's younger brother and my best student, Connal Lee Swinton, who prefers to be called Baby Boy."

Captain Reed smiled and doffed his small cap as he made a slight bow towards the ladies. "A pleasure to meet you, ladies. This young man of yours has just asked for my advice in finding the next novel for him to read." He smiled at Baby Boy, who smiled back, thrilled at the attention. "Now tell me, ladies, will you be buying him the book, or will he need a loaner? Will you be camped long enough outside the Fort for him to read one if I help him find one?"

Lorna returned the handsome officer's pleasant smile. "I'm not exactly sure how long we will remain here replenishing our provisions, but Baby Boy is an avid reader. I suspect he could finish most any novel before we pull out. Will the store really lend a book to someone just passing through?"

"Yes, ma'am. But if you are not one of the local community or a member of the armed services, the sutler will ask you to put down the cost of the book to borrow it. He will refund the money in full when you return the book."

Lorna nodded her head. "Well, that makes sense, doesn't it, Sister Swinton? Well, sir, if Baby Boy finds a book, I will be pleased to vouch for the cash deposit. Now come Sister Swinton. Let's finish our shopping while the good captain advises Baby Boy on his next novel to read."

As she drew Sister Woman away by the arm, she clapped Baby Boy on the back in congratulations for finding the books.

With his arm still over Baby Boy's shoulder, Captain Reed turned them to face the bookshelves again. "Now, what do we have here, eh, Baby Boy? What do you think you would like to read next?"

"Ah jus' loved readin' about David Copperfield growin' up in England. Does ya know any other books about boys growin' up in strange places?"

Captain Reed chuckled as he looked down at Baby Boy. "You think the great city of London is a strange place?"

Distractedly, the captain mused, to himself, *If the boy had a good bath and a haircut, he wouldn't look like such a wild street urchin. These poor, white trash Americans. How do they ever manage to grow up to be productive citizens? Well, I guess most don't. Look how he's outgrown his pants and his sorry boots, too. Yet he somehow reminds me of little Donny, my darling baby brother. If I still lived at home, Donny would be around this boy's age. Blond and blue-eyed and just starting to grow up, too.*

"Well, London is strange tuh me, Captain Reed."

"What? Oh...yes, I suppose it would be. For a country boy, a huge metropolitan city in Europe would be a strange new world, indeed. Being an American born and bred, I find myself partial to American writers, although I do enjoy British writers as well."

They examined and considered several books. Most had been handsomely bound in leather with gold stamped lettering. A few were bound in fabric glued to paperboard. They looked at the recently published book *Walden; on, Life in the Woods* by Henry David Thoreau, but Captain Reed decided it might be a little deep and philosophical for a young boy just starting to read. "Well, too bad they don't have a copy of *Robinson Crusoe*. You would have enjoyed it."

They ended up with the collected stories of *Oliver Twist; or, the Parish Boy's Progress*. "You said you enjoyed *David Copperfield*, Baby Boy, so I think maybe you will like this one, as well. It was also written by Charles Dickens. He published it one or two chapters at a time back in England until he finished writing the whole novel. Poor young Oliver had a hard start in life, but after lots of struggles, he made good in the end. Does that sound like something you would like to read?"

"Oh, yes, suh, Captain Reed. It surely does sound interestin'."

"All right then."

The captain picked up a well-worn copy of *History of Tom Jones*. "Well, I've found the book I want to read next. It's been years since I read *Tom Jones*. Come with me, young man, and I'll introduce you to our good sutler, Mister Samuelson."

Captain Reed spotted Lorna Baines and Sister Woman talking to the sutler's wife at the board counter set on big wood barrels. Baby Boy ran over to them. "Look, Sister Baines. Look, Sister

Woman. Ah've found me a new book tuh read. Captain Reed says it's real interestin'. Can Ah get it, please?"

Sister Woman frowned. "How much is it, Baby Boy?"

Captain Reed raised his hand to get her attention. "Don't worry about that, Missus Swinton. It would be my pleasure to advance the deposit for this fine novel." He turned and gave Baby Boy a stern look. "You do promise you will return it before you decamp the Fort, do you not?"

Baby Boy grinned and nodded his head enthusiastically. His right hand flicked a cross my heart over his chest.

Sister Woman scowled. "Why, Ah don't know, Captain Reed, suh. That's real nice o' y'all, but..."

"No, no. I really must insist, ma'am. The boy reminds me of my little brother, who is about Baby Boy's age. I miss my brothers and sisters. I would take it as a kindness if you would give your permission for me to do this for Baby Boy."

Lorna touched Sister Woman's shoulder. "I really think it would be all right, Sister Swinton."

"In fact, with your kind permission, I happen to have the day off duty today and planned on doing a little reading of my own. How about I invite Baby Boy to join me for dinner at the Old Bedlam, our commissioned officers' quarters? Afterward, he can read to me. When he gets tired, I can read to him. It would be like a touch of home, having the company of my little brother for the afternoon. Would that be agreeable, Missus Swinton?"

"Oh, no. Ah don't think so. What would Zeff say?"

"Sister Swinton, I believe we can trust the good captain to see that Baby Boy gets back to us, safe and sound."

"Yes, ma'am. Thank you. Would you like me to return him to your camp before dark or before supper? Does he have chores to do in the evening?"

"Well...jus' make sure 'e gets back tuh the camp safe afore dark. All right, Baby Boy?"

All excited, Baby Boy could only nod his head, thrilled at the idea of spending the afternoon with this interesting, good-looking officer. He gazed up at Captain Reed with hero-worship shining in his big, blue eyes.

Lorna pointed over to a small counter where a sign hung from the ceiling. "Let me post a letter to my son in London, then I'm ready to return to camp. Are you ready, too, Sister Swinton? Goodbye, Baby Boy. It was a pleasure meeting you, Captain Reed. So long, now."

Sister Woman shook her finger in Baby Boy's face. "Y'all mind yer manners, now, ya heah?"

Baby Boy happily tagged along behind the dashing young captain. They walked southerly past the officer's magazine. "This is where we store ammunition and other explosives close at hand for the officers to draw down as needed." They approached a handsome, symmetrical, two-story building with balconies running along the front. "This is Old Bedlam, where I am stationed when I'm in the Fort. Come on in, young man."

Captain Reed led Baby Boy into a hall near the end of the building, then up a flight of stairs to another hallway. He knocked briskly on a neatly painted door. It opened almost instantly. The captain removed his small blue cap with its shiny, narrow black bill and tossed it onto the neatly made bed as he strode in. "Ah, Ned. Thank you. This is my guest, Connal Lee Swinton. Baby Boy, this is my body slave, Ned. My grandfather, General Reed, gave him to me, along with my pride and joy, Paragon, when I received my commission. Grandfather informed me in the note Ned brought when he delivered my stallion that an officer and a gentleman need a superior horse to ride in front of his men and a good manservant to keep him clean and orderly at all times."

Baby Boy found himself speechless. He had heard of slavery. He understood that many of the darkies he had seen back in Missouri were or had been slaves, but he had never met a Negro before, much less a slave. He didn't know what to say. He nodded at the tall thin black boy. Ned nodded back with a big white grin.

"Help me change my shirt, now, Ned. Then I'll need a jacket so I can take my young friend to a hot luncheon."

Ned stepped up and removed the captain's bow tie. He unbuttoned the three little shirt buttons below the neck. As the captain raised his arms, Ned smoothly pulled the shirt up out of his pants

111

and over his head. He threw it down on the bed beside the hat and tie. He would put them away when the captain wasn't waiting. Baby Boy caught a glimpse of the captain's bare chest and had to stop and stare. *Why the captain's as beautiful an' as strong as that Pawnee warrior back on the plains. Ah sure hope Ah grows up big an' strong an' handsome like them. Maybe Ah should be a soldier, too, when Ah grows up.*

Baby Boy watched as Ned withdrew a clean, folded shirt from a chest of drawers and shook it out. The captain raised his arms. Baby Boy's eyes zeroed in on the nests of curly armpit hair, finding them very attractive and masculine. Ned slipped the shirt over the captain's arms and head. The captain loosened his belt buckle and tucked the shirttails into his thin, light blue wool pants. Ned refastened the belt. While the captain stood tall, like at attention, Ned tied the captain's dark blue bow tie, then used both hands to smooth down and tuck in the shirt until it lay free of wrinkles.

Ned picked up a silver-backed boar's hair brush off a tray on the bureau and brushed the captain's hair neatly back behind his ears. He reached for a vest, but the captain shook his head. "It's too warm today. Besides, I'm off duty. Just the jacket if you please."

"Yessuh."

While the captain changed his clothes, Baby Boy gazed in amazement at a room larger than Zeff and Sister Woman's home back on the mountain. He walked over and touched the glass window pane. He had seen glass but hadn't realized how smooth it would feel to the touch. He looked out over the balcony and down onto the parade ground, busy with people coming and going in all directions. Baby Boy ran his fingers along the white glossy paint on the plaster walls. He examined a heat stove set off to the side of a big brick fireplace. Its tin chimney disappeared into the wall above the mantle. "This is all yers, Captain Reed? Wow. Ah never knew a home could be so nice! And it's so clean, too."

The captain chuckled as he watched Baby Boy explore his simple room, completely lacking the luxurious, decorative refinements of his parents' elegant Edwardian home back in Boston.

After Ned finished grooming the captain, he picked up a horse hair valet brush with a silver handle and brushed down the jacket.

The young cavalryman plopped his hat back on his head at a jaunty angle. "Come along, then, Baby Boy. Let's see what our own Missus Whinton has prepared for us today. Shall we?"

Baby Boy followed, still clenching the book in his hand. They walked back down the steps to the dining hall built into an extension off the back of the building. The view out the window drew Baby Boy's attention. He walked over and looked out at the stables where the commissioned officers billeted their horses. He saw the Fort's vegetable gardens to the left of the stables and the big Laramie River twisting and bending around the far side. Low mountains raised their treeless sides to a nearly flat plateau above the river's plain.

A young teenage private walked in from the kitchen, dimly visible through the opposite door, carrying a small white towel neatly folded over his arm. "Good afternoon, Captain Reed, sir." He gestured towards a small table already set with a white tablecloth. "Luncheon for two today, sir?"

"Yes, Mannford. Thank you."

The private held out a nicely turned colonial-style chair for the captain. Baby Boy helped himself, although he pulled his chair up too close to the table. He gawked unabashedly, taking in the fine hanging brass and glass lanterns, the cold fireplace, and the varnished wood floor. Suddenly, he felt lost and out of place. Frowning with worry, he glanced across the table at Captain Reed, who watched him with an amused grin. "So, how do you like the officer's mess, Baby Boy?"

"What? The officer's mess? What's that, Captain Reed?"

"Why, a mess is what we in the army call our dining halls. This mess is a closed mess. All of us officers contribute money for Missus Whinton, our head cook, to buy special foods and prepare them for us. Our mess is private. It's not open to those who do not subscribe. We even have a few bottles of respectable wines, believe it or not. We're almost civilized. Well, not quite, but we do try. Let's face it, we are a long way out from the States after all, way out here in the western wilderness."

"A mess, huh? This looks pretty darn neat fer a mess, doncha know."

113

The private brought them a platter of yeast rolls fresh from the Fort's bakery that morning and a saucer holding a wedge of fresh-churned sweet butter. Baby Boy, always hungry, didn't need any encouragement to dig in and start eating.

A leisurely hour later, the captain pushed back from the table and tossed his napkin on the tablecloth. "Let's take your book outside and find a quiet place where we can read, shall we? It's not far down to the riverbank. I know of a cluster of trees we might sit under in the shade."

The captain led Baby Boy to a quiet grove of young plains cottonwood trees growing close to the river's edge. The captain removed his jacket and pulled his tie and collar loose. He gestured for Baby Boy to sit on the ground, leaning against the rough tree trunk. "This is nice, don't you think? Now, how about if you start reading. When you get tired, I'll take over. All right, Little Brother?"

Baby Boy propped the book up on his knees and smoothed open the cover. He coughed self-consciously, then swallowed with a gulp. "Chapter One. Treats o' the place where Oliver Twist was born an' o' the circumstances attendin' 'is birth." He paused and glanced over at the captain reading along beside him. The captain smiled and nodded. "Among other public buildin's in a certain town..."

Baby Boy read for nearly an hour. He had to stop often to sound out unfamiliar words like consolatory, passionately, and perspective. He also stopped to ask the captain the meaning of several new words. They didn't make fast progress through the book, but it fascinated Baby Boy.

The captain took a turn reading, patiently answering Baby Boy's hesitant interruptions as they came across more new vocabulary. After a couple of hours, the captain stood up and brushed off the seat of his pants. "Let's take a break and walk around a bit, shall we? I could use a drink, couldn't you?"

"Oh, yes, suh. Readin' out loud is dry work." Baby Boy carefully noted the page number, closed the book, and leaned it against the tree trunk. They walked down and knelt beside the running water. Using their cupped hands as drinking cups, they lifted cold water up to their lips. When they returned to the tree, Baby Boy's curiosity got the better of him. He sat down close to the captain and leaned his shoulder over against the captain's like when he sat with Zeff or Gilbert Baines. "So, Captain Reed. Where did y'all come from afore ya became a captain, anyway?"

The captain put his arm companionably around Baby Boy's shoulder and pulled him into a light hug. His eyes gazed into the distance. "Well, Baby Boy. I was born back in thirty-seven in Boston, Massachusetts. My father was a successful attorney with a big law practice. Now, he's a prominent judge in Boston. My mother was the daughter of a United States congressman. Both of my grandfathers served with distinction in the Continental Army. They both served as officers during the Revolutionary War, which is how my parents met."

The captain leaned his head back against the rough bole of the tree. Baby Boy pushed his long blond bangs out of his eyes when he looked up to admire the captain's handsome profile. "My older brother and I enrolled in Hahvuhd Univasity right after I turned fourteen."

"Sorry fer interruptin', Captain, but what's a hahvuhd univasity?"

"Why, that's the name of the college I attended back in Boston. Hahvuhd. You haven't heard of Hahvuhd? The campus was too far away from my parent's estate to travel to classes every day, so father arranged for us to board in a fashionable private boarding house within walking distance. I graduated three years later, in May of eighteen fifty-five. At my father's urging, I began reading law in father's law firm, but I discovered that as much as I love reading novels and studying, I did not enjoy reading dry old law cases.

"I wrote General Reed, my father's father who had retired to Virginia just outside of Washington, and asked his advice. He still had connections in the war office. Because of my education, he managed to wangle me a commission as a second lieutenant. With all the trouble along the Overland Trail, the army sent me to Fort Riley in Kansas, where I studied cavalry tactics and precision drilling for the summer.

"That fall, I received orders to take my platoon and present ourselves to Brevet Brigadier General William S. Harney. The general's orders were to punish the hostile western Sioux Indians for raiding white settlers on the Overland Trail. We arrived just in time to join up with the general's other five companies under his orders. We attacked and destroyed a Lakota Sioux village on Blue Creek, right around halfway between North Platte and Scotts Bluff in the Territory of Nebraska. I believe your handcart train passed that way on your journey here. I will never forget that day, the third of September, eighteen fifty-five. It was the first time I fired live ammunition at humans and killed a man."

Baby Boy pulled away so he could look the captain in the eye. "Y'all've killed Injuns? Fer real?"

"Yes, Little Brother. For real. It was a sad but important day for me. General Harney took note of my skills in leading my men into a successful battle. He lauded my valor and cool head under fire. He gave me a field promotion to captain to fill one of several vacancies resulting from the action. He then ordered me to Fort Laramie with all my new command. You see, Baby Boy, back years ago, the army thought that just maintaining a presence in force would keep the native tribes in line. But, unfortunately, we've seen time and time again that wasn't enough. We sometimes have no choice but to defeat the tribes by force of arms to compel them to accept living on the reservations the government has so magnanimously set aside for them as required by treaties. Regrettably, the native tribes remain a problem, even to this day."

Baby Boy gave the captain a gentle hug, then rested his head against his shoulder. Captain Reed looked down at Baby Boy's messy long hair and tattered clothes. *My little brother should be about the same age and size as this young man. Of course, Mother would have sent him to a barbershop long before he ever became this shaggy and unkempt. He would never be allowed to be seen out in public looking like Baby Boy.* The captain affectionately brushed Baby Boy's bangs off his forehead. When Baby Boy looked up, and their eyes met, the captain smiled and gave him a nudge. "I feel like riding for a while. Would you like to see my stallion?"

Baby Boy stood up. "Ah loves ridin' horses, Captain. Let's go!"

They dropped Baby Boy's book off at the captain's lodgings for safekeeping. The captain tossed his jacket on the bed. "Ned, my spurs, if you please. We're going for a ride."

Ned knelt and fastened shiny brass spurs to the captain's knee-high polished black boots. Baby Boy had never seen anything so detailed and ornate. He had to lean down to look more closely. He examined cast brass sculptures of eagle wings coming off the spurs' black leather straps. The eagles' mouths held the pointed spur wheels.

The captain led the way back behind Old Bedlam. Ned accompanied them to saddle the captain's stallion. Ned spent a good portion of his day grooming and tending to Paragon's well-being and appearance, in addition to his primary duties of maintaining the captain's quarters and wardrobe. He also shaved the captain and dressed him.

Ned rushed ahead, put a halter on Paragon, then led him out of his spacious, clean stall. Baby Boy took in a breath in amazement. "Wow! Captain! That's yer very own horse? Wow! What kind is 'e?"

Captain Reed clapped Paragon affectionately on the neck. "He's a Thoroughbred Breed, fast as the wind, and strong like you would not believe. Such stamina. He can trot for hours and still be fresh enough to ride into battle." He took the reins and held Paragon steady while Ned saddled him. Baby Boy admired the stallion's proud, classic lines. The horse's Arabian heritage clearly showed through in the arch of his neck, raised tail, and long, muscular legs. Paragon's back stood taller than Baby Boy, even when he stood up on tiptoes. "Look, he has a white star on 'is forehead. Isn't it beautiful?"

"Yes, Baby Boy. He's a beautiful glossy black except for two white socks on his rear feet and the star on his forehead."

"Oh, Captain. He's the most beautiful horse in the whole wide world. An' so shiny, too."

"I happen to agree, young man. He *is* the best horse in the world. Now, would you like to join me for a ride?"

117

The captain leapt up on Paragon, then reached down and pulled Baby Boy up behind him. "Hold on now. Paragon needs some work today." The captain shook the reins. "Walk on, Paragon. Walk on." After they cleared the huge stable doors, he gave Paragon the spurs. The great horse took off running as Captain Reed gave him his reins. Baby Boy grabbed the captain tighter around his trim waist and shouted, "Yahoo!"

Baby Boy loved pressing his face against the captain's strong back, riding on the great black stallion in the sun. After reaching the crest of the hills overlooking the Fort complex, the captain slowed them down to a walk. When they arrived at a good vantage point, they stopped and dismounted. The captain kept hold of the reins with his right hand. They strolled along for a while. Baby Boy impulsively took hold of the captain's left hand. The captain looked down at the top of Baby Boy's windblown hair but didn't withdraw his hand. He enjoyed having friendly company, like being with family. He hadn't held hands with anyone for ages.

On the ride back to the stables, they chatted amiably. Baby Boy regaled the captain with his first time shopping in a big store. His descriptive observations had the captain chuckling in amusement. He mentioned that his Sister needed winter coats for Zeff and himself. "Ah don't think Sister Woman has enough money tuh buy coats, though. We're kinda poor when it comes tuh money, doncha know."

"Well, Baby Boy. If she didn't find a coat for you, then tomorrow I want you to go over to the commissary and ask for Sergeant Tomlinson, the quartermaster. I would bet that if you told him I sent you, he could find a used coat that someone traded in. He would probably let you have it for cheap, too. Most all the enlisted men are poor, so that's nothing new for the sergeant. Can you remember the name Tomlinson?"

Baby Boy nodded, happy at the thought of helping Sister Woman find him a coat.

When they dropped Paragon off at the stables, the captain ordered the two privates, detailed to work as stable hands that day, to leave him saddled. "We will require his services after supper. Just loosen the cinch so he can rest comfortably and remove the bit from between his teeth."

"Yes, sir, Captain!"

That evening while eating supper, the captain once again pushed Baby Boy's hair off his face so he could see his eyes. Baby Boy grinned bashfully as he gazed up at the captain's nicely trimmed and brushed hair. "Does y'all think maybe Ah should get muhself a haircut, Captain?"

"If you were one of my men under my command, I would order you to get it trimmed. The army doesn't have any firm regulations for hair length for cavalrymen like for other soldiers, but still, a gentleman should be clean and well-groomed, even when working at the hardest physical labor."

The sun began setting when Private Mannford served them apple pie sprinkled over with heavy cream and white cane sugar. Baby Boy glanced out the window and saw a bright moon, three-quarters full, hanging above the stable in the evening's twilight.

"Before I take you back to your camp, I would like to speak to you from my heart, as though you were, in fact, my little brother. Would that be all right with you?"

Baby Boy nodded, suddenly nervous, afraid he might have done something wrong.

"Baby Boy is a cute nickname for a little baby boy. But you are growing up now. You are no longer a baby, so it's not so cute anymore. You are a boy growing up into a handsome and intelligent young man. Maybe it's time for you to start using your real name and leave childish things behind. Didn't Missus Baines tell me your name is Connal Lee? That's a good name for a man. What do you think, Little Brother?"

"Why, Ah suppose. It's jus' that Ah've always been called Baby Boy. If'n someone called me Connal Lee, Ah might not know they were talkin' tuh me."

The captain chuckled. "Well, Connal Lee, let's give it a try. If you asked them nicely, I bet your brother and sister would be glad to start using your real name. I'm certain Missus Baines would prefer to use proper names. She seemed the type that would be particular about social amenities."

"Oh, that she is, Captain. She's mighty particular."

"Come on, Connal Lee. Let's get you back to your family's campfire."

When they rode up, Zeff and Sister Woman stood up to admire Paragon. "What a beautiful animal! What a big stallion!"

The captain lowered Baby Boy to the ground, then dismounted. He held his hand out to Zeff. "Captain Reed at your service, sir. You must be Baby Boy's older brother he has told me about."

"Thas right. Zefford Ray Swinton. Nice tuh meet y'all."

"Missus Swinton, it's good to see you again. Here's your baby brother back safe and sound just like I promised."

Sister Woman smiled and nodded her thanks.

"Well, I must be off now. Thank you for pretending to be my little brother this afternoon, Connal Lee. Keep up the good work with your reading!"

Baby Boy impulsively ran over and threw his arms around Captain Reed's waist for a big hug, his book still clasped in his hand. The captain mussed up his windblown hair affectionately. "So long, now, Connal Lee."

"Thanks, Captain Reed. Yer the best friend Ah ever had!"

"You are most welcome, Little Brother."

The captain climbed back up onto the saddle. "Don't forget to see Sergeant Tomlinson, our quartermaster, tomorrow about a warm coat. So long, now. I'm on duty tomorrow, so I don't know if I'll see you or not. In any event, I wish you safe travels as you continue on with your journey. Bye, now."

The captain gently nudged Paragon in the stomach with his spurs and a snap of his reins. They tore off, racing back to the Fort.

Baby Boy couldn't stop chattering excitedly about the captain and his home and horse and reading all afternoon and learning new words and making a new friend. Finally, he wound down, to the relief of both Zeff and Sister Woman.

He grabbed a quilt to wear like a shawl as the night cooled down.

Chapter 10: Winter

After eating his favorite breakfast of hominy grits with butter and molasses, Baby Boy strolled over to see Lorna Baines. "Good mornin', Sister Baines."

"Why, good morning, Baby Boy. And how are you this fine and glorious morning?"

"Ah'm good, thanks. An' y'all? Good morning, Brother Baines."

"And the top of the morning to you, my fine young man. I hope you don't want to see my shoe tongues again. I just barely got my shoes tied."

Baby Boy chuckled and shook his head no. "Ah jus' wondered if y'all were plannin' on goin' up tuh the Fort again today. Sister Woman says she got ever thin' she needed yesterday an' won't be goin' over again." Baby Boy lowered his voice and leaned in confidentially. "Ah think maybe she don't like big crowds o' people. Makes 'er nervous."

"Frankly, I hadn't planned on going to the fort, Baby Boy. I want to finish sewing up my new dress today."

Baby Boy sat down on the ground beside Mr. Baines. "Oh. Well, Ah guess Ah'll jus' mosey on up by muhself, then. Ah've gotta buy me a winter coat. Captain Reed tol' me tuh see his friend, the quartermaster at the commissary. What's a quartermaster, Sister Baines?"

"Why, I believe a quartermaster is the officer in charge of provisioning, you know, supplying uniforms, blankets, weapons, and so forth."

"Oh. Tell me, Sister Baines. Do y'all think Ah needs a haircut?"

"Well, you are a bit shaggy, now that you mention it. Why do you ask?"

"Oh, muh new big brother tol' me yesterday that Ah should always be neat an' clean. The captain has a real nice short haircut.

Did y'all notice it when ya met 'im at the store? He looked so handsome what with 'is clean shaved face an' short hair. Ah wants tuh grow up tuh be jus' like 'im."

"That's nice, Baby Boy. You really took a liking to the good captain, then, I take it."

"Oh, yes, ma'am. He lives in a really nice place. He has what he called a body slave, a young black boy who keeps his room, an' clothes, an' war stallion all clean an' proper. Oh, an' didja see 'is stallion, Paragon, when he rode me home last night? He's the most beautiful horse in the whole wide world."

"I take it you had a good time with the captain, then."

"Oh, yes, ma'am! He's so kind an' so smart. Ah wants tuh be jus' like 'im when Ah grows up. Maybe Ah'll even be a soldier."

"Is this your roundabout way of asking me to give you a haircut, Baby Boy?"

"Well, Ah did see y'all cuttin' Brother Baines hair the other evenin'. Ah wouldn't want tuh bother ya none, but all Sister Woman ever did was put a bowl over muh head an' cut off ever thin' below it with 'er scissors. Maybe that's good enough fer a little kid, but the captain tol' me Ah was growin' up an' needed tuh start takin' care o' muhself better. Would y'all mind, Sister Baines?"

"No, I wouldn't mind. It only takes a minute with the clippers. Gilbert, would you please be a dear and fetch us the hand clippers and a dishtowel from the handcart?"

"Yes, my dear, it would be my pleasure, indeed, to contribute in my own small way to the sartorial improvements of our maturing, young friend here." A moment later, Gilbert Baines handed the steel clippers and towel to Lorna.

Baby Boy stood up, feeling very self-conscious. Lorna tucked in the towel around Baby Boy's neck. "This will keep the hair from falling down inside your shirt and itching you all day long."

"Oh. Thanks. What does Ah do, now, Sister Baines?"

"You just stand up straight, right there, while I work my magic. Would you like your hair as short as Brother Baines'?"

"Well, maybe not that short. Jus' like the captain will be fine, if'n y'all can manage it, please."

122

Lorna pulled a thick comb through Baby Boy's unruly hair. He flinched a couple of times as she had to tug through some real snags and snarls. She began by lifting a section of hair with the comb and then snipping off the ragged ends. When she squeezed the handles, the blade moved back and forth over the clipper's fine-toothed edge, cutting off the captured hair. Dirty blond hair drifted down all around them.

"Ya know what else muh new big brother tol' me?"

"What's that, Baby Boy?"

"He tol' me that Ah'm too growed up tuh keep usin' muh nickname o' Baby Boy. He said Ah'm not a baby no longer, but a growin' young man. He advised me tuh start usin' muh real name o' Connal Lee. He even said 'e thought y'all would approve, too."

"Well, young Master Swinton, as a matter of fact, I do agree wholeheartedly with the fine captain. Good advice, young man. Shall I start calling you Connal Lee, then, Baby Boy?"

"Yes, ma'am. If'n y'all would, please. Ah guess Ah'm gonna have tuh ask Zeff an' Sister Woman tuh call me by muh real name, too."

Lorna pulled the small flannel towel out of his collar and flicked it over his shoulders to remove the stray hair. "Well, there you are, Connal Lee. All trimmed up and ready for inspection by the good captain. You look very handsome, too, if I say so myself."

Baby Boy turned around and gave Lorna a hug. "Thanks a lot, Sister Baines. Now, Ah'm gonna go wash at the river then head on up tuh the Fort fer a winter coat. See y'all at class this evenin'. Thanks again."

"Good luck with the quartermaster, Connal Lee."

Baby Boy grinned and took off towards the Swinton handcart for a towel.

Two hours later, a much cleaner, better groomed, and more mature-looking young man strode into the Army warehouse. When he asked for Sergeant Tomlinson, they told him he could find the sergeant in the commissary next door where they stored food. Connal Lee went to the other building. "Sergeant Tomlinson? Ah'm Connal Lee Swinton. Muh new big brother, Captain Reed, tol' me tuh look y'all up an' ask fer yer help findin' a old used coat fer the winter."

"Oh, the captain told ya that, did he? Well, what the hell were ya doing talking to the great high lord and master himself?"

"What?"

"Our great and noble captain is so gol-danged high and mighty, he normally wouldn't be seen talking to riffraff and poor white trash like yew. Why, he even has a slave to kiss his boots – I mean, shine his boots. He doesn't have the time of day for common people like us."

"He tol' me y'all were 'is friend an' that maybe ya could help me find a coat. Muh sister tried tuh buy me one yesterday at the sutler's store, but even the used ones there cost too dang much money. We don't have a lotta money, ya see."

"So, Captain Reed called me a friend, huh? Well, when I went on patrol with him under his orders, he sure didn't treat me like a friend. He ordered me around more like another of his slaves, truth be told. But, who knows, maybe that's how rich folk treat all their friends. Well, come along, young man. We store the used coats over in the main warehouse, though I'm not sure I'll have much that will fit. You are younger and smaller than most men joining the army. Well, let's go see what I can find for a friend of my friend, the great and important captain."

The Sergeant led Baby Boy next door to the back of the big one-story sod warehouse. Dozens of interior cedar posts supported its low roof of sod. "When a man outgrows or wears out his clothes, he turns in the used ones for a credit against his new uniform. We store them all over here."

Baby Boy smelled old dirt and sweat on the used clothing as they drew near. Sergeant Tomlinson picked up a coat that looked newer than the others. "Here. Try this on for size, young man."

Baby Boy pulled on a blue wool frock coat. The bottom of its skirts fell below his knees. The sleeves hung down over his knuckles. The Sergeant shook his head. "No, no. That's too big."

Baby Boy shrugged. "Oh, don't worry none 'bout that. Ah jus' started muh growin' spurt, so I'll grow into it jus' fine. How much is this one, anyway?"

124

"Well, for a good friend of the most illustrious Captain Reed, I can let ya have it for four bits."

"What? Why so cheap? This looks like a fine, warm coat."

"Oh, it is, but nobody wants to wear it. I can't even give it away to an enlisted man."

"Why doesn't anyone want to wear it, Sergeant?"

"Take it off, and I'll show ya." The Sergeant turned the coat over and showed a stained bullet hole in the middle of the back. "This'll need some work getting it cleaned up and the hole patched, but the coat's nearly new, otherwise. This is why nobody wants it. The previous owner died in it. You aren't squeamish or superstitious, are ya, young man?"

"Why, no. An' muh sister knows all about sewin' an' cleanin' blood off clothes. This will do right nicely, Sergeant Tomlinson. Right nicely. Thanks!"

"Now, while we're at it, I think I might have some old trousers over here that aren't too ragged. You've pretty much outgrown those dungarees. And we've got to have some used boots that will be better than your poor, decrepit old boots. Just look at the sorry state of your clothes. I'm surprised the fancy Captain Reed would even talk to ya, dressed the way you are."

Connal Lee looked down at the ground, now embarrassed, hoping his new big brother hadn't been offended at his poor clothing. He had never given a thought to what he wore or how he looked before. It took another hour to find him a pair of used boots and a pair of old pale bluish-gray corduroys, intended to be worn for work, not as part of a dress or parade uniform. The legs bunched on the floor, but Connal Lee just rolled them up in cuffs. The smallest pants the Sergeant could find had a waist four inches too large, so he cinched up his knife belt tight enough to hold them up. By the time he finished shopping, he had paid the Sergeant all four quarters Sister Woman had given him to buy a coat.

He felt like a rich man as he marched across the parade ground wearing new boots and pants. He carried a gunny sack filled with his old boots, dungarees, and his new coat folded up neatly. His happy smile welcomed everyone he saw.

His path took him past the front of the whitewashed army head-quarters. He gazed up and admired the enormous American flag fluttering in the breeze at the top of the tall flagpole. He heard a man call out, "Connal Lee. Is that you, Connal Lee? Hey, Baby Boy! Yes, you. That *is* you, isn't it?"

Baby Boy's heart skipped a beat when he glanced over and saw Captain Reed standing on the porch of the headquarters building. His eyes lit up. He jogged over and stopped in front of the porch. "Captain Reed, Ah was hopin' Ah would see y'all today. How are y'all doin'?"

"Why, I'm doing just fine, Connal Lee. What have you done to yourself, young man? You look so much more grown-up and mature just since yesterday."

Baby Boy looked down at his new boots and shuffled his feet. "Well, Ah guess Ah got me a haircut, Captain Reed, like ya tol' me tuh do."

"Looks very nice, young man. Very smart and neat. I wasn't sure it was really you, especially when you didn't answer when I called your name."

Baby Boy smiled bashfully. "Ah tol' y'all that would happen, Captain. Ah recognized Baby Boy when Ah heard it, but not the Connal Lee part."

The captain harumphed with a grin. "Yes. You did tell me that would happen. I take it you saw Sergeant Tomlinson?"

"Oh, yes, suh. He was most obligin'. He didn't believe me at first when Ah told 'im y'all was muh friend. But, he finally believed me. He helped me get a mostly new coat, too. It only has one bullet hole, an' a little blood stain Sister Woman can fix fer me. It's real nice. Thanks fer sendin' me tuh see 'im, Captain."

A man stepped out of the office and tapped the captain on his shoulder. Captain Reed nodded at the other officer, then looked at Connal Lee. "Duty calls, Connal Lee. Good job with the haircut, young man. When do you pull out, do you know?"

"Ah don't knows yet, Captain."

"Well, goodbye for now. Maybe our paths will cross again."

"Thanks fer ever thin', Captain Reed. Ah sure hopes tuh see y'all again soon. Bye, now!"

The bargains Baby Boy had made without her help impressed Sister Woman. That evening as they ate supper, Baby Boy asked them to call him Connal Lee from now on. "Ah ain't a baby no more. Ah'm a growin' up."

He spent the rest of the evening reading about the sad life and troubles of Oliver Twist until it became too dark to see.

Around midafternoon two days later, Connal Lee finished reading *Oliver Twist*. He sat thinking about Oliver's adoption by the Brownlows. He loved reading that Oliver had a home at last without Fagin forcing him to do bad things. Happy, he closed the book as Captain Hanover walked up to their fire pit. The Swintons stood up as he shook hands with Zeff. "Well, Brother Swinton, it looks like we'll get back on the trail in the morning. Do you have everything in order for an early morning departure?"

"Yes, suh, Captain Hanover. We'll be ready. Never yew fear."

Connal Lee frowned at the book he held in his hands. "Oh! Ah promised Captain Reed tuh return this here novel afore we hit the trail. Ah've gotta rush up tuh the sutler's store afore they close." He looked over at the angle of the sun, all concerned.

Sister Woman nodded at Connal Lee. "An' Ah finished checkin' muh stores this mornin', an' figure Ah better get some more bakin' soda an' bakin' powder afore we leave fer the pass, or Ah might run short. Ah would hate not tuh make muh soda bread on the way. Ah'll come along with ya, Baby Boy. Oh, sorry. Connal Lee."

"Let's stop by an' see if Sister Baines needs anythin' while we're on our way."

"All righty then, let's git a goin'."

Zeff loaded Chester Ray into the knapsack on Sister Woman's back, then gave her a kiss goodbye with a smart slap on her behind. She jumped and giggled. "Oh, yew!"

Together, Sister Woman and Connal Lee strode over to the Baines cookfire. Obviously, the Baines had already received word about leaving. Gilbert had the contents of their handcart laid out on the ground around their camp, all organized, busily repacking it efficiently. Lorna stood up with a big smile when she spotted Connal Lee and Sister Woman approaching.

"Hiya, Sister Baines. We're goin' tuh the sutler's store fer some last-minute things an' so Ah can return *Oliver Twist* like Ah promised. Y'all wanna go with us?"

"Oh, thank you, Connal Lee. But I completed my shopping list yesterday, just to be on the safe side. But thank you for thinking of me. My, but I must say, you certainly look all grown up in proper britches and boots, young man."

Connal Lee grinned bashfully as he looked down at the ground. No one ever complimented him, and he didn't know what to do or say in response. Sister Woman examined Lorna Baines' new day dress and nodded her head. The simple top had long sleeves fastened at the neck and belted at the waist with a skirt that ended just above her ankles. "Thas a real nice new dress, Sister Baines. Oh, an' Ah jus' love how ya gathered up the sleeves at the shoulders. It looks so purdy."

"Why, thank you, Sister Swinton. I even had enough material leftover to sew up a matching bonnet for traveling in the sun." She reached down and picked up her new hat and deftly tied it on with a flourish. Smiling proudly, she turned to show the ruffles gathered in the back to cover her neck.

"Right nice, Sister Baines. An' such fast work, too. It looks almost too elegant tuh wear fer ever day."

"You are too kind, Sister Swinton. I've always had a knack with needle and thread. My mother taught me when I was very young. It has always come in handy."

"Come on, Sister Woman, Ah gotta get tuh the store afore it closes. Let's go! Bye, Sister Baines. See y'all later, Brother Baines."

"Goodbye, Sister Swinton. Goodbye, Connal Lee. See you later in class."

Sister Woman and Connal Lee hiked up to the Fort complex. Connal Lee rushed up to the counter close to the bookshelf, holding the book up high to get the attention of the sutler or his wife. Mr. Samuelson saw him and waved him over.

"Hello, Mister Samuelson. Does y'all remember me? Captain Reed borrowed me yer book tuh read, an' here it is back, jus' like Ah promised 'im."

"Yes, young man. I remember you. Now, let me find the register for the good captain's account, and I will enter a credit for the return of the book. Thank you for bringing it back so promptly."

"Would y'all please tell Captain Reed that Ah kept muh word an' returned it? Ah really loved readin' it. Please tell 'im thanks, again, fer the recommendation. Ah'm so relieved Oliver got adopted an' Fagin got what 'e deserved. It was a great book. Did y'all like it, too?"

"Yes, young man. I enjoyed it a lot. I'm sure the captain will be delighted to hear your review and approval of his choice. I'll be sure and let him know the next time I see him."

"Oh, good. Thanks, suh." He turned and pointed to his sister. "We needs some stuff fer the road as we leaves tomorrow in the mornin'. Thanks again, Mister Samuelson. Bye, now."

"Happy trails, young man. Safe travels, Missus Swinton."

Sister Woman crossed over to the food section and completed her minor purchases. As they walked through the Fort on their way back to the camp, Connal Lee kept looking around, hoping to see Captain Reed so he could say goodbye. But he never found him. They made it back to camp in time for Connal Lee to hear Lorna Baines ringing her handbell, announcing the five-minute warning before class began. He headed towards the center of the camp to attend class while Sister Woman cooked their supper and Zeff finished packing the handcart.

Chapter 11: Vocalization

One step at a time, they climbed slowly higher and higher, drawing closer to South Pass, now only two weeks away. They crossed the northwestern edge of Nebraska Territory, which would eventually become Wyoming Territory and later the State of Wyoming. Connal Lee found the going harder than back on the flat plains. The whole company did. Their speed slowed down the higher they climbed. The nights began turning cooler with the higher elevations.

One morning shortly after they began the trek, Connal Lee spotted an oak chest of drawers sitting off to the side of their trail. At midday, they passed three empty travel trunks cast aside and deserted. Before they reached their next campground, Connal Lee spotted a small sheet-iron cook stove sitting alongside the trail. At first, he couldn't identify it, but as they passed, he could make it out.

When Zeff and Connal Lee handed off their surplus kills to Captain Hanover that evening, Connal Lee asked him why people had discarded valuable items by the wayside. Captain Hanover chuckled. "There's gonna be a lot more o' that the higher we climb, Baby Boy. That stuff's what we call leeverites."

"Please call me by muh grown-up name, Captain. Muh name is really Connal Lee."

"Very well, Baby...um, sorry, Connal Lee."

"Thanks. Now, what the heck's leeverites, Captain? Is it a religion like Canaanites and Israelites?"

The captain laughed a great belly laugh. "Naw. Ya see, when the great covered wagons start goin' uphill, the beasts an' the people are already worn out from the long trip. So the pioneers have t' lighten their loads. They have t' leave 'er right here t' lighten the wagons. That's why we call them leeverites. Treasures back in Missouri became burdensome an' start slowin' 'em down by this point. So, they leave everything they can right here."

Connal Lee understood but didn't find it funny. He heard Lorna Baines ring her little brass bell calling the children to school. He said his goodbyes and headed for the commissary wagons.

That evening, Lorna Baines talked about the proper pronunciation of the English language. She discussed local accents and dialects, both in Great Britain and the United States. She gave examples of upper-class speech spoken by the British aristocracy and Cockney spoken by the working class in London. Some of the children chuckled to hear the differences. She explained how a Boston accent sounded similar in many ways to some English accents, then she gave examples of southern accents. To make her point, she called on Connal Lee. He stood up to answer her. Lorna picked up her little slate board and chalked in the capital letter I. "Connal Lee, what is this letter I just wrote on the slate?"

"It's the letter Aye."

"Correct. Please use it in a sentence, now."

"Ah'm pretty sure that letter's an Aye." Just as he said, Aye, his voice broke. He jerked upright, shocked at the bass croak that came out of his mouth. The boys and girls sitting around Lorna giggled and pointed.

Lorna smiled knowingly. "Don't worry about it, Connal Lee. It's just your voice starting to change now that you are growing up. No need to be embarrassed. It will soon settle down to your adult man's voice." She took a deep breath and nodded reassuringly. "Now, did you just hear what you did when you spoke, other than your voice cracking? Rather than saying I'm pretty sure, you said, Ah'm pretty sure. That's the southern accent you learned to speak back in the Ozarks. Like most accents, the pronunciations don't always follow along with how we spell words. Do you remember how Captain Reed pronounced Harvard University in his Boston accent?"

Connal Lee nodded. "Yep. Hahvuhd Univasity, Sister Baines."

"How do you spell Harvard? Do you remember?"

"Yes, Sister Baines. H-A-R-V-A-R-D."

"That is correct, Connal Lee. So, as we learn to read and spell, we all need to be aware of how people pronounce words differently. The correct way is most usually closer to the way a word is spelled, except those words with silent letters." She paused and gave Connal Lee a wink. He grinned back. "Now, Connal Lee, please repeat after me: I am going hunting."

"Ah'm goin' huntin'.""

"Let's try it again, but this time rather than eating the ends of the words like so many Irish, Scottish and English speakers do, try to pronounce the words properly. Try again. Listen hard. "I am going hunting.""

"Ah..."

Lorna held up her hand imperiously. "No. Not Ah but Aye. Try it again."

"I am goin' huntin'."

"Say going."

"Going."

"Good. Now say going hunting."

Very slowly, concentrating hard, Connal Lee recited, "I am going hunting."

"Correct. Very good, Connal Lee. Now that you are aware of it, please pay attention to how you say your words. Children, let's all practice being precise, despite whatever accent you learned growing up. It will make your communications clearer, and it will help your spelling when you write things down for others to read in the future."

The students all nodded, whether they understood or not. Connal Lee had a serious look on his face as he thought to himself, *Harvard University, not Hahvuhd Univasity. I am going hunting, not Ah'm goin' huntin'.* As he walked Lorna back to her cookfire, he mumbled, "That's hard, Sister Baines, not talkin' regular like." His voice broke again. The end of his comment came out louder and deeper than the beginning of his sentence. Connal Lee shook his head, irritated at his changing voice.

"Talking, Connal Lee. Not talkin'."

"Oops. Yep, yer right. Still, tain't natural, though."

"Yes, you are right. Still, that is not natural, though."

"Oh."

The handcart company maintained a westerly heading, always traveling west towards South Pass, steadily traveling uphill at a gentle grade. The ground grew increasingly dry and rocky. The dirt took on a whitish alkaline color. Stunted sagebrush grew low to the

132

ground, seldom higher than twelve inches. Dried grasses and little else grew around the sagebrush. Everyone found it cooler than expected for so early in the fall, primarily due to the higher elevation. The days stayed in the comfortable low seventies, but nights became quite chilly, especially when the wind blew. The wind blew more often than not.

Lorna Baines changed her teaching schedule. She merged the two small groups of students into one class. She spent the first quarter-hour reviewing basic spelling and vocabulary, often based on what they read out loud the day before. She devoted the next quarter-hour to addition and subtraction exercises. They spent the balance of the class reading aloud from *David Copperfield,* taking turns among the better readers. Connal Lee ended up being called upon only every other day.

The entire class made progress in speaking more correctly and not swallowing the ends of their words. Lorna's students learned not to contract their words but to speak each one out clearly as they were more often written. "Do not allow yourselves to have lazy tongues, children. Speak clearly and distinctly at all times."

When Connal Lee had free time during daylight hours, he wandered over to Lorna and Gilbert Baines' fireplace. They welcomed him and made him feel right at home. He read to them from *David Copperfield*, then spent many enjoyable hours discussing the book's vocabulary, different lifestyles, and philosophies. Lorna prepared supper as they chatted.

In Gilbert Baines' younger days, he had studied divinity and geography at the ancient University of Edinburgh, known throughout the world for its medical college. Later, he came to realize he lacked a true calling to be ordained a priest. His time spent there tamed his Scottish accent into an educated manner of speaking before he moved to London. While Lorna prepared food and cleaned up, he spent an increasing amount of time with Connal Lee. Connal Lee affectionately leaned his shoulder against Gilbert's while they shared a book between their laps. Gilbert ended up having a greater influence on Connal Lee's improving speech patterns than Lorna. Connal Lee not only began to lose his lazy hillbilly Ozark accent, but his speech took on a crisper accent, more like Gilbert's smooth flow of words. Occasionally, Lorna heard a touch of her husband's Scottish brogue coming through as Connal Lee imitated his alternate teacher's lilting manner of speaking. Lorna had always been charmed by her husband's bright, light Scottish brogue. It tickled her to hear it from Connal Lee.

Within just a couple of days of the first time his voice broke, it stopped flipping between high and low and settled into a pleasant, grown-up baritone. After supper one evening, Zeff sat down beside Connal Lee and gave him a warm, one-arm hug. "Hey there, Baby Boy, yer really a growin' up now, ain'tcha? Jus' listen tuh yer manly voice. Ah guess yer gettin' hair on yer body, now, an' ever thin', huh? Ah'm glad yer becomin' a man, Little Brover. Now we definitely cain't be a callin' ya, Baby Boy. Sister Woman an' Ah're plumb proud o' y'all, Little Brover. Yer growin' up right afore our eyes into a good man. We're so glad yer part o' our family, doncha know. We both loves ya, Connal Lee."

Connal Lee looked down, feeling embarrassed yet proud, too. "Thanks, Big Brover. Yew'll always be muh older brother an' muh foster paw. Ah love both o' y'all, too."

Zeff stood up and walked away to draw down a bag of buckshot from the freight wagons. Connal Lee sat thinking about how his testicles were hanging low now. Sometimes he felt them moving when he walked. He had also begun growing hair a couple of weeks ago. Unconsciously, he reached down and fondled his penis. Seemingly overnight, before he quite knew what to think of it, it had grown twice as big, drawing his attention more and more to the man parts swinging between his legs.

He remembered the unpleasant way his father had used his stiff shaft to hurt and humiliate him. He knew firsthand the pain and degradation of being penetrated against his will. He also knew Zeff and Sister Woman made love using their man parts and woman parts. Back in their old home, they used to be quite enthusiastic, moaning and shouting and having great fun. Connal Lee always smiled when he saw them under the quilts and heard their cries and sighs. Now, on the trail, they made love very quietly and only whispered their endearments. Neither Zeff nor Sister Woman had ever invited Connal Lee to join them, so he knew nothing about the pleasure of making love. He only knew about using sex for pain, dominance, and humiliation.

Zeff once told him they had produced Chester Ray by making love, but he couldn't quite understand how that could have happened. Connal Lee knew he had his newly grown penis for more than just urinating, but he found himself confused with all the new feelings rushing through his maturing body. He had begun waking up every morning with an erection poking up in his pants. Sometimes it tented the quilt. The thought of Zeff or Sister Woman noticing it embarrassed him. If they ever saw anything, they didn't make any comments or jokes, to his relief. When it happened, he poked at it until it went down before he dared step out from underneath the quilts.

When Lorna cooked more food than Gilbert and she could eat, and since it wasn't practical to cart most leftovers the next morning, she invited Connal Lee to take supper with them. They enjoyed many lively conversations during their meals, discussing life in England and Scotland and their travels across the Atlantic Ocean. As soon as Connal Lee finished eating supper with the Baines, he hightailed it over to the Swinton fireplace for a second meal. He always felt hungry anyway. Sister Woman teased him he ate so much he must have a hollow leg.

Connal Lee grew in spurts and bounds, both in height, in muscle, and in intellect.

Chapter 12: Reconnoitering

A couple of weeks' journey west of Fort Laramie, everyone in the company became alert when they saw a cloud of dust rising in the air ahead of them like would be stirred up by a large body of mounted horses riding towards them from the west. Even though only midafternoon, Captain Hanover ordered everyone to form up camp in a tight defensive position, just to be on the safe side. Wagon trains didn't travel fast enough to stir up great clouds of dust in their tracks. The minute the Swinton handcart stopped, Connal Lee chocked the wheels with a couple of stones so it wouldn't move. They had camped that afternoon on the side of a gentle hill and didn't want their cart to roll unattended. Then, quick as he could, he grabbed his double-barreled shotgun, loaded two lead slugs, and took off running towards the west side of the camp.

By the time they organized the camp, Captain Hanover could identify the riders as Federal cavalrymen, not an Indian war party. His tense posture relaxed as he sat his favorite big piebald gelding. He watched the cavalry draw near at a reasonably good pace but riding slower than their regular business-like trot.

Connal Lee walked up and stood beside the captain's horse. He shaded his eyes with his hat in his left hand to see more clearly. "Who do ya think they are, Captain?"

"Why, it appears they're a cavalry patrol returnin' from reconnoiterin' further west along the trail."

"What's reconnoiterin', Captain?"

Captain Hanover drew his eyes away from the riders and the dust trail rising behind their path to glance down at Connal Lee. "Reconnoiterin' is when the military ventures into enemy territory an' checks out what they're up to. They determine the enemy's size and intent so we can prepare for 'em."

"Oh. I wonder if they're the same patrol we saw leave Fort Laramie the day we arrived and set up our camp there?"

"Most likely. We haven't seen any other patrols pass us goin' either east or goin' west, so it's almost gotta be them."

"Ah wonder where they went an' – and – what they learned?"

136

"Well, stick around. I'm sure they'll stop an' brief us on the trail ahead before they continue on back t' Fort Laramie. Do me a favor, Bab...uh, Connal Lee. Go spread the word t' the Sisters that I'd like 'em t' prepare plenty o' hot food an' drink fer the soldiers, like a early potluck supper, if ya please. They're bound t' be tired an' hungry, bein' out on patrol like they are, ridin' hard all the day long."

"Yes, suh!" Connal Lee took off running back into the camp. After he rushed around spreading the word, he jogged back to stand beside the captain again. He didn't want to miss anything.

As the patrol drew closer, Connal Lee didn't understand why they looked sloppy and disordered. They looked nothing like the crisp military parade he had watched riding proudly out of Fort Laramie in precise formation three weeks earlier. "Captain? Are those bandages? Have they been in a fight, do ya think?"

"Looks like ya might be right. Looks like they might have some wounded men among them, doesn't it?"

They watched while the patrol slowed their approach to a walk. A couple of men rode hatless. Several soldiers wore blood-stained and filthy bandages tied around their legs or arms. One wore his jacket over his shoulders like a cape, exposing a dressing black with blood wrapping his bare chest. Soiled compresses wrapped another cavalryman's head, covering his left eye. One man rode slumped over his horse with his hands clinging to the saddle horn. A young private riding beside him held his reins and led his horse. The last six soldiers at the tail of the patrol each led horses piled high with provisions. Four big draft horses brought up the rear, carrying food supplies and cooking utensils for the patrol. Two horses carried saddles piled high with the possessions of the wounded and deceased soldiers.

"Oh, this don't look good, does it, Connal Lee?"

"Nope. They surely do look beat up an' wore out, don't they just?"

"Run an' tell the cowboys an' guards t' grab their canteens an' get up here on the double. I want 'em t' help the soldiers dismount an' set up their camp. Some of these men look like they're gonna need some help if ya ask me."

Connal Lee wanted to do what the captain requested, but he also wanted to stay so he could see and hear everything that happened. Finally, he jumped into action and scampered to the center of the camp. He delivered the message, talking fast and loud, hoping he could return before the patrol arrived.

The handcart company's men and boys headed out to where the captain sat his horse. Connal Lee returned as fast as he could jog. The three older teamsters tagged along behind to offer their help, as well. Connal Lee reached Captain Hanover just as the first riders turned off the trail, heading directly towards them. Captain Hanover rode forward to meet the young officer leading the patrol. Connal Lee jogged alongside, now out of breath, carrying his shotgun before him in both hands.

"Greetings, Lieutenant. I'm Captain Philip Hanover. Welcome to our camp."

"Thank you, Captain Hanover. I'm First Lieutenant Lucas Anderson of the First Contingent of Mounted Riflemen, Company G, Sixth Infantry out of Fort Laramie, at your service, sir."

"Please, Lieutenant, bring your patrol on in an' join us over alongside our camp by the creek. The ladyfolk are preparin' an early supper fer yer men even as we speak. Here, now, please let me boys help yer troop get dismounted an' settled in."

As he wearily climbed down off his large gelding, the lieutenant turned and saw the small group of young men walking towards them. "Thank you, Captain. Mighty kind of you. My men are exhausted, and more than a few are riding wounded, as you may have noticed."

Connal Lee rushed over with a big smile and held out his hand to take the lieutenant's reins. "Here, let me get yer mount settled in for y'all, suh."

"Why, thank you, young man. And what would your name be?"

"Oh, Ah'm Connal Lee Swinton, suh."

"Nice to make your acquaintance, Connal Lee." The Lieutenant turned to his men and shouted out orders to bivouac alongside the handcart encirclement. While the dusty riders pulled themselves off their weary mounts, more men of the camp strolled over and offered their assistance.

An hour later, they had unsaddled and watered the horses. They hobbled the horses and turned them loose to graze for fodder outside the military camp, wearing only lead harnesses. Captain Hanover walked over to join the lieutenant. "Would ya like t' come sit down a spell. We're dyin' t' hear the news o' the road an' about yer skirmishes on patrol."

Bright-eyed Connal Lee nodded his head, all excited about hearing the news. One of the younger wives, her face barely visible beneath a fabric sunbonnet, strode up to the captain. "Captain Hanover, we have hot coffee and hot food ready for your guests over by the support wagons if you would like to invite them to join us."

"Oh, thank you, Sister Collings. Well, Lieutenant, you heard the young lady. Please invite yer men t' head towards those white tops over there in the center of our encampment. Yew and yer men can rest up an' grab a bite t' eat there. Follow me, an' I'll show ya the way."

"Thank you, Captain Hanover. It is very gracious of your company to go to all this trouble. We can certainly use a bite to eat and a rest, that's for certain. We have wounded to tend to, as well."

The lieutenant turned and shouted orders to set up their one-man tents, then head over to the wagons for an early supper. Connal Lee heard a cheer break out when the men heard about the food. Several of the immigrants volunteered their shoulders or arms to help the wounded walk to the wagons. Connal Lee stuck close behind the captain and the lieutenant as they wound their way through the family campsites to the freight wagons. He didn't want to miss a single word.

After everyone helped themselves to the spread the ladies had prepared, they sat down on the ground to eat. Connal Lee grabbed a plate and loaded it high with meat, beans, and cornbread, always happy to have a chance to eat. He took a seat beside the captain so he could watch the young lieutenant while they all ate.

In between chewing, the lieutenant delivered his report. "We received word back at Fort Laramie two or three weeks ago that groups of renegade Crow war parties were raiding not only the Shoshones, which is nothing new, believe me, but also preying on wagon trains on the Overland Trail. That is against the conventions of several different treaties. Major Sanderson ordered Captain Reed to organize a detail of three squads consisting of twenty-four mounted troops to go check out the rumors. We rode as far as Soda Springs, a couple of days hard ride west of the pass, but we didn't see or hear anything. In fact, we didn't encounter a single soul along our route. We rested a day, then headed back to the Fort to make our report. We rode east and were a day or so past the Bear Lake Valley area when a war party of Crow Indians attacked. They caught us unawares as we made camp after a long hard ride. They were a fairly small raiding party, but they were all worked up. They had painted their faces with white stripes, and they wore big war bonnets. They fought like devils, angry as all hell. They took us totally by surprise. We had no idea they were even in the vicinity. As you saw when we rode up, Captain, a number of my men took wounds during that skirmish, a few of them serious, two of them mortal. Our superior guns finally drove off the war party, but we experienced a lively and deadly altercation while it lasted."

The lieutenant placed his empty white enameled plate on the ground and lifted a tin travel mug of coffee to his lips.

"How didja know they was Crow Injuns, Lieutenant?"

Captain Hanover scowled at Connal Lee for interrupting but didn't say anything.

"You can always tell a Crow by one of two ways. First, they always wear something white when they ride into battle. Usually, it's white feathers in their hair and white bands on their arms above their biceps. Second, Crow men never cut their hair. When they ride into battle, they wear it tied up in large buns on the backs of their heads. If it comes loose, it sometimes reaches clear down to the ground. I've never seen anything like it on man, woman, or child, before."

"Wow. A white feather, white armbands an' – and – long hair. We'll remember that, huh, Captain?"

Captain Hanover put down his tin plate and fork, then looked over at the young officer. "What happened after ya drove 'em off, Lieutenant?"

"Well, sir, we tended our wounded, buried our dead, and rested for the rest of the night. With guards walking the camp's perimeter all night long, of course. One sneak attack a day is one too many, I assure you. Early the next morning, when we broke camp, we saw where three Crow braves lay fallen a short distance away. Crows usually manage to remove their dead and wounded when they withdraw, but they ate a lot of lead during our fierce little battle. I guess they were too debilitated and shorthanded from their wounds to get everyone away. We didn't want to leave corpses on the trail for innocent travelers to come across, so we dragged them over to a small ravine and covered them with rocks. I heard that's how the Crow bury their dead. The ground was too hard and rocky to dig graves, anyway. Then we hightailed it back east." The lieutenant paused for a sip of coffee. "And here we are."

Connal Lee leaned forward and looked the Lieutenant in the eye. "I was just wondering, Lieutenant. Did I hear ya mention the name of Captain John Reed?"

"Yes, young man. He's my immediate superior. Why do you ask?"

"Oh, I met him a couple weeks ago when we was visiting the Fort. He loaned me a book from the sutler's store. He's the best friend I ever had."

The Lieutenant's eyebrows shot up in surprise at the idea that his proud and haughty captain would have anything to do with an impoverished young vagabond. He had always held himself aloof from farmers, the working classes, and the uneducated. "Really? What a surprise."

"Yes, suh. He even took me to have supper with him at the Old Bedlam. It was right nice, too. Will you give him muh regards when y'all see him, please? He was a real fine genelman. He was so nice looking, an' – and – so clean, too. He's the one that told me to visit yer quartermaster to buy me a winter coat. He's the first friend I ever knowed. And so smart, too. He rode me back to camp on Paragon, the most beautiful stallion in the whole wide world."

The Lieutenant found himself speechless. He couldn't imagine the two riding tandem on the captain's magnificent stallion. His snobbish captain never fraternized with lowly enlisted men. "Well, certainly, young man. I will be pleased to extend him your regards personally when I report back from patrol. You said your name was Connal Lee?"

"Thas right. When I met Captain Reed, I was Baby Boy. But he told me I was too growed up for a nickname like that. He also told me to cut my hair an' – and – be more clean and grown-up. We read to each other that afternoon. It was great. He's so smart."

"Really? What did you read?"

"Oh, we started reading *David Copperfield*. Thas a really great book, doncha know. Course, we couldn't read the whole book that afternoon. I had to take it back to camp to finish it. It was a really great story."

"He read to you?"

"Yep. We took turns. Sometimes I read to him, too. He's read a lotta books, so he told me."

"Well, I do declare! The things you learn."

"Does y'all have any books y'all don't want? I don't have nothing to read now that I finished the Bible and the Book of Mormon. Ah already done read the only other two books in the whole company. I prefer readin' stories in novels, don't y'all?"

"Yes, young man. I do, in fact, prefer reading novels over the Bible any day of the week."

Captain Hanover, Lieutenant Anderson, and Connal Lee all chuckled in agreement.

Zeff came by to borrow a horse to go hunting and invited Connal Lee to join him. Connal Lee didn't want to go, afraid he would miss more stories about being a soldier, but he agreed. He knew he had to do his regular duty every evening.

"Bye, Lieutenant Anderson. I gotta go hunting. Don't forget to mention me to Captain Reed, please."

"I will indeed mention your name to our good captain, young man. Good hunting."

After Connal Lee left with Zeff, the Lieutenant suspiciously questioned Captain Hanover about Connal Lee. He hadn't believed a word of the boy's story about associating with his well-to-do, proud, and arrogant Captain Reed. Captain Hanover assured him Connal Lee had told the truth. He had already heard the story of their unlikely friendship from Lorna Baines. The Lieutenant shook his head in complete disbelief. "Well, I'll be! All right then, Captain. Please thank your kind ladies for the hot supper. I must go check on my men. You don't happen to have a doctor among your company, do you? We've got wounds to clean and bandages to reapply. Thank you very much for your hospitality to me and my men, Captain. We'll be breaking camp around five in the morning and on our way by six at the latest."

He stood up. Captain Hanover stood up with him. "I'm sorry we don't have a doctor travelin' with us, Lieutenant. Some o' the ladies would probably be happy t' help out, though. Let me go see who I can round up. I'll send the volunteers over t' visit yer camp right away."

"Thanks again, Captain. When I report to Major Sanderson, I'm going to strongly recommend he send another patrol out right away to escort your company safely beyond the Crow and Shoshone lands, just to be on the safe side."

"That would be greatly appreciated, sir. We're not exactly helpless, but we're not well armed, neither. Good luck on yer journey, Lieutenant."

"You, too, Captain. I can only make the recommendation for an escort, but I suspect the Major will listen. We none of us want any more deprivations by renegade Indians on the Overland Trail. Good luck to you, too, sir."

They shook hands and turned their own ways, going back about their various duties.

After Captain Hanover mentioned the wounded soldiers' needs, Lorna Baines gathered a couple of her friends together to go tend their wounds. After they finished, they took the soiled bandages back to their campfires and boiled them clean so they could be reused. While she sterilized her share of the dressings, she gave her handbell to Connal Lee and asked him to go ring it. She also asked him to take charge of class that evening with the recommendation he invite the older teens to take turns reading aloud to the small group of students.

Late that evening, Lorna returned from delivering the cleaned and folded bandages to the soldiers' camp. She found Connal Lee and Gilbert deep in conversation about David Copperfield returning

143

from abroad only to discover that Agnes Wickfield had been his one true love all along. Connal Lee wasn't sure he understood what Charles Dickens meant by true love.

Early the next morning, before dawn began coloring the eastern sky, the cavalry lieutenant sought out Captain Hanover beside his banked campfire. He handed the captain a well-worn book, *The Count of Monte Christo*. "This belonged to young Private Johansen, who regrettably took an arrow through his eye during the Crow attack and didn't survive. Would you please give it to your precocious young friend, Connal Lee, with my compliments?"

Captain Hanover accepted the book with a solemn nod, though his face looked pleasantly surprised. He chuckled and nodded his head. "Connal Lee will bless ya fer thinkin' of 'im like this, Lieutenant. Yer gonna be 'is friend fer life, jus' yew wait an' see. He's jus' plumb hungry fer the written word ever since Sister Baines taught 'im t' read a couple o' months back."

"I hope he enjoys it. I know I did. It's a pretty serious piece of literature but a really great story. Thanks again for your camp's hospitality last night. We leave immediately. We still have a long ride ahead of us."

"Good luck, Lieutenant. God speed."

"Good luck to you, too, sir. So long." He raised his hand in farewell as he marched back to his cavalry camp.

Chapter 13: Foster Parents

The evening after the cavalry left for Fort Laramie, Zeff and Connal Lee took their surplus kills over to Captain Hanover's campfire. They had each managed to bag a young doe after following a small meandering creek some distance south of the camp. "Here ya are, Captain. Could Ah ask yer men tuh save us three steaks fer our supper tomorrow? Ah'm sure Sister Woman has supper already prepared fer us by now since we're so late."

"Thank yew, Brother Swinton. Would ya please take yer kills over t' the boys at the support wagons fer me? They'll butcher 'em up an' distribute the meat like usual. Jus' ask 'em t' save ya some steaks an' I'm sure they'll be glad t' do so." The Swintons both turned their horses' heads towards the center of camp. "Hold up, there, a minute, Connal Lee. Would ya please wait an' talk with me fer a minute?"

"Sure, Captain." Connal Lee dismounted and handed his reins to Zeff so he could lead his horse with the small doe slung across its withers to the center of the camp. "What can I do for y'all, Captain?"

"Take a seat, Connal Lee. Sit an' relax a spell, why doncha?"

"Thanks, kindly, suh. Don't mind if I do."

The captain's young wife brought them both a tin mug filled with coffee, sweetened with molasses sugar and milk. "Thanks, Sister Hanover."

She smiled and returned to her cooking.

"Well, young man, it appears ya made a bit of an impression on that Lieutenant Anderson yesterday. Before he pulled out early this morning, he found me an' gave me this here book fer ya."

The captain handed Connal Lee the book. Connal Lee's head pulled back in surprise at the same time he eagerly reached out his right hand to clasp the book. "Fer me? Wow! An' jus' look what a fine book, too. Ah should probably wash muh hands before Ah handle such a wonderful book."

Connal Lee turned the book in his hands, admiring the binding of embossed dark blue leather with a blue and gold marbled paper on the cover, edged in gold. He held the luxurious book up to read the spine. "The Count of Montee Christ-oh, Alexander Doom-ass, New York, eighteen forty-six. Why it's plumb beautiful, ain't it, Captain. Ah've never heard of it, but Sister Baines can probably tell me about it."

"I haven't read it yet, either, Connal Lee. Maybe ya can loan it t' me when yer finished with it. The Lieutenant tol' me it belonged to a private killed in the Injun attack."

Connal Lee clasped the book to his heart. "Oh, thanks so much, Captain. Ah wish Ah could thank the Lieutenant myself. This is the best gift ever!"

He jumped up and shook the captain's hand energetically, his grin nearly splitting his face in half. "Wait'll Ah show Sister Baines, and Brother Baines, and Zeff, and Sister Woman!"

He took off running for the Swinton campfire to show off his new book. He couldn't wait to start reading it. While he dodged through the scattered family camps, he glanced up at the lowering sun. *Oh, no! Ah won't have much light left to start reading. Oh, well. There's always tomorrow, Ah guess. Ah cain't wait to read it!*

The next evening, Connal Lee found himself torn with a difficult decision. He wanted to sit by the fire and read more than anything. Zeff expected his company on their usual evening hunt, and Lorna Baines expected him to attend class. *Tarnation, but life is hard! Ah cain't never do what Ah want to do.*

After hunting and class, he only had fifteen minutes of light for reading. He moved close to the fire to see and nearly scorched himself. The flickering cookfire didn't give off enough light to read by. He went to bed wondering what Emperor Napoleon had been like.

Connal Lee woke up Sunday and remembered they had a day off from travel. With a rush of excitement, he jumped up and pulled on his sturdy new army boots. Sister Woman had fried up pan bread for their breakfast. He begged for a big serving and shoved it in his mouth with both hands before it even cooled down. He hadn't quite finished his breakfast before he grabbed his beautiful new book and took off jogging towards the meandering creek. He sought out a private place where he could read to his heart's content.

Even though his stomach growled come high noon, he took a big drink of water from the creek and kept reading. He didn't understand everything he read, but it held his complete attention.

When he finished late that afternoon, he closed the book and lay back, dreaming about the visions of people and places in the book. Eventually, his growling stomach motivated him to return to camp. After eating leftovers from dinner, he took the book over to Lorna Baines' campfire. They chatted while she prepared supper. Connal Lee asked about all sorts of new ideas he had read about, like foster children, the bond market, revenge, and on and on. When he saw Lorna about to serve supper to Gilbert, he stood up. "Ah thinks Ah'm going to need to read this here book again, Sister Baines. There's so much new stuff in here."

Lorna chuckled and shook her head, pleased at Connal Lee's sharp, inquisitive mind and tireless energy. "Good night, Connal Lee. We'll discuss the book's vocabulary more tomorrow. You are doing brilliantly, young man. Oh, and may I borrow your book when you have finished? I'm excited to read it now, myself."

"Why, of course, Sister Baines. Just as soon as Ah finish reading it, again. Good night."

A man's clear tenor voice began singing a solo of the Mormon hymn *I Know that My Redeemer Lives.* Several others in the company added their voices until it sounded like sitting in the middle of a choir. The words didn't mean anything to Connal Lee, but he loved hearing the melody and accompanying harmony.

The next evening at school, Lorna Baines asked Connal Lee to start reading *The Count of Monte Cristo* aloud for the class. He didn't finish the first sentence before she interrupted him. "Stop! I do believe the word is of not o'. Please pronounce the whole word. Now, start again, please."

"On the twenty-fourth of February, eighteen fifteen, the lookout at Notter Dame dee la Gardee signaled..." Lorna winced but decided not to correct his pronunciation of French words during class, so she let him keep reading. However, when she heard Connal Lee say roundin' the, she interrupted. "The word is rounding, Connal Lee, not roundin'. Please try it again."

For the next hour, everyone suffered through Lorna Baines correcting Connal Lee's southern hillbilly pronunciation. He still struggled with pronouncing D at the end of and in his rush to move on to the next thought.

Over the next week, during class and whenever they had spare time, Connal Lee, Lorna, and Gilbert poured over the book. They reviewed its extensive new vocabulary, the unique French names, and all the new ideas about business and family life in big cities, so different from his own simple, backwoods experiences.

Connal Lee concentrated really hard and gradually stopped eating the ends of his words – to Lorna Baines' immense satisfaction and delight.

One chilly evening Connal Lee sat around the Baines' firepit discussing the complicated interrelationships between all the various characters in *The Count of Monte Cristo*. "Do y'all remember when we read about the Count's servant becoming the foster father of Benedetto?"

Lorna and Gilbert both nodded their heads, yes.

"Do y'all remember when ya explained to me about adoption and foster parents?"

They both nodded yes, again.

"Y'all know that Ah've never had me a maw, don't ya? My real maw died when she gave me birth, so Ah never knowed her."

"Knew her, Connal Lee."

"Oops, yep. So, Ah never knew her. In a way, Ah never had a real paw, neither, cause he was always such a drunken mean ol' polecat. He would rather beat on me than look at me. Paw never had a word for me other than do this or do that. He acted more like an enemy than a paw. He always blamed me for my maw's leaving him alone when she died. My older brother, Zeff, and my older sister, Sister Woman, more or less raised me like Ah was their baby. But, Ah wasn't. Not really. So, Ah've never really had me a maw."

Lorna and Gilbert looked at each other in shock as they realized Sister Woman wasn't just Zeff's wife but his sister, too. They had both assumed they were a typical young couple from two separate families. They tried to restrain their scandalized expressions, but when they looked at each other over Connal Lee's head, each could tell the other wanted to discuss if they had actually understood what Connal Lee had just said. Absorbed in his thoughts, Connal Lee missed the non-verbal interactions between the Baines.

Connal Lee reached out and gently clasped Lorna's hand in both of his. "Sister Baines, y'all have been so great to me, first as my teacher, then my friend an' neighbor on the trail. Y'all are just what Ah always thought my real maw would be like if she had lived. What Ah hoped she would be like, anyway. Ah'm so grateful for y'all teaching me both in and out of class. Would y'all like to be my foster mother? Ah would really like to have a mother. Ah know y'all can't adopt me cause my paw is still alive back in the mountains, but maybe y'all could be my foster mother from now on. Whaddaya think, Sister Baines? Could Ah please call y'all mother? Could Ah? Please?"

Lorna Baines felt quite taken aback, more from surprise than anything. She hadn't seen this coming. She didn't quite know how to respond. She patted Connal Lee's hands, then slowly pulled away. She glanced over at Gilbert with a silent plea for help. Then she decided she needed to buy herself some time. "Well, Connal Lee. I'm terribly flattered. That's quite an important request you made of me. It's such a surprise that I really need some time to think about it. It's a serious obligation for anyone to become a foster parent. And, of course, since I am already married, I would need to consult with Gilbert before I could make any such long-term commitments. If I became your foster mother, Brother Baines would become your foster father since we are married. Do you see?"

When her words sunk in, Connal Lee knelt up beside Gilbert. He impulsively placed his arm over Gilbert's shoulders. "Oh, would ya please, Brother Baines? Would ya please be my foster father? Ah somehow feel like Ah need a mother and a father, more than my brother and sister have been, anyway. Y'all are the nicest and kindest people Ah've ever met. Ah would be the best boy in the world if only y'all would be my foster parents. Would y'all? Please? Please?"

While both Lorna and Gilbert admired Connal Lee and cared for him, they didn't know how to respond. Neither wanted to just come right out and say no, which might hurt Connal Lee's feelings, but neither were they anxious to agree on the spur of the moment. They all three sat silently in their little tableau for several moments. Finally, Gilbert reached out, grabbed Connal Lee's shoulder, and pulled him back to sitting between them on the ground. "You've done us both a great honor, Connal Lee, even to think of us like parents. But we've already raised our family. Our oldest child, Junior, grew up to be quite a handful. I'm still worn out from seeing him through to manhood. Oh, but he was a trial and a tribulation all on his own, from the day he learned to crawl until he got married and moved out a year or so ago. Could we please have time to think about this, Connal Lee? I'm not sure if I'm ready to start with a new family, again, truth be told. I think I might be too old to go through being a father again."

Lorna reached out and reclaimed Connal Lee's hand. She gave it a tender squeeze. "Being a parent, even a foster parent, requires quite a commitment and deserves serious consideration beforehand. We couldn't possibly agree casually. That doesn't mean we will say no, but it doesn't mean we will say yes, either. Can you be patient with us while we give it some thought? You know we love you rather like a son, anyway, don't you, Connal Lee? Just using words other than friends won't make any difference to how we deal with each other, will it? You will always be welcome at our fireplace and table, no matter what."

Connal Lee felt extremely disappointed that the Baines hadn't jumped at the chance to become his foster parents. He had thought it such a great idea. He had thought they would welcome him with open arms. When he realized they didn't share his enthusiasm about being his parents, he stood up. Without saying another word, he leaned down and gave Lorna a little hug, then turned and gave Gilbert a brief hug.

He slowly walked away, heading towards the Swinton fire, now burning low in the family camp. Connal Lee felt all alone, like a real-life orphan at that moment, just like Oliver Twist had before the Brownlows adopted him. A tear dripped down his cheek. He passed Zeff and Sister Woman without saying a word and walked on to the little feeder creek. He sat down and gazed up at all the stars shining in the clear, cool air while listening to the babbling water.

As soon as Connal Lee had walked far enough away he couldn't hear them, Lorna and Gilbert leaned into each other and began speaking at the same time. "Did he really say Zeff and Sister Woman were his older brother and sister? We didn't misunderstand, did we?"

"Do you think it's true?"

"Well, when I first met Sister Woman, I asked her what her married name was. When she told me Swinton, it never occurred to me that it might also be her maiden name. What a scandal! Isn't it against the law in Missouri for a brother and sister to marry? It most certainly is throughout the British Empire."

"How could they possibly have obtained a marriage license?"

"I bet anything they never got a license. On, no! I remember Zeff once telling me he had to leave his abusive father in the Ozarks with Sister Woman, Chester Ray, and Baby Boy and go out to seek their fortunes. You don't suppose Chester Ray's father is really their abusive father, do you? I've heard of such awful things before. Good Lord! That would make Connal Lee both the baby's brother and uncle." She paused and stared vacantly into the distance. "On the other hand, Zeff and Sister Woman are affectionate and loving, like a young man and wife newly fallen in love. Oh, I don't know. What are we going to do, Gilbert, dear?"

Gilbert leaned over and gave Lorna a hug. "Let's not get carried away, now. Remember the Lord's words. Judge not, that ye be not judged. They are upstanding young people struggling to find their way the best they can. And they seem to be doing a pretty good job of it so far. From what I've seen, they don't have a mean bone between them. Heaven only knows the Swinton boys are generous to a fault, going out of their way to augment the camp's food no matter how weary they are after a long day's travel."

"Oh, if the others found out, they would be absolutely scandalized. They would surely ostracize them. Polygamy is one thing, but not sibling marriage, I'm sure of it. Maybe it's best if we don't say anything to anyone. Oh, the poor dears. Do you suppose they just didn't know any better? How on earth could their father have permitted it?"

"Poor Connal Lee, growing up with such bad examples his entire life."

"Obviously, he doesn't think there's anything wrong with their being married and siring children. Poor thing."

"Lorna, I really don't think we should be the ones to tell him it is against the law and God's wishes."

"Maybe we should carry on as though he hadn't said anything to tip us off."

"Perhaps that would be for the best."

"Oh, my. The mind just reels! I'm flabbergasted. Truly flabbergasted, Gilbert dear."

"Me, too! Just imagine! Well, it's getting late. Shall we turn in?"

"Yes. Although I'm sure I'll not be able to sleep a wink."

"Come on, dear. It's been a long day."

Chapter 14: The Continental Divide

For the next five days, the little handcart company struggled up the slope leading to South Pass. Everyone looked forward to crossing the continental divide and beginning the downward portion of their journey. The countryside became increasingly dry and barren. The land barely had enough dry grass to feed the milk cows and horses.

Zeff and Connal Lee, weary from pushing their cart uphill all day, rode out every evening, searching for game of any kind. They rode out further and returned later without success. Night after night, they returned empty-handed. One evening while out riding, Zeff and Connal Lee spotted a herd of pronghorns a mile or so away. They took off in hot pursuit. Connal Lee thought they looked like small antelopes. They all had short light brown fur with white bellies and rumps. They had narrow white bands across their throats. The males had black horns that curved artfully inward over their heads. As they grew closer, the pronghorns took off running, stampeding fast as the wind. The boys gave chase but couldn't catch up. The pronghorns ran much faster than their horses.

They went home empty-handed, yet again.

Connal Lee found fried salt pork a poor substitute for fresh meat, no matter what Sister Woman or Lorna Baines did to make it more palatable. They were all getting tired of beans.

Several times they dry camped with no natural water source at hand. The support wagons doled out rations of barreled water each morning for the ladies to use for drinking and cooking. They had none left for personal hygiene. Everyone felt increasingly gritty and dirty.

A day short of making the crossing, a strong windstorm blew straight into their faces from the west. They had to halt their journey because the flying sand stung their faces. Thick dust made it nearly impossible to see or breathe. Everyone's eyes became red and irritated. Tears streamed down their faces in muddy runnels as they huddled on the leeward side of their carts and wagons, trying to keep down out of the stinging wind.

153

Nine hard weeks after leaving Independence, Captain Hanover led the company into the wide barren valley of South Pass. Connal Lee bent over the back of the cart, contributing his part by pushing as usual. A movement to the north caught his attention. He turned his head and saw a large herd of pronghorn antelope on the near horizon.

He told Zeff he wanted to try hunting them again. He grabbed his double-barreled shotgun, loaded two lead bullets, then scampered back to the freight wagons at the rear of the train. He leapt up on one of the already saddled horses and shot away like an arrow, straight for the mottled brown animals. The pronghorns' pale, reddish-brown backs and light bellies camouflaged them so well against the dry, alkaline landscape they nearly disappeared.

When he drew close, he slowed down. He remembered how fast they ran and didn't want to spook them again. Connal Lee slid off the horse and tied its reins to a low sagebrush so it wouldn't wander off. He crouched down and crawled closer. He fired. The herd jumped and turned, all heads alert, as they moved away from the fallen buck. He managed three more shots and brought down a total of three. It took some doing alone and with only one horse, but he gutted them and dragged them back to camp.

That evening, everyone shared a feast of tender pronghorn steaks in celebration of reaching the continental divide. The lean meat had a mild venison taste overlaid with a wild gamey sagebrush flavor. Captain Hanover and all the camp waxed verbose in their thanks for Connal Lee's efforts.

After supper and class, Connal Lee lounged on the dry ground beside the Baines' meager cookfire of buffalo chips and scrawny sagebrush. They had no natural daylight nor firelight to read by. Even though weary, they felt a sense of accomplishment for having made it to South Pass at last. When their conversation wound down, Lorna moved over and sat close to Gilbert. He pulled her into a gentle hug until they rested against each other's shoulders with their arms around each other's waists. "Connal Lee, dear, Gilbert and I have been talking. Do you remember the other evening when you asked if we would be your foster parents?"

Now attentive, Connal Lee sat up Indian style. He leaned forward, resting his elbows on his knees as he gazed closely at the Baines in the darkening sky. "Yes, Sister Baines. I recall."

"Well, since our hearts are big enough to love more children than those we have already borne, we would like to offer to be your foster parents. Of course, you will continue living with Zeff and Sister Woman and answer to them just as usual. But we would like you to think of us as Mother Baines and Father Baines. Would that make you happy, Connal Lee?"

In answer, Connal Lee flung himself forward and fell into their arms, wrapping his arms around them in a big, three-way hug. He began expressing his pleasure and thanks, but instead of words coming out, he started crying and couldn't say anything. He had felt so rejected and alone after he asked if he could be their foster son that hearing them say he could call them mother and father lifted a heaviness off his heart he hadn't even been aware of.

Lorna and Gilbert hugged young Connal Lee to them while he cried silently. They both had tears springing up in their eyes, as well, seeing how much this meant to the boy. Gilbert patted Connal Lee on the back. "There, there. There, there."

When Connal Lee regained control of his emotions, he pulled back to sit on his heels in front of them. He looked back and forth at their kind faces with a tearful but happy smile. "Thanks, Mother Baines. Thanks, Father Baines. Now I feel like I have me a real honest-to-goodness family. I'm not an orphan alone in the world without parents anymore. Ah thank y'all so, so much."

He leaned in and gave each one another tender hug. "Ah have to go share the good news with Zeff and Sister Woman. Ah'm sure they will be pleased for me, too. Good night, Father Baines. Good night, Mother Baines."

They both nodded their heads with a smile. "Good night, son."

Hearing this lovely couple call him son at the same time caused his face to light up with joy. He took off running to the Swinton campfire. "Zeff! Sister Woman! Y'all will never guess what..."

From that night on, the company began the slightly easier and mostly downhill trek on the western side of the continental divide.

The western and northern sides of the bleak hills became marginally greener. When Connal Lee shared this observation with the captain, the captain nodded his agreement. "Yep. The rainclouds seem t' drop most o' their moisture as the winds blow 'em up into the higher elevations. They're pretty much dried out by the time they get t' the eastern side o' the mountain range. It's still dry desert up here, but things'll start getting a little nicer now as we head downhill. It's only a couple o' days till we reach the first little feeder creeks. Only on this side o' the divide, the rivers will be runnin' westerly, feedin' all the way down t' the Pacific Ocean."

Two days later, both Zeff and Connal Lee managed to track down and shoot two stringy mountain goats. After that, they returned night after night empty-handed.

One evening, tired, disgruntled, and hungrier than usual, Zeff and Connal Lee returned their borrowed horses to the center of camp. Captain Hanover walked over and helped Zeff unsaddle his weary mount. Connal Lee sighed and looked at the captain with a negative shake of his head. "This ain't a workin' – sorry. This isn't working, Captain Hanover. We're spending time and effort all for nothing. Do you have a minute? Ah've been thinking. Maybe Ah have an idea."

"Sure thing, Connal Lee. Come on back t' me fire, an' let's have a mug o' coffee. We'll discuss it."

Zeff and Connal Lee followed the captain to his campfire on the western side of the camp. "Pull up a chair an' sit a spell."

Connal Lee and Zeff both grinned as they dropped to the bare ground with their legs crossed in front of them. The captain's young wife poured them each a tin mug of black coffee. "Sorry. We're out of milk right now."

"That's all right, Sister Hanover. Ah like coffee black, too. Thanks."

"Yer welcome, Connal Lee."

"Now, boy. What brainstorm have ya dreamed up t' help us solve our meat shortage? I'm all ears."

"Well, now. It seems to me this land has to have some game. It's just not close to the trail. Between the dry desert and all the hunting over the years, there's just not much to be found for us close

156

by." Connal Lee glanced over at Zeff. "Since the goin's a bit easier, headin' – heading – downhill, Ah was thinking maybe Ah could borrow a horse at first light and ride north where the mountains appear taller, and the valleys appear deeper. If Ah were a betting man, that's where Ah would expect to find some wildlife."

Captain Hanover and Zeff both nodded their agreement.

"Ah'm thinking Ah could ride out for half a day, then ride back to meet up with y'all at suppertime. If Ah took along a strong horse with a packsaddle, Ah'd be prepared if Ah ran into some luck. Ah could haul back more than one doe or bison calf or a whole passel o' birds or rabbits. Well? What d'ja – sorry, what do y'all think?"

The captain looked at Connal Lee, then turned to Zeff. "Well, Brother Swinton, could ya manage yer cart without Connal Lee's help? Do ya think maybe we should give his idea a try?"

Zeff nodded yes. "It would be worth it if 'e found some good meat fer the camp, doncha think, Captain?"

"Very good, then. Good idea, Connal Lee. Now, let's put our heads together an' think about what ya would need."

"We already have a canvas water bag. Maybe a little bread or Johnny Cake for dinner before Ah turn back. Ah have everything else. The shotgun you loaned me. Plenty of buckshot and lead plugs for ammunition. Ah would need some sturdy rawhide ropes an' a long lead bridle for the packhorse, then Ah would be all set."

"Do ya have a compass, boy?"

"Nope."

"Do ya know how t' use one?"

"Yep. Zeff taught me to find my way back in the woods using my paw's compass, but we didn't bring it with us when we left the mountain."

"I'll dig one up fer ya. Picture this in yer mind. Ya travel half the day goin' northwesterly. Then ya return half the day goin' southwesterly. Ya should come out close enough t' spot our camp at the end o' the day. It's gonna be a long hard day o' ridin'. Are ya sure yer up to it?"

"Yes, suh. Ah think so. Otherwise, Ah wouldn't have recommended it. Besides. Ah'm hungry all the time! Ah'm a growin' boy, doncha know."

Zeff and the captain chuckled. They all stood up. Captain Hanover clapped Connal Lee on the back. "I'll meet ya at the horses in the mornin' right after breakfast with a compass. Let's give yer idea a trial run. Good thinkin', young man. Get rested up now. Tomorrow could prove t' be a tirin' day. Good night, Zeff. Good night, Connal Lee."

As Connal Lee drifted off to sleep, he listened to a man whistling a Scottish ballad. When he heard a reed harmonica begin accompanying the melody with a mournful vibrating tone, he sat up to hear better. When the whistler led into the song *The Bonnie Banks of Loch Lomond,* several people around him began singing along. Nearly everyone joined in on the chorus. "O ye'll take the high road, and I'll take the low road..." Connal Lee hummed along rather tunelessly, enjoying the songfest. "But me and my true love will never meet again, On the bonnie, bonnie banks o' Loch Lomond."

Connal Lee stuffed himself with cornbread and molasses early the following morning as soon as Sister Woman cooked it. He asked Sister Woman to give him something to eat at high noon. He grabbed their water bag, his shotgun, and ammunition and turned to Zeff. "Wish me luck, Big Brover. Ah'll do my best to bring home something good for our supper."

When he reached the horses, the captain had just saddled a beautiful dark brown mare with black legs, tail, and mane. He nodded at Connal Lee and pointed at a larger older horse. "Take that one as yer packhorse. Ya can find some packsaddles over in that middle wagon. Ya know how t' rig the breast collar an' rump straps t' make it good an' secure, doncha?"

"Yep. Ah always helped Zeff with our pack mule when we walked down out of the mountain. Ah'll get it."

Excited to be free of the dreary plodding boredom of walking the handcart trail, he jumped into the saddle. With a yank on the packhorse's lead rope, he shook his reins and nudged the pretty mare in her belly with his heels. "Let's go. Giddup! Giddup!"

He found it strange not to have someone to talk to for so many hours on end, but he managed to track down a small mule deer and three white-tailed jackrabbits. He returned like a conquering hero to cheers and congratulatory claps on the back when he turned the kills over to the cowboys to butcher up and distribute. After rubbing down his two borrowed horses, he picked up two rabbits by their back legs and took them to Mother Baines and Sister Woman. They both showered him with praises, delighted to have fresh meat for supper.

For the next several days of riding alone, he enjoyed mixed success. Some days he didn't encounter any game. Some days he found plenty. He came to enjoy riding alone, keeping his eyes open, keeping his wits around him, tracking game like Zeff had taught him back in the Ozarks.

He felt very independent and grown-up.

Chapter 15: Crow

Over the next ten days, the Oregon Trail took them southwest a bit to pass below a ridge of mountains, then curved back, heading northwesterly. Connal Lee enjoyed good weather for his daytime hunts, with temperatures around seventy degrees for most of the day. He paid attention to time his return to camp, so he arrived before the sun went down. After sunset, the temperature cooled off quickly, plummeting down to the mid-thirties just before dawn. Daylight evenly balanced the dark of night. The sun rose around seven in the morning and set around seven in the evening.

In between traveling, Sister Woman spent her free moments stitching up a greatcoat for Zeff from the old wool army blankets she had purchased in Fort Laramie. Her tailoring left a lot to be desired, but Zeff ended up with a warm coat for the winter.

Connal Lee enjoyed the longer evenings when they couldn't travel. He thrived on Lorna Baines' classes, then spent most of his evenings with his honorary foster parents. Under Gilbert Baines' urging and instruction, he lost most but not all of his southern hillbilly accent. Lorna felt terribly proud of his progress and didn't hesitate to tell him.

The handcart company entered a broad valley leading northwesterly towards their next major stopping point at Fort Hall. Bear Lake, noted for its crystal blue waters, so different from the muddy brown lakes along the trail, lay a day's journey or more to their south. Their livestock found plenty of grass for browsing, although it had dried out and turned yellow like straw by mid-October. Low mountain ranges rose to the west and east, blued in the distance. Connal Lee rode up into the mountains, exploring places where he might find game to hunt. Sometimes he turned west. Sometimes he rode east.

The Overland Trail kept within a mile or so of several small nameless meandering creeks winding through the broad valley. Very little grew on the valley floor except for scattered sagebrush, scrub juniper, and small mesquite bushes. Even though they found them hard to cut, the ladies liked how the small mesquite branches infused their food with a subtle smoky flavor. Captain Hanover warned the parents to keep their children away from the sagebrushes because of the potential of ticks.

Around two weeks after passing the Continental Divide, Captain Hanover directed them to make camp where a bend of a thin meandering creek drew close to a ridge jutting out of the foothills to their east.

The following morning, Connal Lee buttoned up his army coat to keep out the chill. As soon as Sister Woman served him a bowl of hot hominy and grits, he saddled up his two regular horses and trotted off across the small valley to the taller range of hills rising in the west. An hour later, he topped the crest and dropped out of sight of the camp. The western side of the low hill led down through a stunted forest. He followed the notch for a couple more hours, spotting a few deer and sage hens along the way.

About the same time that Connal Lee rode over the mountain, Captain Hanover led his followers in their morning prayer. After everyone said amen, he clapped his hat back on his head. "This's a good day fer walkin', Brothers an' Sisters. Let's get our train in order an' continue on up through this lovely valley the good Lord has provided us."

The small group dispersed to their handcarts. They took off slowly, pushing their handcarts as they organized themselves into their usual travel positions in the train for the day. Chester Ray woke up a bit colicky that morning, so Sister Woman carried him over her shoulder to settle him down. Without Connal Lee and Sister Woman's help, Zeff struggled to push their cart, even with its lightened load. So far out from supplies, their reserves had dwindled to next to nothing.

A group of around forty Crow braves chose that unguarded moment to ride around the curve of the mountains to their east, yipping and screaming war cries. They thundered down to attack the pioneers strung out on the trail. Captain Hanover dropped his handcart and ran for his horse at the tail of the train. "Circle around. Arm yerselves. We're under attack!"

Everyone panicked. The ladies screamed in alarm. They grabbed their children and carried or dragged them back to the support wagons, all in a panic. The men shoved their carts with new-found strength, struggling into their circular formation. The cowboys and guards ran for the wagons and armed themselves. Five minutes later, arrows began falling into the edge of the encampment. A man screamed when an arrow dropped from above and slammed into his arm. The flint arrowhead thrust through his wool coat, bounced off his upper arm bone, and stuck with its sharply filed barbs caught in his bicep. He dropped to the ground, clutching at the arrow's shaft. More arrows fell as the attacking war party rode closer. The fierce warriors wore white war paint making stripes masking their faces from top to bottom. Many of the attackers wore great war bonnets of mostly white eagle feathers. Their chief and war chief's bonnets trailed several feet behind them down over their horses' backs.

Confusion reigned. Everyone shouted orders at each other in their alarm. The immigrants fumbled at loading their simple weapons while trying to locate their families to make sure they were safe in the center of the lopsided, hastily organized camp.

Captain Hanover and the cowboys began shooting as fast as they could load, aim, and fire. Zeff pushed Chester Ray and Sister Woman underneath their canted handcart, then grabbed his shotgun and ran towards the noise, fumbling to load lead slugs in both barrels.

The speed with which the whooping painted warriors barreling towards the camp could nock and fire off their sharp war arrows shocked Zeff. Everyone ducked for cover. Zeff heard more screams and cries as arrows found targets among their frightened company.

The screaming warriors darted in closer. Zeff saw they almost all wore doeskin smocks, heavily beaded at the neck and along their jagged bottom edges. Long leather fringe hung from their sleeves. They all wore leather trousers with more fringe and beading running up the outside of the legs. Most carried short war bows, made to be shot from horseback, but a few carried tall spears, dripping with rows of scalps proclaiming their prowess as fierce warriors.

One ambitious young warrior drove his pony up next to one of the teenage cowboys riding alongside the encirclement. With a vicious shove of his flint-edged spear, he pushed the cowboy to the ground and grabbed the horse's reins. The Indian took off with a whoop of delight, stealing the horse and its saddle. Captain Hanover saw the close-in attack. He managed to get off a shot, but he couldn't tell if it found its target in all the confusion.

The war party obeyed the shouted orders of their war chief and began riding in a circle around the camp, constantly shooting arrow after arrow. An arrow knocked the captain's hat off his head, but he paid it no mind. He loaded and shot mechanically, totally focused on defending his people by taking down as many attackers as possible.

After an intense fifteen minutes that seemed like hours to the cowering families in the camp, the Crow war chief shouted out a brief one-syllable order. All his braves stopped firing and turned to pick up their two wounded men and three riderless horses. They left the one dead corpse where it had fallen. Still whooping their war cries, the war chief led his pack northwesterly up into the hills opposite those they had hidden behind before the attack. They screamed their defiance and victory over punishing the hated white men for trespassing on their traditional hunting grounds.

Suddenly it grew silent in the camp, the only sound a soft whimpering of some women and children. With nervous eyes watching the path of the departing war party, everyone began standing up. Husbands and wives hugged, checking each other over for wounds. Several of the party, even some of the children, had clothing stained with blood. The teenage cowboy whose horse had been stolen lay dead on the ground.

Lorna Baines called out to her friends to help her set up a field hospital next to the support wagons. They quickly spread out quilts and blankets on the ground. Those without wounds helped the wounded hobble over to the volunteer nurses. Little children, still crying hysterically, clung to their mother's long dresses.

Two men had to be carried to the hospital. One had passed out from loss of blood. The other had been knocked unconscious when a spear shaft slammed down on the top of his head. He never did find his hat.

Gilbert Baines joined three other men to build a fire beside the wagons. They ran to the nearby creek and filled their pans and pots

163

with water to boil. Everyone pitched in to comfort the wounded, clean them up, and bandage their wounds.

Still breathing hard from the exertion and adrenalin, Captain Hanover hugged his wife up to him. Her feet lifted up off the ground. "Are ya all right, me darlin'? Yer not hurt, are ya?"

She assured him she had nothing more serious than scraped knees from crashing to the ground to dodge an arrow. The captain gave her a quick kiss before he hurried off to check on the rest of the company. The sounds of men, women, and children crying from pain and from relief they had survived the surprise attack drifted over the camp. It seemed quiet without fierce war cries and thundering horse hooves riding around the small cluster of pioneers. One lady sat down on the ground with a plop, nearly passing out from relief she hadn't been killed.

As soon as the arrows stopped, Zeff ran for Sister Woman. He found her cowering beneath their handcart, clutching Chester Ray to her breast. The whites of her eyes showed as she stared around fearfully, not knowing from where the next attack would come. Zeff knelt down, reached under the handcart box, and touched her arm. She flinched. "Shh. It's jus' me, Sis. The war party's gone. Y'all can come out now. They didn't hurt y'all, did they? Is Chester Ray all right?"

Sister Woman could only whimper as she ducked out from under the cart, clasping her baby to her breast. Zeff helped her stand up. He gathered her in his arms and held her securely, their little boy nestled between them. Still breathing hard, Zeff savored the smell of Sister Woman's hair as she shivered beneath his chin. "It's all right, now, Sis. Calm down now. Shh. Shh."

Zeff grabbed their old quilts from the cart's box and spread them on the ground. He eased Sister Woman to sit, leaning against the cart's five-foot-tall wheel. He pulled the blanket up to cover her and Chester Ray then knelt down and hugged her again. He whispered in her ear, "Y'all stay here, Sis. Ah gotta go see what Ah can do tuh help. We got us some wounded. When y'all get calmed down, see what ya can do 'bout a fire an' some food. We gotta help those who were hurt. Ah loves ya, Sis."

Zeff gave her another reassuring hug and stood up. He turned in a circle, looking over the shattered camp, trying to see where he could best be of help. *Ah don't believe we made it through without a single scratch. Some weren't so lucky, though. Oh, no! What about Baby Boy? Where's Baby Boy? Oh, Connal Lee, Ah hopes y'all're safe. Hurry back. We needs y'all! We loves ya, Little Brover!*

Chapter 16: Collateral Damage

Close to high noon on the day of the Crow attack, Connal Lee had ridden several miles north along the spine of an unnamed mountain range. He began thinking about changing direction when a glittering of water in a small creek just ahead caught his attention. As he drew closer to the running water, he found small green bushes, grasses, and stunted trees. He turned his mare to walk downstream. *This looks like a good area for hunting. Let's try our luck along here for a while.*

Half an hour later, two small rivulets merged into a slightly larger creek. One adult buck, two juvenile bucks, several does, and three nearly grown fawns grazed the verdant area. A buck with impressive six-pointed antlers stood in water above its hooves, taking a drink. Connal Lee slipped off his horse, tied its reins to a low bush, and eased his way closer, shotgun at the ready. Quick as a wink, he brought down two beautiful fawns with white spots fading on their backs. The rest of the herd jumped and scattered with their white tails raised high in alarm exposing their white rumps.

Connal Lee dragged the corpses away from the water's edge, then scampered back and fetched his horses. He knelt on the slightly damp soil and cut their throats so the blood would drain out of the corpses. When he saw the flow of blood diminishing to a slow drop at a time, he rinsed both bodies in the running water. He tied the larger fawn over the middle of the packsaddle. He loaded the smaller doe to drape over the horse's buttocks just behind the saddle's wooden cross trees. He secured them with rawhide ropes tied through the saddle's metal rings and leather loops.

Happy with the catch, he dug out a piece of Johnny Cake for his dinner and took off back towards the Overland Trail. After he finished eating, he pulled out his compass and corrected his course. He planned on meeting up with the company late that afternoon in time for supper. The terrain steepened slightly as he rode downhill, carefully watching the trail. He let out more lead rein so the packhorse could pick its own footing.

A movement across the shallow valley caught his eye. He whipped around to look. To his shock, he saw two Crow warriors wearing war paint and war bonnets riding along the ridge. He kicked his mare in the stomach. She lurched forward, yanking the pack-horse's lead. Connal Lee focused his attention on moving out of their sight. He heard a whistling sound pass over his head. Another buzz, almost like a giant bumble bee, accompanied the streak of an arrow shooting before his eyes. His head jerked back in an automatic reflex.

Unexpectedly, he felt a shocking flash of pain. A barbed arrow descended from the sky and punctured his left calf just below his bent knee. The arrow glanced off his tibia, exited the other side of his calf, punched through the thin leather skirt of his saddle, and drove into his horse's ribs.

Connal Lee screamed in shock at the horrendous pain. The horse reacted to being shot by screaming, shaking its head, then lurching into a panicked stampede down the ravine. The pack-horse's lead rope dragged loose from the saddle horn, but it followed anyway. Connal Lee doubled over in pain, trying to reach the arrow sticking out from his calf. He lost the reins as his attention focused on removing the source of the agony.

Reacting to the stabbing pain and free reins, his mare tore away. With each lurch of its pounding, panicked strides, the arrowhead bit into the horse's side anew, pricking it on to a faster lunge as it enlarged the bleeding wound. Fortunately, the morning's war dances, attack, and their subsequent flight had left the war party too weary to chase him. When they saw they had wounded the white intruder, they galloped over the ridge to catch up with their war chief.

After about twenty minutes of a scary, excruciatingly painful ride, seemingly endless, the mare began slowing down from exhaustion. Connal Lee ended up more than ten miles away from the site of the surprise attack.

Soaked in both the horse's blood and Connal Lee's blood, the buffalo sinews that secured the flint arrowhead softened. The jostling run shook the arrowhead loose until it fell off the shaft and dropped by the wayside. When the exhausted horse stopped feeling stabbed repeatedly, she slowed down and stopped. She splayed her

167

front legs and lowered her head, gasping for breath. A narrow stream in a shallow valley on the west side of the range had attracted the thirsty horse. Small pine trees, stunted cedars, a few young cottonwood trees, and grayish sagebrush grew along the life-giving water.

Connal Lee tried dismounting, but the white-fletched shaft pinned his bruised calf to the saddle's leather skirt behind the stirrup's thick leather band. He desperately yanked on the arrow to pull it loose from the saddle. The shock of the pain of the movement of the shaft grating inside his flesh caused him to clench convulsively. Gnashing his teeth, he squealed as he fell off the horse, crashing clumsily to the sandy ground. His fall spooked the mare. She jerked back and trotted away, too tired to run. The packhorse followed the empty saddle.

Connal Lee lay stunned, disoriented, trying to cope with the pain. His left elbow ached from catching his body when he slid off the horse. He breathed heavily for several minutes, trying to focus on what he needed to do to survive his wounds.

Finally, he zeroed in on the cedar arrow shaft sticking out the side of his leg. Using only his right leg and right arm, he awkwardly dragged himself closer to the tiny stream and splashed his leg with cold water. He noticed the arrowhead had fallen off the white cedar arrow shaft sticking out the other side of his calf.

Ah have to pull out that arrow before it causes any more damage. Can Ah do it? Ah need some help. Suddenly he burst into tears and lowered his face into the bent crook of his right elbow. "Zeff! Big Brover. Ah needs ya, Zeff. Sister Woman! Help! Help!"

Gasping from the pain stopped his fearful outburst. He splashed away the blood again. He forgot his language lessons in his primitive fear and pain and retreated to the language of his childhood. *Ah've gotta stop the bleedin' fast as possible. Even Ah knows that.*

He sat up awkwardly on his right hip and withdrew his big knife. He grasped the bottom of his army coat in his left hand and cut a notch an inch above the seam. Using both hands, he pulled on the notch with a yank. The fabric ripped away in a straight line. He wriggled around until he could reach and pull off the strip of dark blue wool from all around the bottom of his jacket. He dampened his improvised bandage in the cold stream.

Gritting his teeth, he bent over and slid his knife from the rolled-up pants cuff to where the shaft stuck through his calf just below his knee. Fearing even more pain, he took a deep breath and grabbed the white feather fletching on the pale hardwood shaft with both hands. He scrunched his eyes closed. And yanked. He couldn't help it. He screamed loud and long. He nearly passed out before he cast the shaft away and lay panting.

Bind the wound, Baby Boy. Stop the bleedin', quick!

Through eyes blurred with tears, he picked up the wet wool bandage and wrapped it around the bleeding wounds, covering the livid bruises encircling the blunt entry point. He wrapped the dressing around again and somehow managed to tie off the ends in a simple knot that wouldn't slip undone. He fell back, nearly comatose from his tortuous exertions. He broke out in a cold sweat from the non-stop pain. He rolled over onto his back, exhausted. The pain turned to a constant dull ache, only a little less than when the shaft lay impaled in his flesh. He felt scared and homesick, so all alone without his family, horse or rifle, only a knife.

Connal Lee struggled to splash a little water on his face and only then discovered he had lost his hat. He lifted a handful of water to his lips and sucked it in, thirsty. He began shivering. He flopped back on the grassy, weedy ground alongside the little stream. "Zeff! Ah needs ya, Zeff. Sister Woman, Ah needs y'all. Oooh."

He rested with his eyes closed, struggling against the constant domineering burn in his left leg and the minor throbbing pain in his left elbow. He forced himself to breathe deeply. "Oh, Big Brover. Sis. Where the hell are y'all when Ah needs ya. Oooh, what am Ah gonna do? Is this where Ah'm gonna die? Zeff! Help!"

Connal Lee lay unmoving, focused on breathing, trying to plan and think. He heard horse footsteps. He lurched up on his elbows and glanced around. He watched his brown mare meandering back along the creek bed, followed by the big packhorse. *Muh ride. Muh shotgun. Well, thas somethin'. Better than before.*

He staggered to his feet with a force of will and grabbed the mare's reins. He quickly tied her off to an immature pine sapling close at hand. He dropped to the ground, exhausted from the effort. He didn't have the will or energy to go after the packhorse. He lay his head on the ground, panting and sweating again.

Finally, he drifted off into a troubled sleep for a couple of hours. Through his feverish dreams, he heard the horses neighing, trying to break away. He forced himself to wake up. Dusk had fallen close to full dark. His stomach grumbled. His dry mouth tasted of dust. He rolled back over onto his right side and lifted little handfuls of water to his face. He drank and drank. Finally, he came fully awake and began feeling a little clearer-headed. He gazed all around, looking for what had disturbed the mare. She stood staring across the narrow creek, her eyes wide with fear as she pulled against the rope tied to the sapling until it bent. The mare still wore the cinched-up saddle and bridle.

Connal Lee followed the line of her fearful stare but couldn't see anything across the tiny brook. Still exhausted and hurting, he lowered himself down to lay flat on the ground. Suddenly, the mare jumped with such strength she snapped the sapling in two and pulled loose. She and the packhorse, still loaded with two small fawns, took off running upstream in a panic. He struggled to sit up. He had no way to give chase, although he feared being abandoned in the wilderness, unable to walk or ride. He couldn't cross his left leg to sit on the ground like usual, so he rested on his right hip and braced up his torso with his right arm. He didn't know what to do. He could hardly move. He felt helpless.

He heard a snuffling sound from across the water. Without warning, a midsized black bear cub scampered across, sending droplets of water spraying to all sides. Connal Lee pulled back fearfully. His heart began beating fast and hard as fear and adrenaline overcame him. He lay frozen in place. The bear, darker than the evening landscape, followed its snuffling nose. It crawled up and sniffed at the blood on Connal Lee's left pants leg and bandages. It nuzzled the wound, then licked out to taste the blood. When it tasted the horse's and Connal Lee's blood, its hunting and feeding instincts took over. It growled mindlessly, excited as it began salivating profusely.

170

Reacting unconsciously, Connal Lee reared back with a lurch. With a squeal and high-pitched moan at the pain this elicited, he found the strength to stand up. The small black bear rose on its hind legs with him. It lunged forward and reached out its arms to clench its prey in a big hug. Suddenly, the fetid hot breath of the animal wafted across Connal Lee's face. He found it disgusting. Yet somehow, the rancid stench focused his mind as he leaned his weight against the reeking furred animal. The bear lifted its arms and hugged Connal Lee tight. Its sharp claws raked across the slender boy's back, shredding the new army coat, and leaving trails of blood.

When the bear smelled the fresh blood, it lifted its left arm and dropped it heavily over Connal Lee's right shoulder. Without even thinking, Connal Lee grabbed his hunting knife and yanked it from the leather sheath at his waist. The bear snarled loud in his ear, focusing Connal Lee's thoughts on fighting for survival. He felt himself beginning to crumple as his weak left knee buckled under the dead weight of the foul-smelling, wriggling animal.

As he felt and saw the bear open its jaws and pull him closer to its face, Connal Lee stabbed up into the bear's left armpit with everything he had, plunging the sharp blade into the bear's chest just below its armpit. The bear screamed in Connal Lee's ear as it sagged back, trying to escape the shockingly painful sting in its side. The bear collapsed to the ground, screeching its pain and defiance with the knife stuck securely between its ribs.

Connal Lee had no more strength. He fell down, nearly in a swoon, dizzy and disoriented. The riding glove on his right hand dripped with hot blood, although he couldn't see it in the late evening. He yearned to feel the security of his knife back in his hand. His hand clenched and reached, but the bear and his hunting knife lay out of his reach.

The bear's convulsing body stopped shaking. Its pitiful whimpering ceased with a moan. Its chest stilled as it expelled its last breath in a great sigh. It lay still, well and truly dead.

In reaction to the fright, the fight, and his unexpected victory, Connal Lee laid himself out with his bloody hands crossed over his chest. He burst into tears, whipping his head back and forth, denying what had just happened and how badly he hurt. When his back relaxed against the damp sandy ground, he realized the bear had clawed open his back in their clenching struggle. He rolled over onto his right side to ease the pressure on the deep bleeding scratches and rested his weary head on his folded right arm. *Zeff. Sister Woman. Ah loves y'all. Ah loves y'all, an' Ah misses y'all, so, so much.*

Eventually, he cried himself to sleep.

Chapter 17: Chance Encounters

The morning after the Crow attacks dawned cold, clear, and bright on the traumatized handcart company and on Connal Lee by himself miles away to the northwest on the other side of the mountain range. Before the sun lifted over the low ridge of hills to the east, three young Shoshone crawled out from under their shared sleeping furs. Quick as they could, they laced up their buffalo hide moccasins, then dragged on their buckskin leggings trimmed with fringe and beadwork. Shivering, the younger warrior and the young shaman girl pulled on heavy long-sleeved smocks with beading across the shoulders and along the bottom edges. The older twenty-two-year-old warrior pulled on a sleeveless rabbit skin vest with the fur turned inside. His spouses had painted and beaded the outside of his vest with symbols of protection. He wore wide cold-pounded silver armbands below his bulging biceps, just above the bend of his elbows, proclaiming his wealth and prestige in the tribe.

The tallest of the three spouses, a warrior named Screaming Eagle and a nephew of Chief SoYo'Cant, had been named the apprentice war chief to the Shoshone tribe. A Crow raiding party had recently raided their camp, making off with over fifty horses. Chief SoYo'Cant had ordered his nephew to take a raiding party and reclaim their tribe's valuable horses. Screaming Eagle had led his troop to a victorious attack, returning with eleven more horses than they had lost. He had also severely punished the Crow raiders, leaving five dead and more wounded. Regrettably, he had lost two of his braves during the bloody skirmish.

After the young warrior delivered the recovered livestock, the chief required him to follow the intruders to make sure they left Shoshone lands. Should he observe them returning, the chief ordered him to rush back and raise the alarm. The warrior dashed to his tipi and told his young wife and their younger brother husband of his orders. They decided they should travel together as a family. Screaming Eagle's wife ran off to find her sisters. She asked them to move her tipi if the chief ordered the clan to move out before they returned from their patrol mission.

The little family saddled their strongest horses and two pack-horses to carry provisions for the cross-country journey. They didn't know how long they would be gone, so they packed plenty of preserved meats, pemmican, dried fruits, nuts, and berries. They also laid in a stock of barbless hunting arrows and sharply barbed war arrows. Each rider carried water bladders, spears, and warm sleeping furs behind their saddles. They trotted away without any ceremony, backtracking the warrior's path when he returned with the stolen horses.

The morning after the invading Crow war party shot Connal Lee, the Shoshone family loaded their packhorses. Their overnight camp sat less than a mile southwest of Connal Lee. They ate a quick breakfast of bison jerky moistened with hot sage tea and mounted up. Screaming Eagle led his spouses towards the trail of the fleeing Crow warriors. Their path brought them near the creek where Connal Lee had killed the yearling bear cub.

They trotted over the crest of a ridge overlooking Connal Lee's impromptu bed. Screaming Eagle's young brother husband, White Wolf, spotted two horses standing in their saddles below them beside a tiny creek. "Screaming Eagle. Look to your left, down by the river."

All three riders turned their war mounts towards the horses. As they rode closer, they found white man saddles on a lovely mare and a big packhorse burdened with two dead fawns. Screaming Eagle and White Wolf looked at each other, puzzled.

Before they reached the horses, they noticed a body sprawled out on the ground next to a bear across the meandering creek. White Wolf stood up in his stirrups. "Careful. Look across the water past the horses. It looks like a wounded man and maybe a wounded black bear. Screaming Eagle, please make certain the bear is not a threat before we go closer. Short Rainbow and I will attend to the stranger's horses."

Screaming Eagle enjoyed superior strength, but White Wolf had the sharpest mind. He could analyze new situations and devise a course of action to protect their family and further their interests. Without a word, Screaming Eagle nudged his stallion's stomach and crossed the creek. He pulled his long spear loose from its ties on his

174

saddle as he approached the fallen bear. He couldn't see it breathing or moving but didn't take a chance. He prodded it with the long sharp flint blade bound to the end of his spear. When it didn't move, he hopped down off his big horse. "The bear is dead. Come on over. It is safe."

White Wolf and Short Rainbow led their horses across the narrow creek and joined Screaming Eagle. After they tied the horses' reins to small pine saplings, White Wolf rushed over to Connal Lee, still sprawled on his right side. He checked over the fallen boy, noting the bandaged leg and clawed back. He couldn't tell if the young man lay unconscious or asleep. He walked over to the horses and pulled Short Rainbow and Screaming Eagle close to him so he could speak softly. "There is a badly wounded young white boy over there beside the dead bear. He's breathing. I don't know how badly he's wounded, but I think we should attend to him. Chief SoYo'Cant wants us to be friends with the Long Knives. He's probably a member of a Mormon wagon train or handcart company. If he's a Mormon, the Chief would definitely want us to extend our help since he was baptized a Mormon himself. Do you agree?"

Short Rainbow and Screaming Eagle glanced over at the fallen boy and nodded their agreement.

"Screaming Eagle, please take the deer off the white boy's packhorse. Leave the other horses saddled and loaded for now until I can examine the boy and decide what we should do. Short Rainbow, please bring my sleeping furs and fetch my medicine bags from the packhorse. Screaming Eagle, if you would start a small fire. I will need to make sage tea to bathe the boy's wounds and willow bark tea to ease his pains and aches."

The three nodded at each other and walked away to their assigned duties. White Wolf returned to the boy. He knelt down in front of Connal Lee and gently touched his shoulder, trying to rouse him from his sleep. The boy lay curled up in an attempt to stay warm, despite the pain across his back from re-opening the clawed cuts around his spinal cord. He lay shivering from the cold. The sun hadn't yet reached the ground where he lay. White Wolf felt the young man's forehead, checking for fever. He picked up Connal Lee's left hand and gently chafed it to help warm him up and rouse him. A few minutes later, Short Rainbow spread a warm fur over the white boy. White Wolf smiled his thanks.

While the injured boy didn't awaken, White Wolf took the opportunity to remove the blue wool bandage wrapping his left leg. He could tell from the bruises around the perimeter of the puncture in the calf that the boy had taken an arrow wound. He rinsed out the bandage and loosely bound up the entry and exit wounds until he had hot water to better clean them.

He stepped over the fallen body and carefully lifted the fur blanket. He leaned down and examined the four parallel cuts starting at the boy's lower left back, going up across his spine, and ending in four puncture marks caught just below the boy's right shoulder blade. The center scrape of the bear's claws had dug quite deep. It still seeped blood. The claw mark above the deep center cut and the two lower scratches hadn't cut as deep and had already begun to scab over. Screaming Eagle wanted to clean the cuts so they would not get infected. His teacher, Medicine Man Firewalker, had cautioned him that bear and cougar claws carried filthy diseases from their dead prey. Their cuts often became infected. Skin infections could turn into grave threats quite quickly.

White Wolf sat back on his haunches, considering the best steps to help the boy recover. Screaming Eagle built a fireplace not far away from the boy. He lit the blaze using his flint fire starter on a handful of dry grass tinder. He added a handful of small branches as kindling. Once the flames caught fire, he stacked small dry deadfall branches around it like a miniature tipi. He soon had a hot fire burning.

Short Rainbow filled two water bladders with fresh water from the creek and placed them close beside the firepit. Screaming Eagle found four flat rocks beside the creek bed. Using a green branch, he pushed them into the center of the fire, where the wood had burned down to glowing coals.

White Wolf opened small doeskin pouches from his medicine bag. He tipped out some carefully prepared chips of dried wood scraped from the inner bark of a willow tree into one of the bladders. He then crushed dried sage leaves he had harvested and dried over the summer in the other bladder. He often used sage in treating in-flammation and infections. The three young Shoshone had worked as a team before, assisting White Wolf's medical treatments. Si-lently, Screaming Eagle lifted the hot stones with more green branches and slid them into the bladders to heat the water.

Short Rainbow knew White Wolf would need bandages. Alt-hough training as a Shaman focused on spiritual healing, she had learned about healing the body as well. She retrieved several strips of soft absorbent leather made from mountain goat hides, prepared for use as bandages. She rinsed them out in the running water and set them down beside the young man. When she noticed the boy had stopped shivering, she smiled approvingly.

She returned to their packhorses and dug out two buffalo horn drinking cups and an undecorated bowl made from a large dried gourd. She handed them to White Wolf, kneeling beside the fire. After he determined the sage tea had seeped enough to be beneficial, he filled the bowl with its transparent golden earthy water. He picked up a scrap of soft goat hide chamois and began washing the boy's arrow wounds. He carefully examined the entrance and exit wounds to ensure no foreign materials remained inside to fester later and cause infections. When satisfied, he bound the leg with his chamois bandage and then secured it with Connal Lee's bandage of dark blue wool. "Please give me a hand. We need to remove the boy's clothing so I can tend to his back."

They removed his lacerated coat without any trouble. White Wolf didn't want to risk pulling the boy's cuts open, so rather than lifting the young man's arms to drag the shirt off over his head, he pulled out his valuable white man steel knife and slit the shirt up the back, through the collar, and lay it open. Short Rainbow pulled the dirty cotton shirt off his arms. She picked up the shirt and coat and walked over to the creek to wash them. While scrubbing them, she thought about how she could mend them so they would not be wasted.

White Wolf and Screaming Eagle gently settled the boy on his stomach on a buffalo hide sleeping fur. White Wolf pulled the fur blanket up over his legs to keep him warm. "Please fetch more hot sage tea, Screaming Eagle. I need to work on his back, now."

White Wolf leaned in closer to inspect the deepest center cut, scraping across the pale white skin. "Short Rainbow, please bring me your smallest needle. I'm going to have to sew up these cuts. I'll also need horsetail hair to use as thread. Oh, thank you, Screaming Eagle. Just set it down here beside me. I see now we will be here at least a day tending to this young man's wounds. Would you please unpack the horses? When you are done, it might be best for you to find the track of the Crow party, so we don't lose them. After I bind the boy's wounds, Short Rainbow and I will set up camp. We'll butcher the boy's two little fawns and set the meat to cooking and smoking. No need to let it go to waste."

On her way back from the creek, Short Rainbow bent over and picked up an arrow shaft. Silently she handed it to White Wolf. He examined it and gave it to Screaming Eagle. "Crow war arrow, missing its arrowhead. Note the white feather fletching." Short Rainbow and Screaming Eagle nodded their agreement, then turned to their work.

Two hours later, White Wolf had cleaned the boy's wounds, sutured them closed, and bandaged them. They had the horses unpacked and the first doe skinned and butchered. The three Shoshone sat around the campfire and ate a little pemmican and deer jerky.

White Wolf thought out loud while the others chewed on the dried jerky. "So, what do we know? What do we have here? We have a wounded young white man. Despite his youth, I believe we can say he is brave. He fought the Crow and escaped with an arrow in his leg. He's a survivor who, even though badly hurt, had the presence of mind to remove the arrow shaft before it could cause further complications and begin to fester. He had the strength to bind his own wound. Then, even though hurting, when his blood attracted that yearling bear cub, he managed to fight it off and kill it. He is also a fairly wealthy young man, owning two excellent horses, a fine leather pale face saddle, and a sturdy packsaddle. He is armed with a shotgun and steel hunting knife with ample ammunition for his rifle. He is well dressed in warm clothes. I think we have a smart and strong young white man on our hands. I suspect he is someone we can respect when we get to know him. Don't you think so?"

Screaming Eagle and Short Rainbow nodded their heads in agreement, their mouths full of venison jerky and sage tea.

"I believe Uncle SoYo'Cant would want us to take care of him until he can return to his people. Do you agree?"

Again, they both nodded their heads.

"We'll talk more tonight when you return from tracking the Crow raiders. I only hope the boy wakes up soon. Even though sleep heals, I don't like him remaining unconscious for so long. I think I'll try to wake him up soon if he doesn't stir on his own. In the meantime, I need to clean myself up and organize my medicines. I'll also need more bandages for later in the day."

They all three stood up. Short Rainbow turned to skinning the second doe. Screaming Eagle leapt up on his warhorse and trotted away, riding uphill away from the creek in a northeasterly direction.

After White Wolf washed his hands and face in the cold creek water, he sat down beside the sleeping boy. He pushed the boy's short blond hair back off his face. He rubbed the hair between his fingers, amazed at its thin, fine texture and pale color, so unlike his own beautiful thick black hair. He tucked the edges back behind the boy's ears to see his face more clearly. He picked up Connal Lee's pale, slender right hand and held it gently between his two warm hands. He felt callouses on the boy's palm and fingers, which told him the young man was no stranger to work. He guessed it might be from pushing a handcart for weeks on end.

White Wolf concentrated his meditations on sending healing into the boy's flaccid body, willing him to feel better and wake up.

179

Chapter 18: Healing Touch

An hour or so later, after Short Rainbow finished butchering the fawns, she set their meat to smoking into travel jerky. When finished, she washed her hands and cleaned the volcanic glass blade she had bound to an antler handle to make a knife. She walked over and sat down beside the patient, joining White Wolf's quiet bedside vigil. She picked up the boy's free hand in her left hand, then gently stroked his bare arm with her right hand, from shoulder down to the wrist. White Wolf began stroking the wounded child's right arm. Short Rainbow and White Wolf looked at each other and smiled warmly.

Speaking very softly, keeping his voice calm and peaceful in case the boy heard him, White Wolf reviewed his concerns with Short Rainbow. "Two things, when he starts to come to, Short Rainbow. He's going to be in a lot of pain. As soon as you see him regaining consciousness, please bring willow bark tea. I wouldn't be surprised if he's extremely thirsty and hungry, too. My biggest fear is that he will be frightened, seeing people beside him who will appear like the Crow who wounded him. He is bound to lurch away, which could do mischief with the stitches in his back. When he opens his eyes, keep a warm smile on your face. Quietly assure him we are friends. Repeat the English words friend and peace over and over. If you can, gently hold his hand or stroke his hair like a mother would with a hurt child."

"I understand, White Wolf. Burning Fire has taught me how to focus and calm my mind, to be open to the world and experiences as they happen. I will follow your lead in all respects."

"His eyes are beginning to flutter open. Keep touching him but don't clutch or grab. We don't want to make him feel threatened."

"Of course. Listen."

Connal Lee slowly shook his head no. He became aware of a throbbing pain in his left calf and a dull ache in his left elbow. As he started to move, he felt a sharp stinging pain shoot across his back. "Oooh. Did those Crow Injuns kill me? Am Ah dyin'? Oooh."

When he felt hands holding his, he sighed in relief. "Oh, Zeff, y'all found me. Ah was so worried."

He blinked his eyes. They didn't seem to want to open. He blinked a couple of times and focused on the faces close over his. He looked up into White Wolf's guileless face and his warm brown eyes watching with a gentle smile on his face. He whipped around and glared at Short Rainbow's young pixielike smiling face. Connal Lee pulled his hands back and tried to scoot away. "Yer not... Oh, no! Injuns! Where's Zeff? Zeff, Ah needs yer help, Big Brover!"

"Shh. We are your friends. Peace. You safe. We friends. Not Crow. Friends."

Short Rainbow leaned over and smiled. "Peace. We friend white man. We friend Mormon. Peace. Peace." She tentatively reached out and softly, soothingly stroked Connal Lee's hand.

White Wolf raised his right hand in Plains Indian sign language. "Peace, friend. Peace." He also reached out to smooth Connal Lee's floppy, short bangs to the side off his forehead. He smiled again as he nodded his head up to Short Rainbow. "Willow tea, please."

Short Rainbow rose gracefully to her feet and walked noiselessly over to the bladders beside the dwindling fire. She dipped a drinking horn and carried it back. White Wolf accepted it with a nod of thanks. "Tea. Medicine. Help pain. Thirsty? You have pain? Drink. Help."

White Wolf gently raised Connal Lee's head and held the cup to his lips. Connal Lee stared fearfully at these strangers, but he needed water. The warm tea had a mild bitterness but went down easily. After a couple of sips, White Wolf pulled the cup away. "Slow. Slow. Good."

A little at a time, Connal Lee drank the entire cup. He began feeling better just from the water.

White Wolf handed Short Rainbow the cup. "Sage tea, now, please."

He leaned over and looked at Connal Lee. "Hungry?"

Connal Lee suddenly felt famished. He nodded his head. "Yes."

"Food?"

"Please."

In a spatter of Shoshone language Connal Lee didn't understand, White Wolf asked Short Rainbow to bring dried serviceberry cakes and a little fresh venison. She handed him the sage tea and walked back to the fireplace. When she returned, she knelt down beside Connal Lee. She broke off a piece of the little cake, popped it in her mouth, and chewed. A big smile lit up her face as she nodded her enjoyment. She broke off another small bite and held it up to Connal Lee's lips. He opened his mouth. She popped it inside. The serviceberry cake had a dry, grainy texture with a mild, sweet flavor that reminded him of raisins, except for the color. He chewed. "Good. Thank you. More, please?"

She hand-fed him the remainder of the cake. White Wolf helped him sip more tea. Short Rainbow picked up a small liver from the young doe she had butchered earlier. She had roasted it on a heated rock beside the fire. She pulled it apart and began feeding it to Connal Lee. He recognized it as liver with the first bite. "Mm. Good. Thank you."

Connal Lee began feeling a little more human. He relaxed back onto the sleeping fur rolled up into a pillow, lounging on his right side, guarding his back and wounded leg. He went to roll over onto his back when he felt the claw cuts. "Ouch! Oh! Ow! My back!"

He instinctively kicked out his left leg to help lever himself over onto his right side when the wound in his calf flared up from the motion. "Oooh. Ah hurts somethin' fierce. Ooow!

White Wolf glanced over at Short Rainbow. "Willow tea, please."

White Wolf remembered the advice of Chief SoYo'Cant's respected Medicine Man, Firewalker, who was White Wolf's teacher in the healing arts. He reached out and began rubbing Connal Lee's leg with one hand above the bandages and one hand below. He squeezed and rubbed, distracting Connal Lee's focus away from the painful wounds. "Rest. Heal. Pain go. You safe. You good."

Short Rainbow lifted and tilted Connal Lee's head to help him sip more mildly bitter tea. It tasted the way willow bushes smelled in the hot summer sun. When he finished drinking, she gently lowered his head back on the soft buffalo pelt. She patted his head and softly stroked his hair. "Good. Good."

Connal Lee sighed and closed his eyes as the stabbing pains receded into mere throbbing aches.

"Good. Rest. You safe. We friend. You heal good."

Connal Lee didn't feel like he was healing good, but he appreciated their binding his wounds and helping him eat and drink. "My thanks. Mighty neighborly of y'all."

Screaming Eagle and Short Rainbow sat quietly, sharing their strength and peaceful healing thoughts with the wounded boy. About ten minutes later, Connal Lee's eyes popped open. His bladder threatened to cause an accident. "Sorry, but Ah need tuh pee." He looked embarrassed.

"Pee? What mean pee?"

"Oh...uh...to urinate. Make water. Go to the toilet?"

"Ah, yes. I understand."

In Shoshone, he asked Short Rainbow to help him lift the boy to his feet so he could take care of business. They each grabbed the boy around an arm with one hand and lifted him to his feet by lifting up on his buttocks with their other hands. Connal Lee stood swaying between them with his face scrunched up as his back and calf screamed with pain. He began panting through lips pursed from the agony.

"Hold our shoulders. We walk."

They carried his slender body between them over the couple of steps to the creek. His feet hardly touched the ground. Careful not to touch his lacerated back, White Wolf pulled down Connal Lee's corduroy britches. "Good. Now."

With a great sigh of relief, Connal Lee let loose. His strong yellow stream arched out into the creek. "Oh, thanks. Ah appreciate y'all's help."

When he finished, White Wolf tugged Connal Lee's britches back up. Slowly, they moved him back to the sleeping furs and eased him down onto his right side. He collapsed, exhausted. "That's so much better. Ah thanks y'all for yer help."

Half an hour later, Connal Lee woke up. Short Rainbow sat beside him, carefully stitching beadwork on white rabbit fur riding gloves for Screaming Eagle. When she saw Connal Lee move, she smiled and set her work aside. "Hunger? Thirst?"

183

Connal Lee stared at her for a moment as if he had never seen her before. His body betrayed him by befuddling his mind. He focused, then nodded his head. "Yes. Please."

Without a word, Short Rainbow gracefully stood up and glided over to the fire with an athletic strut. Connal Lee watched her, fascinated with her dancelike movements. White Wolf removed a small venison steak from the green stick he had used to broil it over hot coals. Short Rainbow gave the boy a drink of sage tea, then White Wolf held the thinly cut meat to his lips. Connal Lee took a bite and then rested against the pillow as he chewed.

White Wolf decided to clean and dress the wounds again. Connal Lee watched the young shamans tend to him for the next half hour. He began feeling a little clearer and refreshed by the time they bound up the arrow wound again. Short Rainbow stretched out beside and behind Connal Lee with her head propped up on her bent elbow. She rested her hand on Connal Lee's lean shoulder comfortingly. Connal Lee gazed up at her black eyes, then glanced over at White Wolf. "Thank y'all. Yer good at the doctoring. Ah really appreciate it."

White Wolf merely smiled and nodded. He knew the boy had a nasty bruise on his left forearm and elbow. He carefully picked up Caonnal Lee's arm and gently massaged it as he rubbed echinacea root salve over the bruise.

Struggling to communicate in English, White Wolf frowned in concentration. "My name White Wolf in English. What name you?"

"Oh, Ah'm Connal Lee. Connal Lee Swinton."

White Wolf pointed at Short Rainbow. "Sister wife name Short Rainbow."

Short Rainbow leaned over and smiled at Connal Lee. She tried repeating his foreign-sounding name, but it came out quite garbled. A smile twitched his lips up a bit for the first time since getting shot.

"Con – nol – Lee."

She repeated it better, only she said it like one word. "Conalee."

"Huh, uh. Connal," he paused, "Lee."

"Ah! Connal Lee."

"That's right. An' you are Short Rainbow. What a lovely name. Ah've never known anyone with a musical name before. Short Rainbow."

They both nodded at each other. Then Connal Lee turned to White Wolf and dipped his head in acknowledgment. "White Wolf."

"Connal Lee."

They smiled at each other. White Wolf patted Connal Lee's shoulder. "We friend. All friend. Rest now, Connal Lee. We eat again later. Rest."

Connal Lee let his eyes drift closed. "Don't mind if Ah do."

Before sleep enveloped him, a feeling of homesickness over-whelmed him. Tears leaked out of his closed eyes. *Zeff, Big Brover. Where the heck are ya, Zeff? Sister Woman, Ah misses y'all. Don't y'all worry none. As soon as Ah'm back on muh feet, Ah'll find y'all. Stay safe. Ah loves ya, Zeff. Ah loves ya, Sister Woman. Ah loves ya, Mother Baines an' Father Baines. Oh, how Ah loves all of y'all."*

Without a word, White Wolf leaned over and wiped the tears away with his bare hand, then patted Connal Lee on the cheek, trying to infuse his touch with a comforting reassurance that the child was safe and well looked after.

Later, the sun began lowering behind the barren sides of the low hills west of the camp. Connal Lee heard a horse trotting towards them and opened his eyes. When he looked up, he found a muscled warrior astride an enormous war stallion. The brave wore a tall feathered war bonnet on his head, like the Crow warriors who had shot him. Connal Lee scrambled up, ignoring the pain in his leg and back. He frantically searched for his shotgun. "Oh, no! Where's muh rifle?"

Screaming Eagle brought his horse to a halt on the other side of the fire from Connal Lee. Before his feet had quite touched the ground, Short Rainbow ran up and threw herself into his arms. They hugged and laughed while Screaming Eagle spun Short Rainbow around joyfully. When he set her down on her feet, her arm went automatically around his waist. They gazed warmly at each other.

185

Connal Lee saw the love they shared between them. It left him feeling lonely and homesick again.

White Wolf heard the horse arrive. He had been fishing upstream. His efforts had only resulted in two immature bass. He rushed up and gave Screaming Eagle a big hug. "Screaming Eagle! It's about time you returned to your family. Did you find the war party's trail? Are you hungry? Short Rainbow, please take care of the horse. I want to introduce him to Connal Lee."

White Wolf pulled Screaming Eagle by his hand to Connal Lee's bedside. They knelt down. Seeing a looming tall warrior, a muscled stranger who looked so intimidating in his feathered war bonnet, shocked Connal Lee.

White Wolf reached out a hand and touched Connal Lee's arm. "Connal Lee. This Screaming Eagle in English. Screaming Eagle, this Connal Lee."

Screaming Eagle remembered the manners drilled into him about white man customs by Chief SoYo'Cant's language teacher, Teniwaaten. He held out his big strong hand for a handshake. Connal Lee's right hand lay pinned under his side, so he awkwardly held out his left. They squeezed their fingers together, then let go. "Nice tuh meetcha, Screamin' Eagle."

The warrior removed his feathered bonnet, nodded his head, and smiled at the recumbent patient. "Connal Lee. Good meet."

White Wolf pointed at Screaming Eagle. "Warrior. Brother husband. We family. Me. Screaming Eagle. Short Rainbow wife. We share tipi. We share life."

"Wow. Y'all are married? Ah thought y'all were brothers and sister or something since y'all look so much alike."

"We in love. We cousin. We papoose together. We happy family."

"Ah see. Screamin' Eagle sure is a tall, strong man, isn't he?"

"Yes. Strong. Brave. Warrior. Much honor. Much good man."

"So Ah see. Wow. Plumb amazin'."

Chapter 19: Language Lessons

That evening, White Wolf and Short Rainbow pulled their sleeping furs up alongside Connal Lee. They snuggled up next to their patient to keep him warm and to be on hand if he needed them during the night. Connal Lee had settled in, sprawled comfortably on his stomach, already asleep. White Wolf and Short Rainbow turned towards him and rested their hands across his unwounded shoulders. Screaming Eagle didn't want to be left out, so he snuggled up behind Short Rainbow and fell asleep, most contented.

Bird song woke them up just before dawn as the sky began to lighten above the eastern hills. Short Rainbow gently extracted herself from her husband's big, warm body. She stirred up the fire and then added more deadfall branches to build up a good hot flame. She brewed up a water bladder of sage tea and one of willow bark tea while she prepared breakfast.

Connal Lee felt disoriented when he first woke up, sensing warm furs rather than tattered old quilts covering him. His face felt chilled from the cold night air, but the rest of him felt toasty warm. After White Wolf and Screaming Eagle walked downstream to relieve their bladders, White Wolf walked over and stood by Connal Lee. "Pee?"

Connal Lee nodded as he struggled to push himself up with his right arm. White Wolf pushed him gently back, then glanced up at Screaming Eagle. "Help Connal Lee to creek, Screaming Eagle."

Screaming Eagle effortlessly leaned down and lifted Connal Lee to his feet. Careful of the claw scrapes on his back, he helped Connal Lee walk downstream by holding him by his elbows. Connal Lee's feet shuffled lightly along their path. When they reached the damp side of the creek, Connal Lee balanced on his right leg. "Please put me down. I need to do more than pee this morning."

Screaming Eagle didn't understand. He reached for Connal Lee's pants, thinking he needed help pulling them down to urinate. Connal Lee shook his head. He felt more than a little embarrassed as he pantomimed squatting over the water for a bowel movement.

"Ah." Screaming Eagle understood. Though worried about Connal Lee bending his leg, he helped Connal Lee remove his trousers. White Wolf had removed Connal Lee's boots the morning before when he first cleaned his wounds. Screaming Eagle faced Connal Lee. He placed his big hands around Connal Lee's ribcage, up in his armpits, and carefully lowered him to a squat. Connal Lee's face scrunched up in pain as his left leg stretched the arrow wound. When he finished vacating his bowels and bladder, Screaming Eagle lowered him so he could kneel on all fours. Screaming Eagle used his bare hand to lift up cold water and clean Connal Lee's crotch. Connal Lee's face burned with embarrassment, but he appreciated the help. With one arm around Connal Lee's waist, Screaming Eagle helped him step into his pants.

They returned to the fire and settled Connal Lee on the buffalo hide bed. Short Rainbow brought him a drinking horn of warm willow tea. White Wolf served tender roasted venison and a dab of pemmican on a green leaf. After they all ate breakfast, Short Rainbow and White Wolf took their time bathing Connal Lee in warm sage tea and dressing his wounds with fresh chamois bandages. White Wolf gently smeared bear fat over the cuts on his back to keep the skin soft and pliable while it scabbed over. Short Rainbow carried the soiled bandage leathers over to the creek and washed them.

"Oh. Many thanks, White Wolf and Short Rainbow. My pains hurt much less today. Ah can even think more clearly after a good night's sleep. Ah hope y'all know how much Ah appreciate y'all taking in a stranger and making me feel safe and cared for. The past two days have been mighty scary for me. Ah've never been shot before. Nor have Ah ever wrestled with a bear before. The pain was almost more than Ah could stand."

White Wolf, who spoke English better than his two spouses, didn't understand everything Connal Lee said, but he caught the gist. He bent down and gave Connal Lee a little hug. "Rest. Sleep. We here. You safe."

"Thanks, White Wolf."

The three Shoshone turned to straighten up the little camp. The horses had eaten almost everything green growing around the far side of the creek where they had been hobbled. Screaming Eagle

188

moved them further downstream to fresh fodder. He checked them for stones in their hoofs or other ailments. They all seemed to be in fine shape. When he returned to the firepit, he found White Wolf working on the bear hide over a small log, using his precious white man steel knife to remove all the fat and meat before tanning it.

Short Rainbow had rigged a tripod using green branches to hold their small gourd bowl. She placed the bear's brains and creek water in the bowl, then squished them up to make a viscous paste. When satisfied the mixture had the correct consistency, she placed the bowl of her concoction over the low flames to heat.

Screaming Eagle squatted down beside White Wolf and affectionately squeezed his neck. "Unless you have something more important you need me to do, I think I should ride out and make sure the war party hasn't turned back. I don't want them to surprise us."

"That's a very good idea. We'll see you tonight for supper. Be alert. Be safe. We love you, you great big wonderful eagle."

They smiled at each other, then Screaming Eagle saddled his big war stallion and rode off.

Connal Lee slept a couple of hours. When he woke up, he asked for help sitting up so he could see around the camp. White Wolf and Short Rainbow moved him over to a small tree where he could lean his right side against the trunk. He watched his two new friends return to their chores. He felt strange not lending a hand. "What are y'all cooking, Short Rainbow?"

She understood the question but didn't have English words to answer. White Wolf looked up from scraping the bear hide. "Bear brain. For tan leather."

"Y'all can tan leather with animal brains? Ah never knew that. We always used tree bark for tanning our hides. Ah wish Ah had known that a whiles back. Ah needed to tan me a deer hide but couldn't find any of the right trees."

He watched, interested in their process. "White Wolf, how do y'all say hide in Shoshone?"

Connal Lee heard a short word that sounded like pee-he. He repeated it and spelled it out in his mind to help him remember.

"How do y'all say tan?"

He heard soa with the ah sound repeated after a quick break, almost like two words. He visualized it spelled soa'a, and memorized the word. "How do y'all say you?"

Hesitantly he strung the words together. In Shoshone, he asked, "You tan hide?"

White Wolf responded with a nod and a big smile. "Ha'a. Yes."

Connal Lee silently repeated ha'a to himself. "How do y'all say no?"

"Gai'."

In between occasional short naps, Connal Lee kept his mind entertained as he learned a few essential words in Shoshone. Fire. Tree. Water. Walk. Horse. Ride. He took pleasure in challenging himself. He also silently sent his thanks to Mother Baines for insisting he pronounce his words correctly and distinctly. He could tell it helped his Shoshone friends when he spoke to them in English. He often had to repeat his words with gestures, pantomimes, and explanations before they understood. White Wolf and Short Rainbow picked up new English words quite quickly, too.

When White Wolf finished cleaning the bear pelt, Short Rainbow smeared the brain paste over it, then weighed it down with rocks along the edges so it wouldn't curl up as it dried.

White Wolf changed Connal Lee's bandages that evening just before sunset while they waited for Screaming Eagle to return so they could eat supper. "I like. You teach. I teach. You learn. I learn."

"Yes, White Wolf. There is a lot Ah can teach you. Ah am sure there is a lot y'all can teach me, too. Do y'all know how to shoot a rifle? Ah would love to learn to shoot a bow. Ah've never tried it before."

Their friendship grew as they became more used to each other and spent more time together. While they waited for Connal Lee to heal enough to ride, Short Rainbow tanned the fawn hides, leaving the fur still on them. She ingeniously made them into a simple scabbard to carry Connal Lee's rifle, tied on under the left stirrup of his saddle. Positioned like this, he could pull the shotgun free with his right hand without having to stop riding. Connal Lee loved the long leather fringe hanging off the bottom of the rifle case. White Wolf made Connal Lee a pair of riding gloves with big cuffs to go up over his coat sleeves. He made them out of tanned cottontail rabbit skin with the fur turned in for warmth. Connal Lee admired their handiwork.

Their mutual language lessons progressed very rapidly, especially between White Wolf and Connal Lee.

Short Rainbow helped tend Connal Lee's wounds, then prepared a venison stew for supper. With all her chores completed, Short Rainbow applied herself to repairing Connal Lee's cotton shirt. She didn't want to sew the two halves together invisibly. She always liked to do things artistically. She took her time and joined the edges with a row of beading. Finally, she handed it to Connal Lee. "It's so beautiful, Short Rainbow! Thanks so much. The only trouble is Ah won't be able to see it when Ah'm wearing it."

While Short Rainbow repaired the shirt, White Wolf decided to work on Connal Lee's dark blue coat. He examined the four parallel cuts slashing diagonally across the back. He chose to emphasize the slits like a badge of honor commemorating Connal Lee's surviving a bear attack. He used thin rawhide strings and tied the edges closed with the same stitches he had used on Connal Lee's back to sew up the really deep third incision. Connal Lee loved the look of the repairs across the back of his coat. He wondered how on earth White Wolf had cut his leather laces so thin. To repair the torn hem, White Wolf had simply rolled up the edge and looped the leather strings around and around to tie it closed.

Connal Lee asked for some rawhide strings to close up the cut on his left pants leg. White Wolf handed him several lengths plus a bone awl. Connal Lee made holes along the edges of the incision and tied them closed by weaving the strings back and forth across the opening. It didn't look as pretty as Short Rainbow and White Wolf's, but he felt proud he had taken care of it himself.

It took four days for Connal Lee's arrow wound to heal enough that he could begin walking around. White Wolf chopped down a sapling tree and trimmed it for Connal Lee to use as a crutch under his left arm. The first day up wore him out, but he felt grateful to be

191

able to at least walk himself down to the creek to tend to his business without help.

After supper the following evening, they sat around discussing plans and options. The Shoshone still had their orders to follow the Crow war party until they left Shoshone lands. They explained their mission to Connal Lee and invited him to travel with them until they could return him to his family.

After a week apart, Connal Lee desperately wanted to see Zeff and Sister Woman. As much as he liked his new friends, he still woke up homesick during the night. He shook his head. "Ah think it would be best if Ah leave y'all and backtrack to the Overland Trail. Then Ah can follow the handcart company until Ah catch up with my family."

Both Screaming Eagle and White Wolf shook their heads no.

"Sorry, friend. Not safe. One? Alone? What if Crow find? What if animal find? What you eat? No. Safe with us. No worry. When finish, we ride you to um family."

Connal Lee reluctantly agreed he shouldn't try to strike out on his own. After all, he didn't have any food or blankets, only two horses, two saddles, a canvas water bag, and the wonderful doeskin rifle scabbard Short Rainbow had made for him. He felt over-whelmed with homesickness, again, knowing he wouldn't see his family anytime soon.

Chapter 20: Cavalry to the Rescue

Later the morning after the Crow ambush, Captain Hanover finished making his rounds. His young third wife had accompanied him. As they walked, they discussed how to continue on their journey with so many wounded. By the time they saw and visited with everyone, the captain had made his plans and went to work. He ordered the three supply wagons unloaded. He explained that with low supplies, they could condense their reserves and tools into two wagons and use the third to transport the wounded who couldn't ride or walk. If they rigged two canvas hammocks like on sailing ships beneath the canvas top and piled quilts in the wagon's pine box, they could carry all the seriously wounded together. A couple of the men couldn't push their handcarts but could ride horses. They only had six horses and two saddles, at least until Connal Lee returned, but they would have to make do. His teen guards and cowboys volunteered to help push the carts of the wounded. The captain directed the older children to herd the milk cows. Everyone pitched in and helped as they could, with a strong sense of community and purpose.

Lorna Baines remained the head nurse for the time being. The ladies of the camp lent her a hand, tending wounds, washing bandages, and cooking communal meals. With so many wounded and exhausted, the captain ordered his followers to tighten up the camp formation and settle in for a couple days of rest.

They all said a lot of prayers.

Zeff and Sister Woman kept looking west, hoping to see Connal Lee come riding in, dragging his kills behind him on the packhorse. They knew he would have a big smile on his face to be reunited with his family. Zeff worried so much about Connal Lee it kept him awake that night.

Very early on the third morning of their layover, Captain Hanover strolled up to the Swinton handcart. Zeff and Sister Woman stood up and shook his hand. He reached out and placed his hands on Zeff and Sister Woman's shoulders. "I know yer worried about

Connal Lee, but we have t' move on. We're losin' too much time on this trip that could make problems fer us later on."

The three sat down around their small fire. Sister Woman offered the captain a slice of fresh hot cornbread and a mug of coffee. While eating the simple breakfast, Zeff and Sister Woman expressed their concern about leaving before knowing what happened to Connal Lee. "We jus' cain't leave 'im behind, Captain. We cain't desert our little brover."

"I know how ya feel, Brother Swinton. But let's think on it for a minute. He's a smart boy. He probably finished 'is hunt an' returned ahead of us on the trail, expectin' to find us a day's walk further along than we are. Surely he's clever enough t' see we didn't pass along the trail. He most likely stayed there an' waited fer us. We'll probably find 'im ahead of us."

"But when we didn't show up two days ago, wouldn't 'e have ridden back tryin' tuh find us? Ah'm jus' afeared somethin' happened tuh 'im. He's got yer compass, so Ah don't think 'e could o' gotten lost. Not fer two whole days. Do ya suppose those danged Crow Injuns found 'im? They left here ridin' in pretty much the same direction Connal Lee took that mornin'. They were only a few hours behind him an' ridin' hard. Ah'm real worried. Ah cain't help thinkin' we should go search fer 'im. Maybe he's lyin' wounded an' needs some help. We cain't desert 'im, Captain. We jus' cain't!"

"I know yer worried, Zeff. We're all worried fer 'im. But we gotta move on. We don't have no manpower nor horses nor time t' make a search party. I am so sorry, Brother Swinton. I'm sorry it's come t' this, Sister Swinton. Let's move on an' hope t' run into 'im on the trail."

"Well, Ah'm not sure we can go with y'all, then, Captain. Ah jus' don't feel right abandonin' muh poor little brover out here in the wilderness, all alone."

"Brother Swinton, I understand how ya feel. But, it's not safe fer ya t' stay behind. We need t' stick together fer our mutual protection. Think o' yer baby son."

194

When the captain stood up, Zeff and Sister Woman stood up, as well. "Please douse yer fire an' prepare t' move out. We leave in about half an hour."

Sister Woman burst into tears. Zeff pulled her in for a hug, close to tears himself. He couldn't imagine not having their cheerful little brother in their lives. *Where on earth could he be? Is he hurt? Ah hates the thought o' leavin' ya behind, Little Brover. Hurry back tuh us!*

Before the captain led his company in their morning prayer, he asked everyone to keep an eye out for Connal Lee, who he hoped would be waiting for them up ahead. Lorna Baines gasped and covered her mouth with her hand. "Oh, no. How can we leave without our foster son?"

Gilbert put his arm around her and held her tight while they lowered their heads in prayer.

That evening, after Lorna and her nurses changed their patients' bandages, Lorna and Gilbert walked over to the Swinton's campfire. They exchanged hugs, then sat down around the dwindling fire with glum faces. "I'm sorry, Brother and Sister Swinton. I sure had high hopes we would come across Connal Lee today. Now that we're his honorary foster parents, we feel a duty towards him. We love him, too."

Zeff nodded with a frown. "Yep, we're mighty worried about 'im. Ah cain't hardly think 'bout nothin' else, only findin' muh poor lost little brover."

Sister Woman burst into tears. "Ah miss Baby Boy. Oh how Ah miss 'im. What're we gonna do? We's gotta find 'im, but the captain won't send out a search party nor wait any more fer 'im. He's gonna think we abandoned 'im. That we don't love 'im no more. An' that jus' breaks muh heart."

Lorna moved over and drew Sister Woman's head down to her ample bosoms so she could cry herself out. She patted Sister Woman gently on the back. "He knows we all love him. He's a smart boy. You just wait and see. Soon he'll show up, probably with a big story to tell of his adventures camping out all alone. Anything could have happened, but we're not giving up hope. We'll pray for him constantly until he returns to us safe and sound."

Zeff and Gilbert shook their heads mournfully. They both wished they could think of something, anything, they could do.

The next day dawned cold and clear. A breeze blew steadily from their left. They had only been on the trail for a couple of hours when the captain heard someone shouting. "Hey. Look back! There's smoke or dust behind us."

Captain Hanover had been riding lookout that morning, a little ways ahead of the train. When he heard the alarm, he stood up in his stirrups and looked back. He observed a great cloud of dust blowing low to the ground. He immediately took off racing back towards the train, waving his hat over his head in a big circle. "Round 'er up, folks. Trouble's comin' hard on our heels. Make it tight. Arm yerselves, men!

The train turned back and began winding its way around the supply wagons as fast as they could push and pull their handcarts. They pulled up tighter than their usual night formation. Once they parked the carts, the unwounded men and boys ran for the support wagons and armed themselves. The women followed hard on their heels, dragging their crying children along by their hands. They all clustered around the wagon carrying the wounded. They stood frozen, watching as horses became visible below the cloud of dust in the distance.

"Not again! Oh, no! Heaven help us!"

Captain Hanover galloped past the encampment to place himself between his people and the approaching riders. He shouted for someone to bring him his rifle and bag of ammunition. He stood up in his saddle and twisted his torso back to make certain the camp had circled up. Satisfied everyone had taken what precautions they could, he sat down on his big gelding, cursing silently to himself. He shoved his big hat back off his forehead, leaned forward, and shaded his eyes with both hands. He watched the approaching riders, anxious to determine if they were the Crow war party returning or someone else.

It didn't take long for the galloping riders to draw near enough for the captain to identify a mounted patrol riding down hard towards them. He made out an American flag and the company's triangular banner held overhead, blowing out to the side. He turned his horse around with a huge sigh of relief and trotted back towards the camp. "Don't worry, folks. Looks like the army finally sent us some help. We can all relax now."

The camp sighed a collective sigh of relief. The men ran to the center of the encirclement to find their wives and children. A big cheer went up.

The captain handed his rifle off to one of the boys to return to the supply wagon, then turned and cantered out to meet the patrol. A tall man on a magnificent black stallion led two lines of riders. As the officer drew near, he raised his right hand in an angle similar to the Plains Indian sign for peace with his gloved hand raised palm forward, fingers up. The column slowed down to an orderly halt. A Cavalry captain rode forward. His epaulets with captain insignia glistened with real gold. He wore a black beaver-felt hat with a tall center-trenched crown. A military cockade pinned the right side of the hat's wide brim to its crown, giving it a dashing look. A brass captain's insignia glittered on the front of his hat. A shiny brass and steel sword scabbard hung off his left hip. He pulled up to Captain Hanover, nodded politely then gave him a precise salute. "Good morning, sir. I'm Captain John Reed of Company G, Sixth Infantry, out of Fort Laramie, at your service, sir."

"Good morning to you, too, Captain. I'm Captain Philip Hanover guiding a Mormon handcart company to the Utah Territories. You are a very welcome sight, Captain. Although until we could make out you were Federal cavalry, you gave us quite the fright. You see, three days ago, we were ambushed by a Crow war party."

"I'm sorry to hear that, sir. Let me order my men to stop and tend to their mounts, then we can talk."

"Tell you what, Captain. Have yer camp cooks meet up with our ladies over by the white tops in the center of our camp. We can take a break, have dinner, then continue on fer the rest o' the day. Between the cholera, inclement weather, an' wounds from Injuns, we've lost too much time this trip."

"We brought along a doctor and surgeon's mate in case we ran into trouble. I'll order them to ride ahead and inspect your wounded immediately. Where will they find them?"

"Our good Sister Baines took charge o' the nursin'. She put all the non-ambulatory patients in that big hospital wagon over in the center o' camp."

"Hospital wagon?"

"That's what Sister Baines named it. She has a way with words, doncha know."

They both smiled. Captain Reed nodded his head. "Might that be the same Missus Lorna Baines I met a few weeks back in Fort Laramie when I met Missus Swinton and Baby Boy?"

"That would be her. The one an' the same."

"I look forward to seeing her again later on. We will be along shortly."

"Thank you, sir."

"Thank you, Captain."

The company had parked their handcarts closer together than usual for defense. The camp really felt cramped with a hundred uniformed soldiers walking through it. Everyone introduced themselves and welcomed the soldiers.

Not long after Captain Hanover turned his mount over to one of the young guards, he saw two men riding quickly towards the camp with a packhorse trotting along behind. They dismounted at the edge of the camp and led their horses through to the center. Captain Hanover sent word for Lorna Baines to join the doctor at the hospital wagon. He then asked his people to prepare a communal dinner for everyone.

The medical officers arrived at the hospital wagon at the same time Lorna Baines walked up. Captain Hanover introduced Lorna. The officers introduced themselves in a crisp military fashion.

"Sister Baines, here, took charge of nursin' our wounded. I'll leave you with her. She can show ya the ropes."

"Thank you, Captain." The doctor ordered his surgeon's mate to break out their medical supplies, then turned to Lorna Baines with a slight bow. "And, now, if you would be good enough to start my rounds by showing us the most badly wounded first."

198

"My pleasure, Doctor. We are all so relieved to have an experienced physician to tend to our wounded. Right this way if you please."

Captain Reed dismounted Paragon at the edge of camp and handed the reins to a private. "Loosen his cinches, Private Jackson, and take the bit out of his mouth. Give him some water, then keep a close hold on him until we're ready to pull out right after we eat. Stay close by. I don't want to have to hunt for him when I'm ready to depart."

"Yes, sir, Captain Reed."

The captain strode briskly through the camp, taking in everything as he searched for Captain Hanover. He recognized Sister Woman and stopped to shake hands. "Good morning, Missus Swinton. How are you today, Mister Swinton? It looks like you made it through the Crow attack unscathed. How are you faring?"

"Good mornin', Captain Reed. It's nice seein' y'all again."

The captain glanced around, expecting to spot Connal Lee. "Where's Connal Lee? I don't see him anywhere."

He turned back to look at the young couple standing before him in time to see their welcoming smiles turn to worried frowns. "He rode out huntin' the mornin' o' the Injun attack, an' we ain't seen hide nor hair of 'im since. We're mighty worried about 'im, Captain. Mighty worried."

"Why, I'm sorry to hear that. Let me go meet with your Captain Hanover, then I'll come back so you can tell me all about it. Maybe there's something we can do to help."

"Oh, we would be most beholdin', suh. Ah surely hope y'all can do somethin'. It's plumb killin' us not knowin' where he is or how he's doin'."

"I'll talk to you soon, then."

The Cavalry captain found Captain Hanover over by the wagons where the ladies had already lit their cookfires. The captain's young wife poured two cups of freshly boiled coffee and handed them to the men with a polite nod. "Thank you, dear. Coffee, Captain Reed?"

"Why, yes. Thank you, sir."

"Let's go sit over there out of the way where we can talk a spell."

"After you, sir."

Before they sat down, Lieutenant Anderson found them and marched up. He saluted both men very crisply. "Sir! Everything has been done as you ordered. Is there anything else I do for you, now, Captain?"

"Thank you, Mister Anderson. Please meet Captain Hanover."

The men stepped forward and shook hands. "Yes, sir. We met on my last patrol out here shortly after we were ambushed. His people were a great help to our wounded."

"It's good to see you again, Lieutenant."

Captain Reed sat down on the ground. "Go grab a mug of coffee and join us. We'll be right here."

"Thank you, sir."

When the Lieutenant returned with a tin mug of coffee, he sat down beside Captain Reed. He took a sip of coffee, blew on the cup, then took another sip. "So tell me, Captain Hanover. Where's your young sidekick? I don't think I ever saw you without him glued to your side, curious about everything we were saying. Did he enjoy that book I left him?"

Both captains frowned. Captain Hanover grunted. "Huh! I'm sorry t' be the one t' tell ya, but Connal Lee left the mornin' of our attack by the Crow war party t' go huntin' up in the hills. We haven't seen any trace of 'im since. We're still hopin' t' find 'im waitin' up ahead fer us. But it's not lookin' so good, now. He's been gone too long."

"I'm so sorry to hear that, Captain. I took a bit of a liking to the young scoundrel."

The Cavalry captain pointed at his first lieutenant sitting beside him. "After Lieutenant Anderson here departed your handcart company, he led his men directly back east to Fort Laramie. He dismissed his men on the parade ground in front of Army Headquarters. Still wearing the dirt of the road, he strode into the new army office building and into the fort commander's office. After greetings all around, he made his report to Major Sanderson. I happened to be on duty and heard it. After the Lieutenant reported on his dead and wounded, he finished his presentation, then asked Major Sanderson for permission to speak freely. The major granted him permission.

"Our good Lieutenant drew himself up to attention and told him, sir, with all due respect, that handcart company we encountered is extremely vulnerable with war parties of renegade Crow warriors ranging about the Shoshone lands. I would like to volunteer to take an armed patrol back as soon as possible and offer them protection until they get through to Fort Hall or Great Salt Lake City. The Major sat back in his chair, then thanked the lieutenant and told him to take a seat and relax while he considered the request. The Major looked towards his doorway and shouted for his orderly to bring them three cups of coffee."

Captain Reed went on to tell how they discussed the pros and cons for nearly an hour. Finally, the major ordered Captain Reed to muster his troops, take his entire company, and ride at top possible speed to the aid and assistance of Captain Hanover's Mormon handcart company. The major remembered the attack on his men on the last patrol and assigned them two medical officers. "Leave at first light. Lieutenant, go get yourself cleaned up and rested. You are back on patrol immediately. Good luck, gentlemen. God speed."

Captain Hanover nodded when Captain Reed finished his report. "Well, we're all mighty glad ya came back, Lieutenant. Too bad it couldn't have been three or four days ago, but it is as God wills it. It sure would o' saved us a heap o' trouble. We all appreciate what yer troops're doin' t' keep the trail safe, Captain, Lieutenant. Now, let's go grab us some grub before it's all gone, then we'll get back on the road."

After they ate, Captain Hanover took his leave. "Please let me know if there is anything we can do fer ya."

"Likewise, Captain. Send me word if you need anything we can help with. Otherwise, I will ride out with my platoon at the head of the handcart train. Lieutenant Anderson, take your platoon and have one of your sections ride left guard and one ride right guard, with your other two sections riding rear guard. Let's keep these poor travelers on the road without any more adventures."

"Yes, sir. Thank you, sir. So long, Captain Hanover. I look forward to speaking with you at the end of the day. I want to hear all about young Connal Lee. I'm going to go check on my men. See you later, sir."

"Goodbye, Lieutenant. Until tonight, then."

It didn't take long to clear away their pot luck luncheon and get back on the road. Everyone felt much safer with armed soldiers guarding their handcart train.

Following is a preview of the continuation
of Connal Lee's adventures in

PIONEER SPIRIT
Book Two: Indian Affairs

Available now in paperback and on Kindle

Chapter 1: Missing Connal Lee

Around 6:30 the evening after the Cavalry joined the handcart train, Captain Hanover ordered the company to pull off and set up camp near an unnamed stream of water. Captain Reed ordered his troops to set up their pup tents about thirty feet out from the handcart camp, surrounding them on all sides. "Lieutenant Anderson, after setting up your camps, have one of your sections take all the horses downstream. Stake them out where they can reach grass and water. Set a rotating guard even across the creek. Then divide up your remaining squads into rotating guard duty during the night, walking the perimeter of the entire encampment. Assign three men to sleep without standing guard duty so they can get up before dawn and ride ahead. I want them to spread out and scout the trail ahead of us to make sure we don't ride into any trouble. Tomorrow night, I'll have my squad take a turn at guard duty."

"Yes, sir!"

"When you have the men in order, come join me in the handcart camp. I'll either be with Captain Hanover or with the Swinton family."

"Very good, sir. Right away, sir. Thank you, sir."

Dusk settled over the now quiet camp. The ladies gathered beside the supply wagons to begin cooking a communal supper. Captain Reed ordered his men assigned to cook for the patrol to join them. When the soldiers arrived with more food, they exchanged noisy rounds of introductions before the camp fell quiet as everyone focused on their work. With inevitable sighs, the two privates ordered to peel the potatoes sat down on the ground, knives in hand, and sent a flurry of potato peels flying through the air.

The ambulatory men and boys fetched water to the hospital wagon and the cooking fires. Lorna Baines met the doctor and surgeon's mate at the hospital wagon, where they attended to the wounded. When Captain Reed sought out Captain Hanover just as dark settled in, he found him by the support wagons speaking with Lorna Baines. The Cavalry captain shifted a small yellowed canvas package to his left hand, then stepped up and shook hands with Captain Hanover and Lorna Baines. "Good evening, Captain Hanover. Lovely to see you again, Missus Baines."

Captain Hanover shook hands with a firm grip. "Ah, Captain. Glad ya could join us. We were jus' thinkin' about moseyin' over t' visit Sister Swinton's tent. Brother Swinton told me she's pretty depressed about Baby Boy – Connal Lee, an' is jus' sittin' there mopin'. Let's go see if we can cheer 'er up, shall we?"

"Excellent, Captain. I am anxious to hear the whole story of how Connal Lee went missing. I share your concern for my young friend, whom I affectionately called little brother back in Fort Laramie. I was looking forward to discussing books with him again."

Captain Reed offered his arm to Lorna Baines. She laid her hand on the bend of his elbow. They followed Captain Hanover through to the north side of the camp.

When Zeff saw them walking towards his little campfire, he stood up, then reached down and pulled Sister Woman to stand beside him. She held Chester Ray over her left shoulder. Zeff put his arm around her shoulders and pulled her into a hug. After rounds of handshakes and polite greetings, Zeff gestured everyone to take a seat around his little firepit. Gilbert Baines saw them and strode over to join the conversation. Lorna scuttled back to her handcart to find a blanket to sit on. As she returned, Lieutenant Anderson strolled up carrying a small package wrapped in brown paper and tied with a string.

They all settled in with friendly nods and smiles. The flickering flames of the small mesquite fire reflected in their eyes. Captain Reed peered at Zeff, then at Captain Hanover. "So, please tell me everything you know. How did Connal Lee come to be separated from your company?"

Zeff looked at Captain Hanover. The Captain nodded for Zeff to answer. "Well, suh. A while back, we was gettin' hungry fer some fresh game. But night after night, we returned empty-handed from our usual huntin' after we stopped fer the day. There jus' weren't no game close tuh the trail in this here desert. So, Connal Lee came up with the idear o' him headin' out ever mornin' tuh ride up in the hills. Captain Hanover lent 'im a good mount an' a pack-horse. Some days 'e did real good. Though once in a while, 'e returned with nothin' fer the pot."

Sister Woman began sniffling, which drew everyone's eyes over to her. She gently set Chester Ray on the ground beside her, tucked his scrap of quilt over him, then dropped her face to both hands. "Ah'm sorry. But Ah miss Baby Boy so, so much."

Zeff scooted over close enough to put his arm around her again. "The day those damn Crow braves attacked us on the road started out jus' like any other day. Connal Lee rode out towards the western range that day, headin' out on 'is usual huntin' trip. Last Ah saw 'im, he rode over the foothills an' disappeared outta sight. It was what, oh, about the same time as we got organized an' hit the road jus' like we do every mornin'. Only them Injuns rode out from around the hill ahead of us an' rode us down. They started shootin' arrows an' a whoopin' an' a shoutin' an' a carryin' on somethin' fierce. We was all scared plumb tuh death. That war party circled around us an' shot us up pretty dang good. Captain Hanover led the men what had weapons tuh defend the camp. They did a good job, all of 'em. After what seemed like ferever, they finally rode off. They came down on us from the east, but they rode off goin' west, pretty much in the same direction Connal Lee had takin'. We're plumb worried they might o' run 'im down out there in the mountains. Who knows what could o' happened tuh 'im."

Zeff shook his head, imagining all the horrible things that might have befallen his little brother. Everyone frowned, worry clearly evident on their faces. Captain Hanover looked over at Captain Reed and Lieutenant Anderson. "Ya see, men, we were plumb busy tendin' our wounded under the kind direction o' Sister Baines, here. I set everyone to tightenin' up the camp, then set up a system o' guards fer the rest o' the day an' that night. Everyone was too beat up an' hurtin' t' leave fer the next couple o' days. While the wounded rested up an' started healin', the rest of us reorganized the supply wagons so Sister Baines could have 'er hospital wagon. Everyone pitched in to cover fer the wounded. We all kept expectin' t' see Connal Lee ridin' in from up the trail, lookin' fer us. But 'e never did. The problem is, that was four days ago, now. He should o' found us by now if 'e were able."

Zeff spoke up. "He's a smart kid, doncha know, plus 'e had 'is compass, too. He would o' figured out that we were behind 'im when we didn't show up down the trail at the end o' the day. Yes, suh, 'e would o' thought 'is way through it an' found us by now, if'n 'e was able. Ah'm so afraid somethin' happened tuh 'im. Ah cain't stand the thought o' me poor little brover out there all alone, maybe wounded or dyin'.""

Sister Woman began sobbing loudly, interrupting the conversation. Zeff pulled her face down to his chest and patted her on the back, trying to offer her some comfort. The lieutenant turned to Captain Hanover. "Did you send out a search party, Captain?"

Captain Hanover shook his head with a sad look on his face. "Lieutenant, we were short o' horses. We only had two saddles left. We were short o' men who could ride. Much as I wanted t' lead a search party, meself, we had t' stick together fer protection an' t' tend t' the wounded. I couldn't see anything else t' do. I felt real bad about it, though. Tough decisions. Tough times."

Captain Reed glared angrily at Captain Hanover but held his tongue. Captain Hanover had command, not him or the army. He leaned forward and rested his elbows on his knees. "So, he's a little more than a day's journey back along the Overland Trail, and he's been gone for over four days. Plus, who knows how far north and west he managed to ride that day or since. Even with a full company of men, that leaves us a huge amount of territory to cover if we were to mount a search party."

He looked Captain Hanover in the face, then nodded his head. "Plus, any men we sent out would leave us short of optimal protection here. If I sent out too few, they could be at risk from packs of renegade Indians roaming the countryside. If I sent out enough for them to be safe, we couldn't guard your handcart train properly. Damn it all!"

"Ya see me dilemma, then, doncha, Captain? No matter what I could figure out, I couldn't come up with a good solution all around. Right or wrong, I prayed on it an' chose t' keep the main body o' me company together an' safe. Tough decisions. Tough times."

They all fell silent. Lorna picked up the edge of her long apron and wiped tears from her eyes.

Lieutenant Anderson held out his paper-wrapped package to Zeff. "I remember Connal Lee telling me how much he enjoyed reading *Oliver Twist*. So I thought he might enjoy this book. It's my favorite book by Dickens. *Nicholas Nickleby*. I brought it along for him since he complained he didn't have anything new to read."

Lorna smiled warmly. "He would really have enjoyed it, Lieutenant. You would not believe how he immersed himself in *The Count of Monte Christo*. He surely did enjoy it. It opened up whole new worlds to him. He often said he wished he could have thanked you in person for leaving it for him."

"I'm glad to hear that, Missus Baines. Here, Mister Swinton. Please take this book and keep it for when he shows up. I know things look bleak right now, but I have faith that he is clever enough to survive and find his way back to you."

"Why, thanks, Lieutenant. He will love readin' another story by Dickens, Ah'm sure. Mighty neighborly o' y'all."

Captain Reed coughed into his hand. "It appears we were all thinking the same thing, Lieutenant. Here Mister Swinton. I brought Connal Lee my own favorite book, *The Three Musketeers*. I hoped he would like to read a rousing adventure story about a young man growing up to become a soldier. He seemed interested in everything having to do with soldiering when I met him. Please keep it for him. I found a scrap of canvas waterproofed with boiled oil and wrapped it for him so it would stay dry. I hope he enjoys it. Please tell him I will expect to discuss this novel with him the next time I see him. I agree with the good lieutenant. Connal Lee is smart enough to think his way out of whatever difficulty he finds himself in. I'm sure he will return to you as soon as he can. Good night, everyone. I'm going to take my leave to go check that my men are in good order for the night."

When he stood up, Lieutenant Anderson also rose to his feet. "Good night, friends. I'm so sorry about Connal Lee going missing. If I may, I will accompany you on your rounds, sir."

"Certainly. I would welcome the company, Lieutenant."

Captain Hanover stood up next. "Well. I think I'll make my own rounds an' seek out my bed at the end of 'em. Good night, Brother an' Sister Swinton. Pleasant dreams, Brother an' Sister Baines."

The Swintons and Baines sat, two sad couples snuggled in each other's arms, staring into the fire as the flames dwindled. Finally, Gilbert stood up and offered a hand to pull Lorna to her feet. She bent back down and picked up her blanket. "Good night, Brother Swinton. Good night, Sister Swinton."

"Good night, y'all."

Chapter 2: Desert Survival Course

The small Shoshone family and Connal Lee saddled up their horses to continue their mission to keep an eye on the Crow war party. The beautifully beaded and fringed saddles the three natives put on their large war steeds fascinated Connal Lee. The front and back of their saddles looked almost like Connal Lee's saddle horn but taller, with one rising in front and one behind the seat.

Screaming Eagle tied his war bonnet over his long black hair. Delicate downy eagle feathers tied to the tips of the large eagle wing feathers standing up around his bonnet fluttered on the slightest breeze or movement he made. Connal Lee found it very beautiful.

They loaded up their three packhorses and rode northeast away from their campground. Screaming Eagle had ridden this path before, so he confidently led the way. They made good time on their strong well-rested mounts. However, about the time they stopped for a noon break, Connal Lee felt his strength waning. He also discovered that his forehead, cheeks, and nose were getting sunburned without his big felt hat. After they dismounted and ate a cold travel meal, Connal Lee pointed out how the red skin on his face.

White Wolf peered closely. "Now I understand why white man wear hat all time. Skin burn. We Newe no burn. We like sun. Sun like us."

Short Rainbow touched his cheek, leaving a white fingerprint on the sunburned skin. "Need hat. Need salve for burn."

White Wolf nodded his agreement and turned to Screaming Eagle. In Shoshone, he told him they would make camp here, but he should ride ahead and check on the Crow war party. He then pointed at Connal Lee. "Please. Unsaddle packhorses. Make fire. I back quick."

White Wolf leapt up on his war stallion and galloped away. He watched for prickly pear cactus out away from the little stream they had stopped beside, where the desert was arid enough for them to survive. He found a small cluster of green and red cacti, bristling with long needle-sharp spines. He carefully cut off three large pads with his steel knife and pushed them into a small deer hide medicine pouch.

When White Wolf returned to the camp, he dumped the cactus pads directly into the flames of the fire. He picked up a stick, then knelt upwind from the smoke to watch the cactus carefully. Once he saw that all the dangerous spines and the tough outer skins of the pads had burned off, he flicked the denuded pads out of the flames. Short Rainbow brought him their gourd bowl from the packhorses and placed it on the ground beside him. White Wolf nodded his thanks. He carefully squeezed the slippery juice out of the cactus into the bowl, then tossed the pulp back into the fire. "Connal Lee. Come. Please."

Connal Lee walked over and sat down Indian-style on the ground beside him. White Wolf reached out his hand and turned Connal Lee's face towards him with a smile. "Red! Now you red man. Ha!"

White Wolf dipped his fingers into the slippery cactus salve and gently spread it over Connal Lee's exposed skin. "Help. Medicine. For burns."

Connal Lee nodded that he understood. "Thank you. Aeshen."

Short Rainbow danced over with a piece of leather in her hands. She wrapped the edge around Connal Lee's cranium and measured the start of a cap. Using a piece of charcoal from the fire, she marked where to cut. When Connal Lee looked at her, puzzled, she twittered a bright laugh. "Make war bonnet white man style." Then she asked in Shoshone, as she shaded her eyes with her hand, "How do you say make shade to cover the face? Shade?"

White Wolf and Connal Lee both answered her at the same time in English. "Shade."

She nodded happily. A few minutes later, she returned with a strip of leather about four inches wide and twenty-two inches long and held it around Connal Lee's head. In Shoshone, she explained, "I'm going to make a hat like an extra big war bonnet, only this bonnet will be topped with a solid crown without eagle feathers. Then, with a brim sewn around the base of the bonnet, Connal Lee will have a Shoshone style white man hat."

White Wolf leaned over and gave her a hug. "So clever. How can I help?"

"Get an awl and make holes to bind the ends together while I cut the crown to top off the bonnet. The bonnet will also need holes along the bottom to attach the brim and along the top to attach the crown."

Somehow, through watching their gestures and picking up the odd word, Connal Lee understood they were making him a replacement hat. He felt awkward not contributing. "White Wolf, I want to help. I don't want you doing everything for me."

White Wolf and Short Rainbow looked at each other with their eyebrows raised. White Wolf shook his head no. "Too much time teach. We do. You good hunt with rifle?"

Connal Lee brightened up. "Yes. I'm good at tracking and hunting. How about if I ride out and find some fresh meat for our supper while you make my hat?"

"Yes. Good. But ride away from Crow. No follow Screaming Eagle."

"I understand. Of course. I wouldn't want the Crow to hear my rifle."

Full of renewed energy at having something to do to contribute to the camp, he strode over, tightened the cinch, and mounted his dark brown mare. He waved cheerfully. "I'll be back as soon as I can."

White Wolf and Short Rainbow waved as he turned the mare around and trotted away, pulling his packhorse behind him.

About an hour later, he spotted a flock of ring-necked pheasants scrounging for seeds in a grassy stretch of land. He nearly missed the well-camouflaged females against the dried grass and weeds, but the brilliant iridescent blue neck feathers and the stark white ring around the males' necks made them easy to see. He quickly pulled out his shotgun and switched out the lead balls for buckshot. With two quick shots directly into the flock, he managed to bring down a large cock and four smaller hens. The rest of the flock flew off in a big whoosh! With a proud smile, Connal Lee pulled a leather string from his pants pocket, tied the birds together by their necks, and draped them over the packsaddle.

He arrived back in camp, quite exhausted – to his surprise – but happy with the hunt. White Wolf noticed Connal Lee's exhaustion and recommended he rest for a while. White Wolf spread out one of his sleeping furs and gestured for Connal Lee to relax on it. Short Rainbow immediately seized the male pheasant, chattering happily in Shoshone about how she wanted to harvest the lovely feathers. White Wolf could pluck, gut, and prepare the females for frying. She didn't care about their dull brown and tan feathers.

By the time Screaming Eagle rode back into camp, Connal Lee proudly wore a neatly sewn leather hat. White Wolf sat beside the fire, frying pheasants for their supper. Short Rainbow sat bowed over her lap, humming a meditation while she crafted a hatband for Connal Lee's new hat out of gorgeous pheasant feathers. She finished it with a three-inch rondel of short, brilliant blue neck feathers to cover the seam where the two ends joined around the hat's crown. Connal Lee shook his head in amazement at her talents and ability to work so fast. "That's plumb beautiful, Short Rainbow. Plumb beautiful. Ah really don't know how y'all do it. Thanks so much. Ah thank y'all, too, White Wolf. Wow!"

Screaming Eagle asked Connal Lee to teach him how to shoot a rifle while they waited for supper. Both White Wolf and Short Rainbow objected, complaining they wanted to learn, too. He gave in to their requests and offered to teach Connal Lee how to shoot a hunting bow. They stepped away from the camp. Screaming Eagle stood behind Connal Lee and instructed him on the correct way to stand, how to nock and hold the arrow, how to aim up a bit higher than the target to compensate for the downward arc of the arrow in flight, and how to adjust for wind. Connal Lee didn't understand all the words, but he caught on quickly. Before it became too dark to shoot, they collected the arrows and returned to the campfire.

As they ate supper, Screaming Eagle complimented Connal Lee on his hunting. Connal Lee thanked him for the shooting lesson. "One good thing about your bows and arrows is that you can make and re-use your arrows. Once I shoot a bullet, it is gone. I need civilization for more ammunition. You know, to buy gunpowder, shot, and lead for casting balls."

The group discussed this problem. White Wolf decided only Screaming Eagle would actually shoot the rifle in practice so they could save their ammunition for hunting and self-defense. White Wolf and Short Rainbow agreed to practice without live ammunition for the time being. "Connal Lee. No problem find lead, find shot. We find Fort Hall. Trade. We give fur. Trader give shot, lead. Trade good. When hunt tomorrow, watch for fur *and* for food."

They had a lively conversation about the most valuable furs. None of them had English words for fox, marten, mink, otter, or beaver pelts, the most highly valued for trade. "Besides," as White Wolf pointed out, "We no find here. Here deer, bear, wolf. No worry. We trade. We get bullets."

The temperature fell quickly after the sun went down behind the hills to their west, so they all snuggled up together on their blankets. Connal Lee noticed his friends making love beneath the sleeping furs. He smiled, happy that his friends loved each other. He fell asleep thinking, *Someday Ah will have someone to love, too. Someday...*

Made in United States
Orlando, FL
08 December 2022

25802534R00136